Hiding Behind The Night

by

Jamil A. Shabazz

Book and Cover Design, Logos, Additional Graphics by Solomon Muhammad http://www.artpal.com/the-solo-rock

Editing by Maurice Gray, Jr.

ISBN: 978-0-9992293-0-9

DEDICATION

To my Aunt Mellissa. The definition of Black and Beautiful

CONTENTS

Shabazz

vi

ACKNOWLEDGMENTS

To God whom all praises are due. Without my belief in him, this novel is not possible. God is love, and so am I.

I would like to thank Valencia and Jamil. The conduits of my life.

I want to thank one of my dearest and oldest friends Ms. Liz. Your constant love and support over all these years, has made my life better. I love you dearly.

To my dear Alane, many people will never get to know and understand the true you; I'm glad I'm not one of them. Your heart is pure, your mouth is reckless and your spirit is fiery. Unorthodox in every aspect of the word. I love you for the best and worst parts of you. BPJ

To my Ms. Margaret, I love you! You manage to stay sincere and down to earth, regardless of what happens to/ around you. I thank you for your support and encouragement. Your spirit and positive energy, has brightened many a day for me.

Whadddup Muzzie! Thank you for saying all the things you shouldn't and making me laugh every time you come around.

Maria! Heeeeeeeeeey gurl! How you doins? Fun-Sized and down to ride, Maria you will always be one of my favorite people because of your rawness and kind heart. The rest of the world wishes they could be fly like you!

To Jennifer B. I know I haven't always been a saint but, I thank you for being a dream supporter. There are very few who are as fiercely loyal and as supportive as you. I love you dearly.

I want to thank Andrea for giving me creative freedom and allowing me to exercise it in this novel. Your life helped inspire my art. It don't get no bettah den dat.

I want to thank my aunts Marlos, Charmon, Linda. My cousin Marlinda. And Gina, Bess and Shana. You ladies were my test and target audience. It is because of you that I realized that there was / is still a market for both literary
style and substance.

To Brother Solo Muhammad. I want to thank you for the magnificent work you did designing the cover. You took my words and turned them into a visual the world can savor.

To Raquel Rhone, I want to thank you as well for the artwork ideas and input that you put into the project. You create beautiful art.

My dear friend Queen Kim, thank you for your tough love, and honest response to every question I ever asked. There are none like you Kim!

To Sharla, you are a better person than most will give you credit for. As the years have passed I've learned to value the quality and loyalty that you embody as a human being. You are a rare woman and I appreciate you you supporting my hopes and dreams the way that you do.

I want to thank Maurice Gray, Jr. for stepping in to edit the project, improving the quality of my novel by allowing me to decipher the forest from the trees.

I want to thank Charles Emmons, my dear brother your words, support and encouragement have been like the street lights that come on in a dark alley; helping me to find my way down a path I had never before been.

I want to thank Heather Melton Fox for being a sounding board and an idea exchanger. I appreciate the fact that you slice through bone, to get straight to the heart of the matter.

I also want to thank Janiece Mackey, for being a bridge that brings people together. You the real MVP!

I want to thank Arnetta Ellinwood for giving Nila a voice. You are a delight to work with! Polite, professional and committed to producing quality over quantity. Listening to you breathe new life into my signature character. Allowed me to understand and reimagine the possibility of Nila's capabilities. One thing I know for certain, when the world hears your voice, they'll be hooked at first listen.

If in my acknowledgements I neglected to thank you, know it wasn't due to malicious intent. I got nothin' but love for you!

CHAPTER 1

"Excuse me sir, but where do I know you from?" I ask the dark brown stranger sitting across from me.

"I was in your dream this one time."

"Really? What did you do?"

He smiles coyly and leans back in his chair. There is a cup of coffee sitting directly in the middle of our round white table. His eyes look at the cup and then up at me; silence fills the space we occupy as I wait for the man to respond.

"You don't remember what happened in that dream?" He breaks the sea of silence.

"Apparently not. I just know you look familiar to me."

"You let me drink your sweet nectar in that dream, and I have been trying to find you ever since." His voice drips with a southern drawl that I'm only now noticing.

"You the man who made my pussy drip all over your shirt."

Dimples form in his cheeks at my verbal recollection of the moment we shared in that hotel room. I look down at the coffee and see that half of it has disappeared. Gazing back up at the Nubian stranger, I see that he is shirtless, chest glistening with what smells like baby oil.

"Is this a dream now?"

"Why don't you reach under the table and find out?"

As I obey, the room begins to flash white. I oscillate searching for the light; finding no trace, I turn back to the table and see that the chocolate mystery is gone. The sound of knocking makes me get up from the table; I take a step and notice that the ground lights up white as well like Michael Jackson in the Billie Jean video. With every little step I take, the knocking grows louder, transforming to a melodic thump that is reminiscent of a heartbeat. In pursuit of the noise, I start to sway with the beat, feeling heat all around me. I feel a caress around my waist- a force pulling me from this space. Eyes still closed, I can feel the fingers in my sugar bowl and hear indecipherable words start to seep from my lips. I feel pressure in my thighs as my fiancé Drian starts to spread my hips.

My man has pulled me from the rapture of my dream and put me in his mouth. His tongue is deep in my coochie while his finger rubs on my magic bump. I gasp for air, because it feels like Drian is sucking it out of me with the way he's resuscitating my vagina. As I work my hand under my shirt to play with my nipples, Drian begins to hum in my pussy like it's a harmonica.

"Ahhhhhhh! Ooooooooohhh!" The vibration of pleasure escapes me as Drian works his tongue and lips in harmony.

The sensation is so strong that I try to retreat toward our headboard with hands on both sides of Drian's neck. I try to push him away from the control he has over me. The attempt is futile because my boo thang is a pro at pleasing me, for as far as I try to run in our king-sized bed, Drian pursues, his tongue never leaving my sugar bowl. Instead of fighting a losing battle, I wrap my legs around his neck and enclose his face in my pussy like it's a Venus fly trap. Determined to lick his way out of trouble, Drian begins to decimate my sex with his thick and powerful tongue, working at my Punani like it's a full time job with all the OT he can handle. I writhe and contort in ecstasy as I feel a squirt coming on. I try to stave off the water show orgasm, as to not drown my lover before I can get some dick in me. I unlatch my legs and shove Drian off me using all my might. Under the light of the moon I look my lover in those Bambi eyes and breathe heavily while caressing his face. He crawls up my body and I lean down to him, our lips meet in the middle, the kiss is lustful and sloppy— saliva and love juice everywhere. I taste my own nectar in our oral exchange. Persistent passion renders words useless, as our nonverbal cues subordinate dictionary definitions.

I push Drian on his back and fish my hand in his boxer briefs. His manhood is ready for me, girthy, long and harder than a diamond, his jewel is destined to shine brightly in my hidden treasure. I snatch the sheath off his sword and throw his boxers somewhere into the darkness, Drian removes my night tee with a single hand. Butt naked, pussy dripping I straddle my lover's pelvis with my Punani hovering inches away from his throbbing desire. Drian sits upright and starts to play with my left nipple, while taking my right breast in his mouth. His tenacity makes my body cave in, I crook myself in his neck and inhale traces of the cologne he wore last night. The leftover pheromones in the fragrance have my pussy hotter than the summers in Bangkok. With Drian under my equator I climb up on his north pole and let his tool break the seal on my coochie lips. I plunge down his shaft and climax immediately. Drian sees the orgasm in my eyes and starts to buck upwards like a Shorthorn at the PBR World Championship. Quick to react, I lasso my right arm around his neck and plant my left palm three inches below his belly button. We rise off the bed with Drian continuing to pound at my pussy at a frantic pace. Not to be bested, I create counter friction when I let my pussy hammer down onto his thrusts, matching his energy stroke for stroke. With all this exertion, I'm surprised that our bedroom is still intact; Drian is knocking down walls like a contractor. His force of will starts to collapse my desire, until the needs meld together to become one in the same, fluid and interchangeable. I am blissfully lost in the stroke of time. Hard, long, soft, short- Drian's dick does every trick inside of me. Ready to be the star of the show I put my hand in the center of his chest and push until he is flat backed on the mattress

"Put your knees up." I command in between gaps of air that reeks of Bodiussy.

Like a good boy, Drian puts both feet flat on the mattress knees upward, with his thighs touching my back. I remount my lover in a modified cowgirl position and squat slightly on his long john. I come down on the dick like darkness over nightfall, absorbing every inch into the crevices of my coochie. Cutting at a vertical angle, my pussy aligns ninety degrees on his manhood, hitting the spot that makes me feel like his dick was custom made for me. As we fuck ferociously, Drian starts to strum on my clit in unison, ratcheting up the pleasure radiating in my loins. Through furious passion I feel the moisture coming on faster with each stroke; Drian's erection grows more and more rigid as we compete to climax. The pressure in my pelvis is traveling to my pussy. Holding off my nut is mission impossible at this point; I acquiesce and fall back into a white space. Powerful convulsions take control and I feel my love juice shoot higher than the fountains at the Bellagio, drenching me and Drian. When I start to come down from the orgasm that took me out of my orbit, I feel wetness underneath me, more than just the tide I overflowed the sheets with, I feel a viscous, warm liquid filling my vaginal cavity. The warm feeling in my love below is the last sensation I remember before the sunlight finds me in the morning, naked in a bed that has no sheets on it

CHAPTER 2

I roll over to Drian's side of the bed and see that he is gone; maybe wherever he is, that's where my clothes and bed sheets are too. I let my skin caress the satin pillow top mattress for a few more seconds before I slide out of the bed. When my feet touch the floor, I have to catch myself to keep from falling; I feel weak in the knees and sore in the hips. My body feels like I did a circuit of squats. I stumble to my dresser, open the drawer and retrieve a pair of shorts and a camisole top to cover up with. Putting on my clothes I shudder at a pang in my pussy a residual sensation of satisfaction in my love below. I don't know when this sea of gratification rained down on me, but I am grateful for God's gift anyhow. I catalog the physical manifestations and meander through the abode in search of my lover. Standing still and wordless, I listen for any sound that would be out of place at this time of morning in my domicile. The buzz of the washing machine clips the air and I head for the basement stairs towards the household laundry room. In the laundry room, in front of the washer and dryer I see a familiar physique.

"Good morning, babe." I gleam as I grab my man by his waist. He turns over his right shoulder and leans down to peck me on the lips before he replies.

"Good morning to you too, baby."

"What'chu doing down here?"

"Your laundry from last night."

I told my tongue and try to think of any mess I could have made last night. I don't remember any. "What mess from last night?"

Drian closes the door on the dryer, sets the timer and turns around to face me before he rifts. "The water works you left on our sheets."

I stare into those big orbs and try to decipher if Drian is kidding or not, until I remember that my man rarely does laundry; something must have transpired that was significant enough to bring him to the basement to clean up the evidence. My glare must have been too focused because Drian asks. "You really don't remember do you?"

A shoulder shrug, explains my position better than any combination of words in the dictionary. Drian leans back on the dryer and begins to shake his dome in slow motion. When he starts to chuckle, the hee hawing pushes me to the edge of my patience for this interaction. Normally I'm too proud to beg, but curiosity is killing me.

"Tell me, please!" I plead as I stand in front of Mr. Yancy, vulnerable and open hands square on my hips and lips jutted out. I imagine I'm sexy even when I beg.

"You really don't remember?"

"No."

He takes his body off the dryer and says. "We had some ol' buck nasty code XXX type sex last night. You jumped me in the middle of the night. It was like the morning of July fifth all over again, except this time you was sleepfreakng me."

That pops the light bulb as to why my loins feel so satisfied this morning, and brings back the memory of the first day I consciously, and physically gave him all of me.

"Sleepfreaking?"

"Yes!" He puts both hands up in the air, like he's praising Jesus at church or raising the roof at the club, before he continues.

"I was laying there sleep and you grabbed my dick, jerked it like we was two kids trying not to get caught in the back of a movie theater. You know I ain't never gonna pass up no puddy, I started licking, rubbing and fingering you and then BAM! It was on! You was cumming like crazy back to back towards the end. Then you had this ol' Exorcist look about you, when you messed around and caught that final nut. That orgasm was so strong you managed to super soak the sheets, squirt everywhere, and get some of that juice in my eye."

I laugh rousingly at the thought of me shooting love juice in my baby's eye. I also have another thought that tickles me in an absurd way. Not that I am incapable of super freakiness, but listening to Drian speak, I am shocked that I have no vivid memory of my out of body sexual experience.

"Awww poor baby," I stick my arms out for Drian to enter. "I didn't mean to stick my love in your eye baby; the Adina in me just wanted you to see where I was coming from! Muhahahahaha!"

Betraying our embrace Drian tries to hem me up, but I elude his grasp like a chicken covered in Crisco and race to the top of the stairs, once I am at a safe distance I scream. "So you just goin' freak me off in the middle of the night like that, huh?"

Drian ventures to where I can see him at the bottom of the stairs puts a hand in his basketball shorts and replies. "Are you gonna ask me a serious question?"

I smile with my eyes. "Sure, what you want for breakfast, MistaLovaMane?"

"You! If you don't get in that kitchen quickly and start making my food woman!"

I slide my short shorts to the side and let my cat out the bag. "Come on up, I got a breakfast taco all ready for ya!"

He walks out of my view without uttering a single word; I take it that he doesn't feel like taking me up on my offer, so I head to the kitchen to fix my baby something else to eat. I pop open the fridge and look for the thick cut maple cured bacon I got at Sam's, some eggs, milk and cheese from the cold pantry as well. Closing the fridge brings the sound of the chimes to the air; convinced I'm tripping I open and close the refrigerator again real fast to rule out the appliance as the source of the noise. My actions didn't generate any sound so I remain vertical and motionless waiting for the sound to repeat. Five seconds pass before three sharp chimes ring the air again, less than a second passes before I hear Drian race up the stairs

"You didn't hear the doorbell, Nila?"

"I'm still semi-sleep; I forgot we had a doorbell!" I yell back in his general direction.

"Girl you betta wake up, I can't have you sleeping through your own wedding!" A friendly female voice shoots back.

"Is that Ms. Vivian I hear in my house?"

"Live and loaded, honey!" The matriarch of the Yancy family calls out

"Pistol or Patron?" I ask Drian's youthful mother.

"Shut up and come gimme some love, girl." She cackles like the wicked witch she was in another life. Thankfully, she is soon to be my fairy mother-in-law.

"Ms. Vivian will you join us for breakfast?" I ask after we unhook from our embrace.

"Does Oprah's guest house, have a guest house?" She eases into a chair at our kitchen table. Before she can call his name, Drian appears in the kitchen wearing a wife beater to go with his basketball shorts and holding a reusable shopping bag with drawings of various fruits on the outside.

"You can set the bag on the table for Mama, baby." Vivian says to her only son.

A man loyal to his mother if there ever was one, Drian stands behind the twenty-three X chromosomes that gave him life. The trip down the birthing canal fortified a bond strong enough to carry them through this lifetime and the next one. The dynamic that they have makes me a tad envious, I can't recall seeing a pair of individuals so tightly knitted that their respective weaknesses are morphed into collective strength, turning two halves into one whole. Untangling my vision from my thoughts I see Drian peeking over Ms. Vivian's shoulder trying to see what she has in the bag. Ms. Vivian shifts the bag to her right side, attempting to obscure its contents. Persistent as a panhandler, Drian slithers his way to the right side of Vivian's body; her reaction is opposite and equal as she moves the bag to her left-hand side. The duo keeps up the Tom and Jerry like shenanigans, until the tipping point is reached, causing them to both start roaring with laughter. The roar becomes a whisper when Drian wraps his arms around his mommy's neck in a tender show of affection.

Looking at the two of them hugging, cheeks touching I see people who resemble each other, but not overwhelmingly so. Ms. Vivian looks a lot like that actress who played Tina Turner's mom in What's Love Got To Do With It, except Ms. V is a tad thicker. Her skin is the color of toffee that was intentionally burnt, smooth and unwrinkled. Her style of hair changes often, but on this morning her hair is asymmetrical and in a bob cut. Her natural brown hair is littered with blonde highlights, making her look feistier than she actually is (which is hard to do). One undeniable trait passed from mother to child those light brown Bambi eyes. I imagine during the final stages of her pregnancy God decided to put a reminder in his work, so he gave Drian those eyes to keep him mindful of the woman who sacrificed her body to give him life.

"Miss Nila, what you over there cooking up for breakfast?"

"Well Ms. Vivian since you're here, I am gonna make French toast, with thick cut maple bacon and some eggs."

She snaps two times in delight before she exclaims. "Hmmmph! Girl you just what to say to make my day!"

"You know I try."

I find my favorite sheet pan, line it with baking parchment and start to lay out the strips of the pork breakfast meat as I wait for the oven I just turned on to heat up.

"You put your bacon in the oven?" Ms. Yancy's voice inquires dripping with astonishment.

"Sure do, it's the only way to keep the whole house from smelling like Waffle House, while I make breakfast."

"I don't know about that honey, I love the way Waffle House smells."

"I do too, when I'm actually at the Waffle House!"

"Touché."

"Say Moms what you got in that bag?" Drian chirps in, tired of being left out of the dialogue.

"Something for ya'll's wedding."

"You goin' let me see it?"

"When the lady of the house joins us at the table I will let her see it, and if you happen to catch a glance, peek at your own risk."

I put the bacon in the oven and wash my hands while the two continue their playful conversation. Part of me wishes she would leave so I could be alone with my fiancé for some quality time, but we don't always get what we want. I swallow my selfishness, fix my emotional face and sit down at the table to join mother and son.

"Iight Ms. V what you got in that bag?"

Knack is the word when it comes to conversing with Ms. Vivian this morning. Accidentally on purpose everything I say seems to be the right words at the right moment. My most recent question lights up Ms. Yancy like a blunt of Snoop's tour bus.

"Lookie lookie here, girl lookie here. I have got for you the one thing that you wanted most for the reception tent. THE same thing that has been damn near impossible to find in quantity, until now."

It is a challenge not to smile with a childlike excitement when I have a good idea what she is going to pull out of that bag. Trying to master the virtue of patience, I sit back in my chair and elect to remain silent, refusing to spoil her big reveal.

'You ready, Nila?"

I nod to let her know that I am. Without saying another word Ms. Vivian digs into her bag at what seems like a molasses pace and comes out with one of the most beautiful man-made instruments I have ever seen. She hands me a single icicle made of plastic, approximately six inches in length, wide at the top and narrowing at the tip; an authentic replica of the real thing.

"Oh. My. Goodness! Ms. V, where did you get these?" I ask pleasantly shocked.

"Oh, you know had an old boo that was an electrician for his side gig. I called asked him if was still bout that life and he told me he would see what he could do—which really meant yes, he just needed some time to locate them. So 'fore I came over here I went by his house to pick those up and tell him good morning."

A twinkle develops in her eye after the last two words off her lips. I suspect her old electrician boo reignited a new flame earlier this morning. Trying to be polite I get up from the table to pretend check on bacon I know is not ready. After she has her mental morning reenactment of mischief, Ms. Vivian relights the conversation. "So anyway, he said that he will install them in the tent if we want."

"Ummm hmmm, that would be wonderful." I whisk the batter for the French toast and get my skillet heated on the stove.

"And he also said that he could hook up an AC unit for that tent, so we won't be so hot that sweat starts to drip down the crack of our asses."

I smile. "The threat of a sweaty ass crack is nothing to mess around with. I watched a documentary on TLC and it said that ass crack sweat is the number one deterrent to getting married in the summer. And seventy-four percent of all wedding planners agreed. That is some scary shit"

The fumes of sarcasm coming off me are overwhelming the aroma of breakfast food, so much so that Ms. V doesn't know whether to laugh or choke, instead she lets out a sound that sounds like the worst of both worlds. Silent at the most opportune times, Drian just sits there staring up at the ceiling trying to stifle his soft chuckle.

"Nila..." Drian's mom tries to calm her fit of amusement, and waits until most of her calm is restored before she continues. "Nila, girl you are crazy. And that's why I like you."

I take her compliment in stride as I beat the eggs and look to see if my toast needs to be flipped yet. Knowing that everything is almost ready I decide to make a request of my fiancé.

"Drian can you start setting the table please, sir?"

"Yes'm, I's get rite on dat, missus." He sounds like a janky Morgan Freeman.

"What I wanna know is, why would ya'll decide to get married on the Fourth of July, any dang way?"

My soon to be mother-in-law's question stops me from flinging a spoon at Drian for sassing me just seconds ago.

"Mom I told you that day is special to us."

'Yeah, but you never said why it was/is."

I turn my head just slightly in the direction of my left shoulder. I'm grateful that my back is to Ms. Vivian so my facial expression can't betray my thoughts, Drian on the other side is not so lucky, out of that head turn I see that he's face to face with the woman who gave him life, those Bambi orbs piercing one another. Vision is always 20/20 in your third eye and that's what Vivian is looking at Adrian with right now I can feel the scorch of them burning a hole through one another with their eyes. She wants a truth he's not ready to tell. He wants her to stop asking about what happened on the Fourth of July that soldered us together. Drian and I almost lost our lives on that day of independence--almost a year ago.

"Okay Baby Ade, I give up." Those six words bring their ocular contest to an end.

Anxious to cool the room down from the heat generated in the staring contest, I lay out platters of eggs, French toast and bacon on the table. With mother and son seated I grab hot sauce and syrup before I proceed to sit down.

"Where's the OJ?" One of the Bambi eyes asks.

"Damn!" I snap. "Knew I forgot something." I get up from the table and grab the Simply Orange Juice with Mango from the fridge and head back to the table. On my next to last step, a knock sounds at the door. I look at Drian, and he looks back at me, then we both look at Vivian while she stares at the both of us. Perplexity abound, I set the juice down and decide to make an executive decision.

"I'll get it. You two go on and eat before it gets cold."

The knocking sounds at the door again as I have my hand on the handle, yanking the door open I see a pale White man in a yellow golf shirt, tucked into his khaki pants. The man is not very tall, maybe five-five he has a slouch in his posture that makes him look shorter and blonde hair only on the sides of his head. The combination of those things make him look older than he might actually be. I put the over-under for his age at about thirty-five. Annoyed with for him interrupting my impromptu family breakfast I elect to use one word to determine the reason for this stranger's visit.

"Yes?"

"I am looking for Yenila Montgomery?"

"She is I, right before your eyes."

The admission makes his head cower; he makes to reach in his back pocket and extracts a manila envelope that he hands to me.

"What is this?"

"Congratulations, Ms. Montgomery, you've just been served."

Despite his shell of appearance, the pale man is gifted with nifty speed as he makes it off my porch and halfway to his car before I can slam the door in his face.

CHAPTER 3

I tuck the envelope under the cushion of my zebra print chair, and try to think of a believable lie on my way back to the kitchen.

"Don't tell me it was one of them Jehovah's witnesses again, baby"

"Okay I won't tell you." I let Drian assume my way out of a lie. The truth of hunger rattles in my belly as I reclaim my seat at the table.

"I hate them damn Jehovah witnesses." Vivian bites down on a piece of bacon. "Them jokers goin' bum rush me one time when I was in the bathroom at a King Soopers, while I was in the gotdamn stall!"

The retelling has her so animated that Ms. V shoots a spittle of bacon on my table. Drian sees the projectile and damn near chokes trying not to laugh. After a sip of juice, Drian's mother is ready to resume her rant. "But like I was saying, I was in the stall TCB'n it and I see a hand come under the stall with one of them lil' Watchtower pamphlets attached to it. And I'm thinking what in the hell? Then this lady goin' ask me if I was prepared for Jehovah's return, I was like, 'Heffa! Are you prepared to wipe my ass, 'cus that's the only thing I can do with that pamphlet right about now.'"

Tapping all my resolve, I manage to not spit juice all over the table as I start to crack up at Ms. Vivian. "Whew! Ms. V, you is something else, you almost made me spit out my beverage!"

"Uh huh, don't put that on me, honey. Blame it on Jehovah!"

"Oh, so you Jamie Foxx now huh, Ms. V?"

"I wish I was in Jamie Foxx right now?"

"What?!" Drian exclaims.

"Oh, I did not mean to say that out loud. My bad ya'll, please continue with this tasty breakfast my future-daughter-in-law has made for us." Sidestepping the comment altogether and needing no further instruction I reply with a nod and dig into breakfast to help quiet the baby tiger like roar circulating through my stomach. Masticating on my sweet, salty and smoky bacon, I feel a set of eyes on me, that are waiting for me to finish chewing so I have no excuse not to answer the question the brain attached to those eyes has in mind.

"Say Nila, how do you do it?" Ms. Vivian delivers the question I knew was coming.

"Do what?"

"How are you able to be so hands off, to a degree about your wedding?"

I put my fork down and push my plate away, realizing at this point it's just not in the cards for me to enjoy an undisturbed breakfast this morning. Drian reads my expression, gets up from the table, puts his dishes in the sink and heads to the master bedroom. I take a deep breath before responding.

"With the work that I do as an event planner, I have a very consuming yet fulfilling job. I spend so much time doing for others that I told myself that if I got married, I would do the least I possibly could, I'd let others do for me. So, when you, my mom and Clarice stepped up and wanted to be in charge of planning, it was like God came down from heaven."

"Amen!"

I smile. "Hallelujah, baby!"

It's funny how life work out sometimes, I always wanted to get married; I came close a few times, but never got to the planning stages. And when ya'll called me and said ya'll was getting married, my first thought was happiness. My second thought was hoping that you would let me help plan the wedding. When you told me and your mom at that brunch that we could plan it how we wanted it, I thought you was BS'ing, but here we a few days from the wedding and up to this point Drian has been more involved in the planning than you."

I run my fingers through my mane before I glibly reply. "I know that's right."

"Nila I just wanna say..."

I am certain she finishes her sentence and starts another one because I see her mouth continue to move at a sluggish pace. Thing is, I selected to tune out her words for a more predominant sound; water. Specifically, a pulsating water stream, the kind that hits the fiberglass that most showers and bathtubs are made of. Drian is in the shower, which increases the likelihood that he is getting ready to leave. I'll be damned if he's gonna leave me here alone with his mother. Now is the time for me to make my escape route.

"... almost died."

"Almost died?" I repeat the two words that distract me from my route and pull me back into the chair that sits across from Ms. Vivian.

"Yes ma'am. I almost died having that boy." She pauses to unlock the vault where her most valuable memories are stored. "Adrian was my firstborn child; I had a miscarriage with the baby before him, so I was excited and grateful that he made it to term. I was in the delivery room all nervous and whatnot so my mama had

19

to come and hold my hand through the whole ordeal. Especially when they gave me that epidural injection; it hurt like hell but once it kicked in, I was in a lovely mood. I'm pushing like a bodyguard trying to get two fat, drunk chicks out of the after-hours spot. It got to a point where all I was doing was pushing and squeezing; I like to break my mama's hand as hard as I was squeezing. Then splat! Baby comes sliding out. The nurse gives 'em to me after they cut the cord and wiped him off, I tell you that boy was so precious, yeshewus!"

Those last few words made the new mommy in her come leaking out again as she rambled in that baby talk jargon, adults speak to kids with. Wanting to hear the rest of her tale, I tap on the table with my French tips to get her to come back to the moment. She shakes before she realizes where she is. Surroundings recognized, Vivian dabs at her eye and resumes her story.

"Anyway, I give him back to the nurse so they can take him to the nursery. By this time my sisters, aunts and even my brother had shown up to see the baby, you know. They were all in the hallway waiting, and when they see the nurse come out of the room with the baby they all follow her like she's Moses. Meanwhile I am in the room dazed and blissful at my accomplishment; my mama said I had done a real good job, and that made me proud. Then the doctor comes in and says it's time to deliver the afterbirth. I was confused by what he meant so I looked at my mama and she smiled and told me that it was normal, it was nature's way of tidying up my womb, so it be ready for the next baby if I want another one. So that made me calm, the doctor told me to give a big push, and he'd tell me when to stop. With my last bit of strength, I push using every fiber in my body, then he yells stop after we hear a big splash on the floor like somebody spilled a pitcher of water. I had stopped pushing when he told me to, but the splashing noise was still going on. He asked me if I had stopped pushing and I told him I had. I look at him and there is a panic in his eyes; he gave me the kind of look told me something was wrong, but he didn't want me to panic. I look at my mama and her lips are curved into a smile, but her eyes have the same look as the doctor's. In a nanosecond, my hearts starts beating rapidly; I am starting to go into shock because the splashing noise is still there flowing as heavy as Victoria Falls. By now the doctor has his whole arm in me all the way up to here."

She points to a space a little bit above her elbow, just below her bicep. I didn't feel it but my mouth must be agape because Ms. Vivian touches me under the chin indicating that my trap is wide open. I close my jaw, swallow my spit to moisten a throat that has gone dry and adjust in my chair anxiously awaiting the conclusion of this story.

"Last thing I remember before I lost consciousness was the doctor yelling about substantial blood loss, and my mama cussing. That's when I knew life or death was in the balance because I ain't never heard my mama cuss before that day ain't heard her cuss since. By the grace of God, I woke up and my mama was on my right and Adrian was in a cradle on my right. Adrie is my miracle baby; I thank God for him helping to make me whole."

There is a question on my lips that I want to ask Ms. Vivian, but I withhold the inquiry because I don't want to spoil the joy and peace that has come over her. Together we sit in a silence that is peaceful, each of us drifting on our own thoughts. A chair rattling against the floor interrupts the solace. Great excitement washes over Ms. V as she flails her arms and leans toward the bag with the fruits on it.

"Ooooh ooh, Nila, you almost made me forget I got one other thing for the wedding." Ms. Vivian ruffles through her bag and produces a cluster of cylinders that look like old time sticks of dynamite, with wicks sticking out of the top. There are six cylinders clustered together, alternating in color from red to white then blue. The clusters are banded around the middle with a shiny silver plastic that is affixed to a latch that is in the shape of a star covered with red and blue rhinestones. My soon to be mother-in-law hands the object to me.

"Ooooh now what is this?"

"Open it."

I turn the rhinestone studded handle and the cylinder pops open like a treasure chest. In one half of the cylinder is a picture of Drian and I that we took specifically for our wedding photo shoot; in the other half of the cylinder encased in foam padding are two water pistols. One is translucent blue with a white handle; the other is a red translucent pistol with a white handle with my name inscribed in red cursive lettering. Peering down at the blue and white pistol I see Drian's name written in the same fashion. Holding the plastic toy, I think about what happened the last time I held a pistol; someone wound up getting shot twice. I am equally moved and suspicious about the memento, it's either one hell of a coincidence or the shade tree has come out to cast its shadow.

"This is really unique and beautiful. Where did you get the idea from?" I opt for neutral flattery, as to not give her any subliminal fodder.

"Well since you wanted pastel colors for the wedding I figured we needed something to pop, since it's the Fourth of July. I was at Hobby Lobby and I saw these and the idea just clicked, we could give these out as a keepsake, you know. These cylinders look like big firecrackers and then kids love water guns and whatnot."

"Ummm hmmm, you right." I'm unable to detect whether or not she is being transparent or if she knows more than she's saying.

"Hey, what ya'll doing?" Drian returns to the kitchen showered and dressed in a pair of navy blue pinstripe slacks, a crisply ironed white dress shirt and as he comes further into he's putting on the Michael Kors watch I got him for Christmas.

"Oh, we were just talking about the wedding and a very interesting story your mom told me about the day you were born."

He turns to face Ms. Vivian before he speaks. "I see you telling the 'I almost died giving birth to Drian' story again. Mom I swear you find any excuse to tell that story."

Ms. Vivian stands up and wraps her arms around her only son's neck and says. "That's 'cus you my miracle, baby. I am just thankful for you, that's all. Is that so horrible?"

"No, it's not." He replies in a soft voice.

Manipulation is a subtle instrument and Ms. Vivian plays it like a master bandleader pulling at Drian's heartstrings like Geppetto does when is still his puppet Pinocchio. I have a bile like taste developing in my mouth from watching their interaction. Reaching for a reprieve I decide to interject in the show they have on display.

"Hey baby you dressed up all fancy like. Where you going?"

"Well I guess I better get going too." Ms. Vivian interrupts before Drian has a chance to respond to my question, jealousy is dripping from her tone.

Drian stands between us, blocking my view of her eyes. I can still feel the holes she is trying burn into me through Drian's flesh and bone.

"Well, lemme walk you out, Mom."

Ms. V grabs her bag and turns toward the door; she stops suddenly, steps around Drian and extends her arms to me. She hugs me close and I reciprocate the embrace. There is a tension in the kitchen, but my heart is determined to keep the peace with all that is swirling my family and soon-to-be family as well. She sheds our embrace and her and Drian head for the door. I stand in the kitchen for a moment to get my wind. Looking down I notice the table filled with dirty dishes. I make up my mind to wash them right now so I won't have to worry about it later. I pick the littered plates off the table and drop them in the sink; as I am going back for the condiments I hear a voice ring out.

"WHAT ARE YOU DOING!?"

I rush to the front door and stopping short I see two police officers have cuffed Drian and pinned him on the wall to the left of our front door.

"Mr. Yancy you are under arrest."

"LET HIM GO!" Vivian yells at the officer attempting to advise Drian of his Miranda rights.

A burly armed officer glares at her. "Miss, step back or you will be placed under arrest too!" I grab her by the bicep and pull her close to me.

"They not goin' Eric Garner my boy!" Ms. V shouts to whoever is listening.

"Shhhhh." I say as I hold her near. "I need to hear what I can hear."

She understands my meaning and her mouth closes accordingly. As she quiets down the burly armed officer restarts. "Mr. Yancy you are being placed under arrest for kidnapping and violating an order of protection against you. You have the right to remain silent.. . ."

My ears fade to the rest of the Miranda rights, as my eyes pick up on a silver Corolla parked across the street, and the woman leaning with her backside on the driver's side door. I'd recognize that squared chinned Scocchie if I was blindfolded. The officers begin to lead a behind-the-back handcuffed Drian to their squad car. Before they get off our driveway, I yell out. "Drian, I got yo' back."

He turns only his head to me while staying in stride with the officers and responds. "I got yo' front."

The trio makes it down to the cruiser and race off down the block. The worthless excuse for a human being smiles like the gremlin she is, while her gaze remains fixed on me. A bit of time passes before Vivian catches on to what I'm starring at, when she realizes who it is two words spew off her lips.

"That bitch."

"A bitch would be a step up for that bottom of the barrel slop faced wench."

The scallywag stands stoic for a few more seconds, projects an acid like spit in our direction, hops in her raggedy Corolla and speeds off in the opposite direction of the police officers. Vivian and I stand on the porch glaring across the street long after Drian's baby mama departs.

"What are we gonna do, Nila?"

"What needs to be done."

CHAPTER 4

L ocks and latches clicking intermittently are about the only sound rattling through the holding lobby at the Aurora Detention Facility. The lobby is only slightly bigger than two jail cells put together. The dingy room is sparsely furnished with two small round metal tables with benches affixed to them. The table and benches have been spray painted with a bright orange color that is starting to fade in various spots. Along the periphery of room are five chairs, Forrest green in hue and made of plastic. Looking down at the floor I don't know if it is a light beige or just dirty. Without question this room has been painted with a somber tone from the day they laid the first brick. The incarcerate drone of the locks and latches engaging and disengaging echo through the hollow lobby. The sounds serve as a constant reminder of freedom capsized by a sea of criminality. Confined behind this intricate maze of concrete and steel are a slew of individuals who picked the wrong answer in the game of life. More than a trivial pursuit the offense was significant enough that the wheel of misfortune sent them straight to jail; where only face cards with dead presidents can purchase freedom. The stench of an institution crushing basic human needs permeates the air; the janitorial crew attempts to cover up the stench with a steady supply of pine oil and sawdust, but the miasma is too powerful.

I hear the echoing sound of dress shoe soles coming down the corridor that leads to the pungent room that I'm sitting in. After ten or so paces, the feet stop in front of me. My attorney Robert Bland appears, adorned in a pair of black ostrich square toe dress shoes, that are part of his obsession with non-leather shoes.

I rise to greet him. "Robert."

"Nila, it's a pleasure to see you again."

I slip out of his embrace and turn to my left. "Mr. Robert Bland this is Ms. Vivian Yancy, Adrian's mother."

"Nila I wish you wouldn't start off our meeting with such a lie. This lady couldn't possibly be Adrian's mother; she is too youthful looking to have full grown children."

Ms. V laughs in a way I've never heard before, like her coochie is one doing the laughing and her mouth is the conduit for the sound. Robert takes her left hand in both of his and kisses it slowly and gently. This elicits another laugh from Drian's mother. Even if he's not trying, Robert can be smoother than satin. Robert chose one of the few careers that aligns ideally with his Type A personality. With charisma and charm more polished than the Hope Diamond, Robert Bland is the ideal litigator. He is intelligent and ruthless enough to cut through legalese with the craft and precision of an instrument created to slice through the hardest material known to man; a diamond. Since only diamonds can cut diamonds, I laud Robert for helping to keep me sharp, since day one.

We met when I had just started at Tyson Taylor's as a receptionist. That first week, instead of hitting the ground running, I hit the ground and face planted into the law firm of Bland & King. At the time, they employed a paralegal by the name of Arthur Ruxby, a persistently annoying human being, driven by his insecurity to be perfect in every area of his life. Ruxby worked exclusively with Robert as his aide, doing a variety of work for him even though his official title was a paralegal.

My first week working at Tyson Taylor's correlated with the organization and planning of Miss Kiffinie Bland's wedding, nine months in advance. Kiffinie is Robert's middle (and I suspect favorite) child. The first fax and email I received on that first day of work were from Arthur Ruxby; both transmissions arrived within minutes of one another. One minute after the fax and email arrived, my phone began to ring. Imagine my surprise when I picked up the receiver and Mr. Ruxby was on the other end asking if I had received the correspondence, and if so why had I not responded.

I advised him that the communications had literally just arrived in, that I was in the midst of reviewing them, and that he would receive a response shortly. I will never forget his reply. In a semi-British accent, he said, 'You need to learn how to anticipate water before it gets wet and plan thereupon.'

I thanked Arthur for the advice and severed the connection before he could utter another word. I sat there at my desk and contemplated quitting for a fraction of a second. After the fraction became a whole second I took a deep breath and got back to what I was getting paid to do. Over the next nine months Arthur and Kiffinie were like two ten pound twins, tussling in a womb designed for none. Working with them galvanized my desire to do as little work as possible when planning my own wedding; after those nine months, I was all planned out.

About a week before the ceremony Robert came to the office to visit with Mr. Weldon Taylor, co-owner of the company and a client of Robert's. That day I was sitting at my desk trying to look like I was working even though I had drifted off into a daydream. Robert strutted out of my dream and into my office, wearing a nice charcoal grey suit with a pastel pink dress shirt that was open at the collar. His hair was sandy brown with traces of gray back then. His mane was parted at the side and slicked back with pomade. Tall, White and handsome would best articulate what I thought when I initially laid eyes on Robert Bland.

He walked to the front desk, put out his right hand and I gave him my left. He kissed it gently and said he's here for a meeting with Mr. Taylor, in French. I responded in the same language and an impressed look lit up his eye. He assumed my panties would melt with that hand kiss and a few words in a foreign exchange and he was halfway right; our exchange did make me a little moist and very fond of him since that day.

When he and Mr. Taylor concluded their meeting both men came out to the lobby and Mr. Taylor properly introduced me as the woman who survived the experience of Arthur and Kiffinie. The words make the three of us chuckle and opened the gate for a business relationship that has been invaluable to this day. As difficult as it was for me to accept, Arthur Ruxby was right. My success at Tyson Taylor's has hinged largely on my ability to foresee inevitability and adjust to a new normal. Not long after the wedding, Arthur suffered a massive stroke at the age of 27, literally almost working himself to death. I heard he spends most of his days at an assisted living facility, trying to re-learn basic human skills. For reasons that only he truly knows, Robert continues to pay for Arthur's residence at the assisted living facility and his private physical therapy treatment. Given his career choice Robert has a relatively stout moral fabric, remaining loyal to people that are loyal to him.

"Robert, dial back some of that silver fox charm, and give me the nitty gritty."

He relinquishes his grip from Ms. V and turns his attention to me, adjusts his pocket square and motions for the two of us to join the already seated Ms. Yancy. I occupy the orange bench opposite Vivian and while I wasn't looking Robert manages to scoop up a chair and seat himself. Once we're situated he pops open an aluminum attaché case, from this he pulls out a tablet, which he hands to me. I scan the screen for less than a minute, finding no new information on the screen I turn my attention back to my attorney.

"How much is his bail, Robert?"

"$10,000."

"You still use Gigi for your bonds?"

"I do, but Mr. Yancy's has already been paid."

"By who?"

The lawyer sits all the way back in his chair, interlocks his fingers behind his completely gray head of hair and looks at me. The smile never leaves his lips.

"Bland, Robert!" An authoritative voice yells from behind plexiglass welded into a cage. The attorney leaps from his chair to answer the call from the authoritative voice.

Ms. V taps my elbow and asks. "What my baby done got himself into, that he done landed in jail with 10,000 dollar bail?"

I consider telling her about the events from last summer, but then I remember she is not my mom and I don't owe her an explanation. Sometimes in life even when we don't owe, we are still held liable for deeds past and present. Standing on the verge of being intertwined forever, I know Drian's problems, are my problems too. Well aware of the worst-case scenario I opt to make a deal with my soon to be mother-in-law.

"Ask Drian. If he doesn't tell you when you ask him, then I'll tell you what you wanna know."

Sated by the offer, Vivian's shoulders descend slightly. The gesture indicates she will accept the only offer that will get her close to the destination of truth she relentlessly desires.

"Ahem." Ms. V and I turn and focus our attention on the attorney. " His bail has posted and he is being processed out now."

Ms. V perks up. "How much longer we have to wait here?"

"In here? Not much longer; when he is processed out, he will come from the back entrance of this building, so if you'd like we can leave now and go wait in the car."

Ms. Vivian doesn't even let the last syllable fall from Robert's mouth before she slides off the metal bench, stands firm on two feet and holds her arm out for the gentleman to pick up. The pair latch arms and start to walk down the corridor towards the exit. Five paces pass before they realize I am still left on the bench.

"Nila? You coming?"

"Yeah, I just need to go to the restroom real quick."

"We'll be with Maurice in the maroon Tahoe out back."

I let out a wordless grunt as I sprint toward the restroom to signify that I heard the words being said to me. Entering the bathroom, I am surprised at what I find, or rather what is missing. Absent is the putrid stench of the slow disintegration of human will. The bathroom is relatively odorless, devoid of the aroma of piss and shit that tend to dominate a crevice like this. The serenity of this restroom is starting to conflict with chaos in my stomach.

Momentum forces me to my knees, gravity leads me to the toilet, violence explodes from my stomach and out of my mouth as I vomit up what little breakfast I had, and the significant amount of alcohol I consumed last night. Spitting out bile while still hunched over the commode, I feel enough composure to make it to the sink about six inches to my left to wash out my mouth. I take one step and retch angrily in the space between the sink and the toilet; except for my ears fluid and regurgitated contents are spewing from every hole in my face. Through a teary gaze, I see a paper towel dispenser with the words "Fuck Da System" written on the side in green marker. The rebellious vandalism makes me laugh all the way down to my pinky toe. Coursing back up the laugh turns to agony in my belly as I find myself leaned over the porcelain making it rain acid.

CHAPTER 5

"May I get the four of you anything?" I hear a female voice ask.

"Can you bring me a ginger ale on ice, please?" The words come out in a rush as I recline with closed eyes on the chaise lounge in Robert's office. Committed to a horizontal position, I struggle with each breath to keep the contents of my stomach where they belong.

"I'll have a water, please." Drian calls out.

"Me too, please." Vivian seconds the notion.

"The usual for you Mr. Bland?" I assume Robert nods his answer because he doesn't speak a word until the door to his office opens and closes.

"All right now that the refreshments are en route, let's get down to what we came here to do. Mr. Yancy will you explain in your own words why they would arrest you for kidnapping and violating an order of protection?"

The attorney in Robert frames the question. I can only see the back of my eyelids, but I know Drian's body language well enough to know how he is squirming like a worm at having to respond. If it were just three of us in this room, my fiancé would be more willing to articulate the issues at hand. The addition of a maternal variable is complicating this equation.

"Drian, baby..." A knock at the door halts my groggy voice.

"Come in." Robert commands.

I feel a presence coming toward me, I tell my body to sit up, but it ignores the instruction. The aide must be feeling my vibe because she serves the other three first then circles back to me. "Okay, I have a ginger ale for the young lady."

I tap my reserve strength to sit up to receive my beverage. "Thank you." I mumble as I grab the carbonated beverage in a crystal glass off a silver tray. If I ever make it off this couch my goal is to make enough money to live like Robert. I hit the first swig of ginger ale and it sizzles in my stomach like drops of water on a hot frying pan. The nausea seems to have subsided, so I drink a little more of the refreshing beverage.

"To answer your question, Mr. Bland, the story of why I was arrested today, stems from events that happened almost a year ago."

Watching Drian from the comfort of the silk velvet on the chaise lounge I see him start to sputter at first, the emotional unpacking a bit too heavy. When he lulls for too long, I clear my throat loud enough for him to know what I mean without having to say a word. He looks to his left, shoots me a "shut the hell up" glance and repositions himself in the burgundy coaster chair he is sitting in. I see that Robert's face has a stoic cast, as if he were sitting before a judge and jury. I shift my glance to Ms. Vivian, who is turned in her chair so she is facing Drian, her eyes glued on him like a kid watching Saturday morning cartoons on television. At his own pace, Drian restarts the retelling of events that took place on a summer night, many moons ago. Weaving his way through verbal traffic, his conversation is moving like a well-oiled machine. Drian is so busy cruising that he doesn't notice that his mother is the only person actively engaged in his anecdote. Robert has heard the most relevant parts of this story a few times over.

Half listening, I fade in and out of Drian's version of events, since it's a tale I've heard more than a few times as well. I slide back into the soft silk of the lounger, put my feet under my butt and sip casually on my ginger ale to keep my mouth from interrupting, before my boo has completed his purge. I am waiting for him to expel the reason that we are all gathered here in Robert's office today. A gurgling in my stomach further tunes out the redundant conversation. There is a burning sensation behind my navel and acid in my throat. Move legs! I knock over my drink on the way to the washroom in Robert's office. Turn handle, turn! The fight with the knob almost suffocates me. Ugggggggggh! most of my stomach contents make it into the brass wastebasket inside the washroom, on the right wall.

What is going on with me? Pregnant? No, can't be. Well maybe I could be. I knew I shouldn't have let that boy skeet off in me, when we went to New Orleans. Too lazy to get a condom, my ass! Too slow to pull out is more like it. Hol' up tho, I think he let off up in me last night, too! That's why my pussy felt some kinda way this morning, had all them semen swimming in my ocean. Could I have gotten pregnant that fast? No. When was the last time I had my period? Last week? Week before? I honestly don't remember. Stop with the shenanigans!

Yenila you are not pregnant, girl! How do you know? How else you explain all the vomiting and dizzy spells? Stomach bug. Yeah that's it maybe something I ate. Damn Ethiopians and their delicious cuisine. Okay girl, let's get together, wash out your mouth and fix your face. Ready? Good, let's go. I feel all eyes on me as I step out of the washroom, close the door behind me and strut towards the Victorian gold trimmed chaise. I don't see the glass I knocked over and I'm in no rush to find it. The struggle is to get comfortably seated, with eyes still glued on me. I want to ask them to carry on with the conversation but I'm afraid that if I open my mouth, I won't be able to stop an unwanted unknown from leaking out. I'm also worried about vomiting all over the place too.

"You good, baby?"

I make a sound while barely opening my lips that sounds close enough to the word yes for the three of them to stare at me a few seconds longer.

"As you were saying Mr. Yancy." Robert cuts the staring fest short. I hear the gulp of swallowed spit before Drian responds. "Somehow the video of the explosion rescue went viral and a few days after that happened, Angela put a restraining order against me, barring unsupervised contact with Adrianne."

"And Monday was my grandbaby's birthday." Ms. V's words answer part of the question rolling through my mind.

"It sure was. My baby turned five on Monday. I have yet to miss a birthday, so I went to her daycare on Monday and pulled her out for a few hours. The two of us went to Monkey Bizness, ate pizza and went toy shopping."

Drian's voice is cracking like the faults that sometimes separate cement. To see him vulnerable like this is an anomaly like the rose that grew from concrete, except Drian's heart is being pricked by thorns. If baby's hurt, then Momma hurts too. His sighs are her sniffles. She grabs him by the hand and gives him her strength to continue. "It was either the people at the daycare or the doll I let Ajae keep that spilled my secret. Knowing Angela like I do, I knew this could come back on me. But I love my baby so much that the reward outweighed the consequence."

"Well, the kidnapping charge is a pipe dream, since you took her back to the daycare, so the violation of a protection order is our only real problem."

The professional side of Robert is loath to deal with emotions, avoiding them like a friend who owes you money. "As of yet, my office has not been notified of any hearing on your behalf. With the weekend of independence on the horizon, I don't believe the legal system will be in any particular rush to hash this matter out. Mr. Yancy it would be in your best interest to abide by every single law, to the letter. We don't want to give any legal authority the ability to capture your freedom. As you well know, it is easier getting into jail than it is to get out, especially on a holiday weekend."

"In that case," I pause to find my balance before I get off the couch. "Since the four of us are free, three of us have work to do outside this office."

"Indeed, I almost forgot about the wedding this Saturday."

Ms. V bats her eyes at Robert. "Will you be in attendance for the nuptials, Mr. Bland?"

"Most certainly, knowing the two of them, there will be fireworks on display, well before a single wick is lit." The esquire chuckles heartily. Vivian swats him playfully, as she laughs from her coochie again. Drian quickly turns his back on the two of them and walks to me. I make it off the lounger, but I'm still feeling dizzy and unsteady on my feet. Wobbling like a bowlegged toddler, I loop my arm around my man's waist, as we drift in the direction of the door

"Nila, you looking pretty bad right now. I think you should go home and get some rest."

"How bad I look?"

"Bad enough to turn ugly into beautiful, because that's what you look like right now."

"Shit, if I can do that then wait until you see me turn wine into water."

"I've seen your water show before; the live version almost drowned me."

"I just wanted to see how long you could hold your breath underwater for, sweet cheeks." My whole midsection is on fire as I begin a giggle that quickly escalates into a laugh. The amusement is literally side-splitting as pain starts to rattle my ribcage. The laughter is torture, but the pain hurts so good I just keep on chuckling at memory of my late-night waterworks anyway.

"Mom, we'll be out in the car." Drian shouts over my ruckus.

"You two go on, I think I'ma stay here with Mr. Bland."

"Mom, you know this man is probably busy and don't have time to be bothering with you." Drian turns toward the two elders in the room. Both my arms are wrapped around his torso, while I let my head peek out from behind his left elbow.

"Mr. Robert Bland, am I bothering you?" Vivian's tone is sweeter than a bag of jellybeans.

He adjusts his posture minutely so that he is inches away from my fiancés mother. "Not yet."

"See, Adrian? I am no bother."

"Mother I am certain that you have a lot of planning and loose ends to finish up before the wedding don't you." I feel a chill come over me after Drian's words to Vivian. The chill turns to ice as she stares at her only son like he is a bouncer that just denied her entry to the club because he said she looks like a hippopotamus in a dress.

"You two go ahead, I'll be down in a minute. I just want to say goodbye to Robert if that's all right with you Adrian." Her tone is flatter than Miley Cyrus' backside and her eyes are still locked in on her firstborn child. Drian spins abruptly, almost knocking me over in the process and attempts to separate Robert's office door from its frame while storming out of the room.

"I'll call you later Robert." I say, before I exit in the space that Drian left open.

***

Drian barely gets outside before Vivian lashes out at him. "Boy! Have you lost your damn mind?!"

"Me? You need to check yourself. What the hell was that up there all up on that man like that? You just met ol' boy."

'Did I Adrian, did I? How you know I ain't been knowing Robert for years?"

"I know who you know, Mom."

"What all you know, ain't all there is to know."

We must be at a red light or a stop sign. The forward momentum of my car has stopped. I hear the two of them sucking up air like a fat dude up a flight of stairs. In the space where they're not arguing, I take notice to how smooth and comfortable the back seats are in my Tesla. I'm half tempted to be sick more often so Drian can chauffeur me around while I lay back and relax on Italian leather. The car starts to move again, and so does Vivian's mouth.

"Mama got needs, baby. I ain't got nobody, tryna marry me or be with me. If I want a lil' attention, a lil' TLC from a man with a JOB then that's just what it is."

"Don't start with that BS, mom. Please don't, you raised me to act like a man about all things, so I'ma need you to be a woman and a mother above all else."

"Drian you ain't my gotdamn daddy! If I wanna flirt I will flirt. If I wanna take a guy home with me tonight, then that is Vivian Yancy's bizness!"

"Mom you kn--"

"STOP! The both of you, please just shut the hell up. ya'll givin' me a headache with all this bitchin' and arguin'." I interrupt, sitting up in my backseat. I have enough chaos inside of me, that I don't need it all around me.

"Who the fuck you think you talking to?" One of them says.

None of us have a chance to respond before Drian slams on the brakes to avoid hitting a father and his young son. The man looks at the three of us before he scurries across the street half dragging, half carrying the child. Rotating my head, I see that we are two lefts and a right away from home. I bite my tongue, making no move until we pull into our driveway. Everyone remains silent until Vivian bursts out of my Tesla and power walks to her automobile. She doesn't pass go or collect two hundred dollars- she just jumps into her Ford, turns the engine over and speeds off down the block.

After helping me out of the car Drian walks straight into the house without saying a word to me. I see him drop my keys on the table before he heads to the basement. I go to the medicine cabinet in our bathroom, down some Pepto Bismol, brush, floss, grab my keys and make a beeline for the door; away from the chaos, or with my fortuity right back into it.

.

CHAPTER 6

Commitment is sanity for a relationship. Commitment keeps you from doing things that society would label deranged or insane. Commitment is a controlled rage, smoldering low and slow like white hot coals on a barbeque grill. Frustration in a relationship will flare up from time to time. Flames of insecurity, jealousy and foolish pride can set even the strongest relationship ablaze and engulf any hope of what was to be, leaving instead the ashes of a lost opportunity. Commitment kept me from following Drian to the basement just so I could cuss his ass out and exacerbate the situation. Commitment has been a catalyst for my maturity; a younger Nila would have doused the situation in gasoline, got all up in his space telling him how wrong he was, just so I could feel right and feed my ego, but sometimes you got to let go like an Eggo. Commitment is tantamount to love on my list of priorities. They both intersect when I have to make important decisions. Asking Drian to marry me on the fifth day of July last year was the most vested decision I have had to make as an adult. I have never loved anyone with my whole heart before Drian came along. Life will sometimes get you to believing that closing of a part of your heart, mind body and spirit will allow more space allotted for love. But that's a lie; a heart is a house for love, and sometimes you got to leave the door open to let love come on in.

A sharp ringing seeps from my purse, pulling me from my thoughts. I decide to call whoever it is later and let the phone ring until it's finished. I head into my office and see a familiar face.

`"Good afternoon, Ms. Clarice." I greet one of the few people in my life who is a river of calm when the tide is determined to turn.

"Afternoon, young lady. I sho' was not expecting you around here today."

"Oh yes you were, otherwise you wouldn't be sitting there doing that crossword puzzle book."

Since Clarice was hired by and works only with me, if she knew I wasn't going to be here, then neither would she. Less than a year ago God put Clarice in my path when I went to breakfast at a Waffle House. Her skill set and personality led me to offer her a job, right then and there. I hired her to work exclusively with me here at Tyson Taylor Enterprises. Officially she gets paid for being an executive assistant at this event planning and management organization. Her real job is to be my gatekeeper, the first line of defense in keeping the unknowns out of my drama-free zone. I was promoted about eighteen months ago and in all that time I never had a full time assistant. I was either stupid or extremely productive, probably a little of both. Life here with Clarice has allowed me to feel comfortable delegating and trusting that the work will get done.

"Well miss missy, we gettin' pretty close to that knot tying time, how you feelin'?"

I laugh for a good minute straight while Clarice stares at me with intrigue and bewilderment. Once the guffawing stops, my conversation starts. "Whoooo! Lady Reese, let me tell you this morning has been so busy, the last thing on my mind has been some daggone weddin.' Aww shucks I've been around you so much, that I am starting to talk like you!"

"Welp, Suggafoots with as reckless as yo' mouth can be at times, talkin' like me ain't the worst thang evah happen to you. Give you a touch of class." She holds her pinky upwards as though she is sipping tea.

"Classy with a C or with a K?" I let the sass drip in my tone for Lady Reese.

"Girl gone now, get to yo' office, an' lemme finish my crossword." She shoos me away with a folded over puzzle book.

I turn and start to my office door before I let a teaser drop. "Oh, so you don't wanna hear 'bout my morning now? Hmmm all right guess I'll just mosey on to my office then."

"Now, now hol' on juss a minute, I may have a moment to hear a few thangs."

The gossip fiend called me back for her fix. I slowly saunter over to Clarice's solid oak desk. If you had an overhead view you would see that her desk is custom made in the shape of a capital C. Before she would come to work for me, she fleeced me for this desk. She said more than anything she wanted a big ol' desk to sit at because it makes her feel important.

Her desk is so large we had to bring the pieces of oak in separately, then construct the desk in my antechamber. Soon as it was completed, Clarice went to work decorating it. The space that she does not work on, is piled with knickknacks, dolls, blocks with sayings on them and her highly cherished collection of snow globes. Twenty of them line the frontal outer edge of her desk. Traditionally that's the place where a client would sit, but since she doesn't want anyone near her snow globes, there is no other chairs at her desk aside from the high-backed throne she sits in. I am grateful she was gracious enough to have a cherry red stool placed behind her desk if I want to sit out there and talk to her for an extended period of time. I was perched on this stool when she told me about her obsession with the globes. Clarice told me she started collecting them when she was a teenager as a keepsake from a family vacation to California. Today I sit here and get ready to tell all my business, expression by confession. If there was a piece of particle board between us, she would be the priest and I the wayward wretch.

"Now is you goin' sit there like a bump on a lump or is you goin' give up the funk?"

"What!?" I can feel my eyebrows crease from confusion.

"You been sittin' there with this faraway look in yo' eye 'fo 'bout five minutes now. Come on with the tea, girl."

I take an extra deep breath because I know I'm going to be talking for a while. I tell Clarice about almost everything that happened this morning; I leave out the part about being served until I can talk to Robert and see what's what. Towards the end of my tale, Clarice is sitting there with both hands on her chin in marvel like a fat kid at a candy store window. She almost has a heart attack when her desk phone starts to ring.

"Hello." She answers in her most professional tone.

"Who? One moment please." She puts the caller on hold and turns to me "They say there is a gentleman named Evander Wiggins, at the front desk for you."

"Did they say what he wanted?"

"No."

I stand there and try to think if I had any appointments or meetings scheduled for today, but I can't think of any. Still drawing a blank I tell Clarice. "Have them send him back. When he gets to you, have him wait two minutes out here and then bring him to my office."

She nods and says. "Yes ma'am."

I hop off the stool and head towards my office. At my office door, I put in the pin code that only Clarice and I know and head inside, I am alarmed and intrigued by the gift bag sitting on top of my desk. I want to look in it, but the male voice talking to Clarice out in the waiting area reminds me that I don't have the luxury of time to investigate. I turn on selfie mode on my phone to check my face and hair, I am not wearing makeup and my hair is slicked back in a ponytail, but I check to make sure I still look professional. I have on a sleeveless skater skirt, which is coral colored at the top and fades to turquoise towards the bottom. I accessorized the dress with a pair white and coral flats. Appearance approved, I hurry to take a seat behind my desk, to make sure the visitor knows who is in control.

As soon as my cheeks hit my seat, Clarice comes knocking on my door, she waits half a second before turning the handle. She walks in before the gentleman and ushers him to one of the two white leather swivel chairs that sit in front of my desk. I stand up to greet my peanut butter colored guest, before Clarice introduces us.

"Ms. Montgomery, this is Mr. Evander Wiggins." She bows slightly and then walks out of the room with military precision. As the door closes me and my peanut butter complexioned guest take our respective seats. My unknown guest is of medium height with bold facial features, thick eyebrows and a beard so black and lush that I have to restrain myself from reaching out and touching it. The black beard is in contrast with the hair on his head, he is mostly gray with a patch of black in the front. His hairline is just beginning to recede, but his low fade does a good job of camouflaging nature. He has on a linen two-piece walking suit covering his starter beer belly. The outfit is canary yellow with a red and white argyle print on both sides of the center row of buttons. The linen two-piece is something that Drian would look in, I think to myself. He carries himself with the bravado of a man that is still young and handsome, even though Mr. Wiggins is closer to old and bloated

"Mr. Wiggins, how may I be of service today?"

The man shifts over to his left side and grabs a Smartphone from his right pocket. After unlocking the device, he taps on it a few times, then hands the device to me. I look at the screen showing images of a box of chocolate bars that kids would sell for a fundraiser.

"Mr. Wiggins, did you come here to give me a craving for chocolate?"

He smiles. "Keep scrolling."

Thumb scrolling the phone I see more pictures of food, popcorn, candy, toffee. All of these pictures have the confections glamorized in a way that would make a person tempted to buy them. Viewing the sugar sweets has put a rumble of hunger in my belly; the feelings of nausea have disappeared. Hungry as a hoe in front of a plate of ham hocks, I hand the phone back to my guest, more curious then annoyed. The rumble in my stomach asks. "What can I do for you, Mr. Wiggins?"

He leans forward in his chair and pauses for a minute before replying. "Sheila McBride."

I let the name process for a second before I recall that Clarice and I planned Sheila's wedding a few months ago. My eyes tell him that I recognize the name.

"I went to Sheila and Thomas McBride's wedding earlier this year and I was impressed thoroughly by the way the event was coordinated and organized. The wedding presentation was top shelf."

"Are you thinking of tying the knot, Mr. Wiggins?"

"Oh, no." He chuckles. "Been there, done that and don't wanna go back. I am here today because of the pictures I showed you. I work for the company that manufactures those items and then sells the stuff wholesale to schools, churches, boy and girl scouts and so forth. Me and the reps at my company work hard almost year around and I wanted to have an event to honor and recognize their hard work and effort."

I let my head bob up and down in admiration of Evander's efforts. "Well, Mr. Wiggins when did you plan to have this event?"

"In September. It's the slowest time of year for us, before business ramps up again."

I look and see that my laptop is not on. I search my frosted glass desktop for my notepad and jot down the particulars that Mr. Wiggins has given me.

"All right Mr. Wiggins, do you have a preferred time of month, beginning or end of September?"

"Does not matter to me."

"Okay, got it. Well Mr. Wiggins after today I will be out of the office for about a week, but when I get back, me and my assistant will get started on this."

"Wonderful!" He claps his hands together. "Are you taking an extended Fourth of July holiday?"

"I wish." I say as I peel from my chair. "I'm actually getting married this weekend."

Evander's eyes widen at my proclamation. "Really? Well let me be the first to congratulate you on your nuptials."

"Why thank you, sir." I pull my office handle at the last word and hold my hand out for the gentleman to follow. Back out in the waiting area Clarice is sitting upright and alert at her desk, with the puzzle book out of sight. Clarice is a master at code switching when we have company. If Mr. Wiggins had been able to watch us on unknowingly from afar, he wouldn't believe that the Clarice that sits before him is the same woman.

"Ms. Clarice, can you collect Mr. Wiggins' contact info and give him one of our cards please?"

"Yes, right away."

I extend my right hand to Mr. Wiggins to bid him adieu. "Thank you for stopping by, Mr. Wiggins. May our partnership be as sweet as sugar."

"I expect nothing less." He laughs at my pun and offers a firm handshake. As I release Blackbeard's grasp, a knock sounds at the door. I look at Clarice in mystery; her eyes tell me she isn't expecting anyone. I affirm using just my eyes and go to answer the door. Standing on the other side of the threshold is a tall brown skinned man with a mustache and triangle shaped hair under his lip. He has on a navy blue pinstriped suit with a white shirt and a navy and white houndstooth tie. There is a red rose pinned in the left lapel of his suit jacket. He holds a derby hat in his left hand; the lid has a dark blue band around it with a gray peacock feather coming out of the side.

"Detective Nash-Cunningham, to what do I owe the pleasure of this First of July visit?"

He stands there with a smile that could illuminate the ball that drops in Times Square on New Year's Eve. His lips never touch as he asks. "A moment of your time, please?"

CHAPTER 7

"**I**t's Lieutenant now, actually."

"Pardon Monsieur, mes excuses."

The newly minted Lieutenant looks at me like I am a foreign exotic animal that he didn't believe existed. His face of confusion at my reply amuses me greatly.

"Well, Lieutenant I think I may be able to squeeze you in. Step into my office please."

I slide out of the way to let the officer of the law cross my threshold. The lieutenant enters with a slow stride, unsure of where to go. He looks to his left and, tips his hat to Clarice and Mr. Wiggins. Clarice nods in kind, while Mr. Wiggins has his posture semi-turned away from the lieutenant.

"It's straight back, the door at end of the hall." The lieutenant resumes his stride in the direction of my office door. I turn to Mr. Wiggins one final time, shake his hand and thank him for stopping by. He nods, and then quickly scurries out the door. I ask Clarice to bring me and my guest some water, as I head down the corridor to investigate the reason for the lieutenant's visit.

"Det— excuse me, Lieutenant please have a seat." I politely order the lawman. Frank Nash-Cunningham takes up residence on my L shaped black and white couch. I purchased this particular couch because it reminds me of my favorite cookie–an Oreo. The couch resembles an Oreo with the top cookie twisted off, leaving only the white sweet cream filling on top of a chocolate cookie bottom. The lieutenant reclines with his back to the window, derby resting comfortably on my oval coffee table composed of smoked glass and elephant ivory. I sit in the same chair that was most recently occupied by Evander Wiggins. For a while there is no vocal exchange between the two of us. I sit, wait, and practice my virtues. In my practice, I see that the lieutenant's gaze has drifted to my flesh. His eyes are on my legs in a manner that is less than conspicuous. I let the lieutenant's eyes linger at a Promised Land he's never going to get to for about two more seconds before I make a quarter turn in my swivel chair. Abruptly his eyes stop on a dime, his full attention is on me, from the neck up.

"While I can't blame you for wanting to soak in all this fineness up close, I know you didn't come all the way down here for that."

After my last syllable, I hear a noise that sounds like a chicken clucking, I rotate my chair left to right searching for the source of the sound. Not finding a henhouse or any chickens I look directly at the lieutenant. In the split-second it takes my eyes to catch up with the speed of sound, I confirm the emission is coming from Frank. I've never heard him laugh before; his vocal amusement catches me by surprise. He carries on that cackle to the point that tears begin to well in his eyes. I clear my throat, attempting to get him refocused on why he is here.

"All right," He waves his hand left to right. "Ms. Montgomery, I thank you I sure needed that laugh."

"I wasn't aware that I said anything that was comical."

"And your obliviousness is what made the comment all the more amusing." He chuckles some more. The taps on my office door put the lawman back on alert. Three seconds later Miss Clarice enters the room with two bottles of Voss on a stainless-steel serving tray. She hands the brand of water that is reserved for special guests to me and the lieutenant.

"Can I get ya'll two anything else?" The waitress in Clarice asks.

We both respond in the negative and the ageless woman bows before us and departs my office, closing the door behind her. "Lieutenant Frank Nash-Cunningham, why are you here?"

He takes a long drink from his mineral water before answering. "The state of Colorado vs. Tyrrell Ramirez-Williams."

The sand in my throat lets me know it's my turn to take a long swig from a bottle of water. I am focused on the wetness of the water until the lieutenant picks up again. "He is set to go to trial in August or September. I am here today to inform you that you are on the witness list. The state of Colorado will request a deposition from you to get you prepared to testify at Mr. Ramirez-Williams trial."

I decide to cut in to clear my confusion. "Wait, around the time that this happened me and my attorney came in and gave a written statement and everything already. Why do I have to go through this again?" The question brings the lieutenant to the edge of my Oreo sofa. Frank leans forward, elbows on top of knees, hands contorted in the space between his pinstriped slacks.

"What you gave us last year was a witness statement, which is common for the witness to a crime. The deposition is a much more invasive exercise. It's like playing a game of tennis; except you are the ball and the lawyers are the rackets. That's why I came here today. The official request for a deposition has not been handed down to your attorney yet, so I came to give you a heads up."

"I see. The events from last Fourth of July netted you some clout and a nice lil' promotion there, Frankie Fantastic." If the Detective promoted to Lieutenant's eyes were fire, this office would be up in smoke after my remark.

"Heaven forbid, I actually did any police work before you and your fiancé fell into my lap on a Fourth of July."

"Lap, huh? At least that explains why you act so stiff every time I see you."

I decide to throw a little kerosene on the blaze. The July heat has gotten the better of the lieutenant. He downs what's left of his water and makes it to his feet. Snapping the lapels on his suit, he looks down on me like he wants me to beg him to stay, or ask him not to leave at the very least. I intend not to comply with either telepathic request until an inquiry hatches in my mind.

"How do you know Drian is my fiancé?"

With his back to the window, the smile on his face is gargantuan enough to eclipse the sun. "You think I worked my way up to where I am now, by not keeping my ear to the streets? Nowadays ya'll make a police officer's job real easy with all the stuff ya'll post on social media."

I smile. "You been Facebook following me, Lieutenant?"

"Not at all. I am still on good terms with Adrian's aunt and she was the one told me about the engagement. Which brings us to the other reason I am here."

He reaches into his jacket, pulls out a manila envelope and hands it to me.

"What is this?"

He smirks. "A wedding gift. On that note I shall depart, since I know you have a wedding to get ready for in a few days."

The lieutenant picks up his derby hat as he begins a slow stride to my door.

"Frank?"

The lieutenant only turns his head and neck in my direction. "Yes?"

"I wouldn't be upset if you came to our wedding."

His smile says more than words ever could as he turns the handle and walks out of my office.

When the hinges on the door tell me it's closed, I tear open the "wedding gift" envelope from Lieutenant Nash-Cunningham. There are only two items inside the envelope; one is a photocopy of a Denver Post article dated April 2, 1982. The other is a sticky note with an address scribbled on it. After reading the photocopy, I have enough puzzle pieces to make a phone call. The phone rings four times before he answers.

"Hello."

"Hey Robert, it's me." I set the envelope contents aside, remembering something I left on the back burner.

"Nila, you feeling better?"

"Yes, remind me not to mess with that Ethiopian food no more."

"Will do. How can I help the soon to be married woman?"

"Uh, I just got a visit from Lieutenant Nash-Cunningham. He wanted to warn me that a deposition is coming down the pike for me."

I lean over in my chair to pick up the gift bag that was sitting on my desk when I entered, determined to do two things at once.

"I see the seeds planted from last July 4th are starting to bear some unwelcome fruit."

I pull out a card taped to a box covered in cream wrapping paper. "Indeed, just call me Nila Appleseed, because I am about to running things from the root to the fruit."

Robert's laugh is a boisterous thing, rich and smooth like dark chocolate.

"You've been doing that since I met you. Without question, you are one of the most take- charge people I know." Looking at the unwrapped gift, joy floods my body and soul. I am happier than a professional athlete who just received a negative paternity test result for a child consumed with a mistress.

"Nila? Hello, Nila?"

"Yeah, sorry Robert I am still here just taken aback by some of the pre-wedding generosity. Speaking of which, the reason I called you is because I got served this morning with a lawsuit from a Hortense Dewart."

"Who?"

"Some more fruit from the Fourth of July tree. On the day that everything went down with Drian last year, earlier in that day I got into an altercation at a Walmart with an ol' decrepit scallywag. No charges were ever filed so I thought the ordeal was dead, until I got that notice this morning. Guess the bitch need money for some Polygrip or something. I wanna wrap up this issue with this ol' Mother Hubbard broad sooner than later."

"I take it you want to settle out of court. Which is a smart move, albeit pricey one too."

"Yes, Robert I do. Now if I can play the cards in the right order, I don't see this costing me a dime, unless you goin' bill me."

"Nila, you know the struggle is real, so I just might have to."

The comment catches both of us at the right time and we get to hootin' like the audience at a Def Comedy Jam.

"Seriously though, I am going to send you an email with a couple attachments that I'd like you to look over so we can strategize. I'll stop by your office in the morning if that's all right."

"Anything for you, Nila"

"Goodbye, Mr. Bland." I break the connection with a single finger and a smile. I then brace for the intrusion. Ten seconds later Lady Reese comes rushing into my office.

"Ooooooh honey, that was a tall glass of sweet tea that just left here!" She exclaims, voice soaked with infatuation.

"He make you wanna take a sip, huh?"

"That man there make me wanna take more than a sip, baby! He handsome enough to make me want a big gulp."

"Welp Reeses Pieces, if you want we can have us a double wedding on Saturday."

She flicks her wrist dismissively before she snaps. "Oh no, Suggafoots! I married one man and when he died, all he left me was alone."

"Was he a rolling stone?" I ask innocently.

She cuts her eyes so fiercely that they could slice through solid steel. I smile and blow her a kiss as I move the gift bag to the side and hold up the small box that contains a Fitbit. She shrugs her shoulders like she has no idea what is in my hands. I keep looking at her, she remains unmoved. I get up from my desk and creep towards her; she crosses her arms against her chest. By the time I wrap my arms around her, she explodes with laughter.

"Thank you Reese's Pieces! I love it." I plant a kiss on her cheek as I remember something else. "Oh yeah! I see the lil' bit of shade you put in that card! I need keep my PHAT ass in check huh?"

"IF and I do mean IF you blessed to get to my age and you don't got a rump in the front then you be thankin' me, for my advice."

"Yeah, yeah, yeah." I snap as I let her out of my embrace. Excited like a kid on the last day of school, I start to tear into the Fitbit packaging until the sound of chimes and bells rings in the air. I grab my cellular from the desk and answer once I see the picture on the display.

"Hello." Annoyance dominating my voice

"Yes."

"When? Uh, no. Fine. Leaving now, I'll be right there."

Borderline pissed off and absolutely inconvenienced I end the call and shove the phone in my purse. Staring straight ahead I let my neck move in slow motion, stirring up the chaos in my cranium.

"Is everything okay?"

"You know Lady Reese, I don't know. But with my luck today I doubt it."

CHAPTER 8

The driveway is empty; that means Daddy's not here. I think about tapping on the horn twice but Mommy Nomie raised me better than that. I turn off the engine and sit in my driver's seat focused on my breathing. Smooth breath in, smooth breath out. My energy is unbalanced; after dealing with that fiancé and his mother. The steady depletion of my spiritual and emotional resources is starting to drain my reservoir. Note to self: go to YogaPilates class before the wedding.

With as much calm and composure as I can muster I exit my vehicle and head towards the house I grew up in. I follow the concrete path framed with lavender tulips planted on the left and fuchsia orchids planted on the right. The path leads to a white security door I know is unlocked. Turning the brass handle on the security door, I pull it open while pushing on the oak and glass front door simultaneously. Once over the threshold, I step into a home that is cool and fragrant with aromas of vanilla musk and honeysuckle. Stepping into the house I hear an unfamiliar sound under my feet as I notice the carpet has been replaced with hardwood flooring. I scan the foyer for any other changes, noticing none I look up at the half spiral staircase that once lead to the bedrooms that me, my siblings and parents used to sleep in. With the nest free of chicklets, only the hen and the rooster sleep up there now. Hungry and impatient I call upstairs for the woman who I had to pass through to get here.

"Mommy! Where are you?"

Receiving no answer to my call. I walk through the hallway connected to the foyer that leads to the kitchen. Starvation leads me straight to the fridge. Rummage do I through the appliance for something I can eat relatively quickly; with the way my stomach is feeling, I could devour a whole honey baked ham right now.

A voice sounds behind me. "You ain't gonna find much in there Nana Puddin. You know me and yo' daddy is on a diet."

"It's cool, I'll eat some of this lunch meat and this tangerine." I say to the inside of the refrigerator.

"Well get it and come on, I wanna get there 'fore they close."

I grab the foodstuffs, close the fridge and turn to see a reflection of myself in the future; Mrs. Nomie Montgomery. When Tupac mused that we all came from a woman, got our name from a woman and our game from a woman, he was talking about my Mommy Nomie. Of her four children, I am the only one that looks like her. Our skin is the color of apple butter, a dark brown with auburn undertones. We have eyes that are set deeply in our face, brown like pecan pie—giving the outside world a glimpse of sweetness they won't find anywhere else in the universe.

Celebutantes have spent a workingman's yearly salary for lips as full and robust that Mommy Nomie and I were born with. If it wasn't for braces in my teens I would have the same gap that helps lend character to her smile. She will swear before a grand jury that she is fat, while she is not as thin as she was when she was my age, she is nowhere near fat. Age has molded her face into a rounder ball of clay, her cheeks are a little chubby after sixty years in the game and she has a small tummy on her; but I know plenty of men outside of Tuskegee Montgomery (and some women too) who think she look good enough to sop up with a buttermilk biscuit.

"What?" I have no inkling of what was just said.

"I said, are you gonna stand there all day or are we allowed to leave yet?"

"You look nice today, Mommy." Flattery is always the best distraction.

"You think so?" She does a short runway walk, with a backwards hair flip at the end. Honestly, she does look very pretty today. The shimmery sequin red tank top she has on match with the red disco ball earrings pinned in her lobes. The reddish highlights she has in her light brown mane add layers of style to her look. She opted to rock a pair of white shorts with red, white and blue gladiator sandals to bring the ensemble together. If nothing else my mother will never lack style.

"Iight Mommy I's ready. Where we goin' again?"

I hear her sigh and see her shoulders shrug mightily from behind; she doesn't even turn around when she mutters. "Stonebrook Manor."

"Oh! Okay. That place is nice."

I see her auburn and brown hair shake in slow motion as she opens the front door and heads out to the July heat covering the nation. She doesn't say another word as I follow behind her in the direction of my Tesla. When the door handles on my baby slide out slowly, she lets out an ooooooh la la type of noise at the futuristics of my automobile. Driver and passenger aboard, seats buckled, GPS programmed and air conditioning on full blast. Mommy Nomie waits until were on the highway before she begins her inquisition.

"So tell me how do you do it?"

"Do what?"

She pops her lips together before she replies. "How have you managed to be so disconnected from planning your own wedding?"

The deja vu feeling from her question sends a chill to my toes. I switch lanes and speed up on a slow-moving minivan before I respond. "In all realness Mommy, I spend most of my time catering to other folks—planning their weddings, bar mitzvahs baby showers etc. I told myself I was goin' kick off my shoes and relax my feet for my wedding, and let ya'll have the headaches."

"I see you meant every word too. Here we are a few days from the nuptials and the groom, the mother, mother-in-law and Miss Clarice have been more involved in the wedding planning than the bride has."

I take my eyes off the road to look behind Mommy Nomie's head and neck area. When I don't see what I was looking for, I take my right hand off the wheel, using it to fondle the same area I was just gazing at.

"Girl!" Mommy Nomie giggles. "What are you doing?"

I take my hand from her neck before replying. "I was looking for the pull string in the back because I wanted to pull it to see what you was goin' say next?"

"What I look like, some ol' Chatty Cathy doll?"

"I'ont know you lookin' kinda snuggly like Teddy Ruxpin from where I'm sitting. But you and Ms. Vivian have asked me almost word for word the exact same thing today."

"When did you talk to her last?"

"This morning/afternoon, she came by to show me some icicle lights; then we had breakfast and ran some errands with Drian."

Mommy Nomie nods as she says. "Good, good. I was hoping she would find those lights it is going to make the reception room real pretty."

"That reminds me, who is catering the food, Mommy?"

Even with both eyes on the road ahead I can see the light of my mother's smile. Radiance is shining through her gap tooth grin, a grin that is traditionally for when she has important or exciting news, with commotion cocooning today's events I am wrapped up in the rapture of ambivalence. I have a subdued anxiousness about what is liable to come out of her mouth next. I cut eyes in her direction and she pops like a water balloon.

"All right, all right you remember that man you used to date back when you had first started college? Tall, handsome fella that me and your daddy really liked."

"You mean Lee."

"Yes, Lee. Well actually it's Papi now. He changed his name, he such a sweet man..."

"Mommy!" I snap at her to keep her from rambling about my past lover.

She clears her throat, regaining decorum with the gesture. "Okay so a few weeks ago I saw him when I was shopping at Sam's Club. We started chattin' and I found out he has a catering business called Table Manners. And since we were still looking for a caterer, it was fate that I ran into him. He gave me one of his cards, a few days later I called and set up a tasting session for me, Vivian and Clarice. Nana Puddin' the food was exquisite, top notch cuisine. I teased him saying that he never should a let you go." She laughs at the memory. "The ladies made me hire him right on the spot in exchange I made them promise not to tell you who was catering.

Absurdity stitches my words together. "Let me get this straight. You contracted my ex-boyfriend to cater my wedding?"

"Partly."

I smash my hands into the steering wheel. "Partly? What do you mean by partly, Mommy?"

"I can't change the history between you two." Her tone is calm and even as she senses the agitation in my inquiry. Breath drawn through her nose exits her mouth and more words quickly follow. "But I always liked Papi; you know that. From where I sit, I'm helping a young Black entrepreneur out there trying to get his piece of the pie."

"A la mode, indeed."

Mommy Nomie laughs at my pun even though she is trying to maintain an air of seriousness in the confines of my Tesla. Swallowing the amusement, Mommy Nomie moves forward. "Since you have been an absentee bride you haven't been privy to all the details and goings on 'roun this here wedding. But another reason I chose Papi was that he fit within the confines of our budget. Everybody else I talked to wanted Michelle and Obama inauguration dinner type prices. Ain't nobody got money for all that. You know me and yo' daddy on a semi-fixed income."

Never one to argue with financial responsibility I nod in solidarity as I prepare to get off I-25. The curiosity in me asks. "What is on the menu, anyway?"

"Ooooooh! Nana Puddin' we is goin' have a five- I say five course meal. For the hors d'oeuvres we are having bruschetta crostini topped with fresh mozzarella. Italian wedding soup to follow then, watermelon, feta and blueberry salad. The main course will be lamb chops roasted with garlic and rosemary, or wine braised boneless beef ribs. Both will be served with cheddar and garlic mashed potatoes, asparagus and broccoli."

"You just made my mouth moist." Slurping excess saliva confirms the diagnosis. "Yep, I do believe I just had a foodgasm."

"Honey, you and that mouth and the things that fall out of it. I swear, I don't know what to do with you Nila."

I offer no response at Mommy's remark. Instead I find a space in the lot, put my vehicle in park, unfasten myself and go around to the passenger side and open the door so she can get out. With her two feet firmly planted on the hard pavement, Mommy and I stand eye to eye. I extend my right arm bent at the elbow; Mommy Nomie loops her left around mine. We stroll silently arm in arm until fear sends a shockwave rippling through me.

"Mommy?"

"Yes."

"How is goin' look with my ex-boyfriend even being at, let alone catering my reception? On a day that is dedicated to me and my husband."

Her feet stop moving as she turns to look at me. "I may be frugal but I'm no fool. While the vows are taking place Papi and his crew will be at the Manor in the kitchen, getting things set up and ready. He will have all the food mostly prepared before he departs. The head chef at the Manor will add the final touches and the wait staff will do all the serving, thus ensuring that never shall you two meet."

Feeling satisfied, we resume our walk about ten feet from the solid glass entry doors two gentlemen dressed like bellhops come out and hold the open for us using the chrome handles welded into the glass. Heads held high, smiling at the servants five feet away, I whisper to Mommy Nomie while smiling like a ventriloquist.

"Are you sure we can afford this?"

"Is water wet?"

***

"Hey Mommy, you wanna come with me to Miss Clarice house for an impromptu wine and cheese tasting?"

"Don't you think you should have asked me that before you pulled up in her complex?"

"I didn't want you to think you had a choice."

I laugh as I get out of the car and open her door before she has a chance to blink. The parking lot at Clarice's apartment complex has been recently reconditioned the asphalt has been sprayed with a coat of black, yellow lines placed on top of the black define parking spaces. The ground is still hot even as the sun starts to set, while not overwhelming the aroma of melted tar permeates the air. From the parking lot to the sidewalk me and Mommy Nomie cut through the man-made grass field on our way to Clarice's apartment.

The field has a built-in sandbox, where a few kids have Jimmy rigged some orange plastic mesh to a pair of metal poles for a makeshift volleyball ball court. "Hotline Bling" by Drake plays on a Bluetooth speaker in the background while the kids compete furiously on the sandy court. I am semi-surprised to see kids outside; playing around doing what was once commonplace among youth. As society is becoming increasingly dependent on technological interaction as the new normal. Face to face interaction for the fun of it; is becoming rapidly obsolete. Kids and teenagers are so busy on Instagram straight flexin' or doin' it for the Vine; that they don't even notice that they are being passed by mankind. The evolution will not be televised, it will be tweeted, retweeted, liked, snapchatted and live blogged until it goes viral. The observation sticks with me all the way to Miss Clarice's doorstep. As I prepare to knock the door swings inward.

"Nila!" A young voice screams.

"Hey Camiko! How is my little buddy?" I grab Clarice's grandson in an embrace.

The eight-year-old wonder beams. "Good, I'm beating Grandma at Uno." Relinquishing my hold on the child, I venture further into the domicile with Mommy Nomie close behind. The living room in Clarice's two-bedroom apartment has more colors than a jumbo box of crayons. Vibrant and bold shades dominate a room that is an assault on the environment.

Clarice designed the room to make the conceptual come alive. The whole room feels like a kaleidoscope with retina display. The eye snatching centerpiece of the space is a fire engine red couch sitting at an angle to the right of her fireplace. To the left is a banana yellow loveseat with matching ottoman. Centered between the loveseat and couch is a rug designed to look like the Twister mat, except instead of circles all the individual colors are in the shape of a square. On top of the rug is a rectangular coffee table painted sour apple green. The table has white marble top and extractable drawers on all four sides. Sitting on top of the marble is a cobalt blue vase that resembles and upside down spade. Inside the vase is a rainbow of fresh flowers designed to look like the real thing.

Like a lot of older Black women I know, Lady Reese has her lifelong collection of Jet magazines neatly organized on the white marble. I am so captivated by the assortment of colors that I don't even feel the lady of the house standing next to me. The chill on my left elbow turns me slightly; a complete rotation puts me face to face with my executive assistant. She is holding two glasses of wine that she hands me and Mommy.

"I see you got my text." I say behind a smile.

"Yeah I was just 'bout to text you back and tell you I ain't have no cheese, but by that time you was already at my do'."

"Guess I'll just have to make do with this here Asti."
Letting the spirit touch my lips.

"I am sho' you will." She nudges me to the left with her
elbow. "Hey, hey, hey! Nomie, come on ovah here and hug my
neck girl!"

They both laugh as they embrace and almost instantly start
cackling like two long lost friends on a midnight train to Georgia.
Tuning the volume of the ladies down, I begin to look at all the
artwork Clarice has on her walls. Most of it is abstract and filled
with colors that match her living room theme, but there is one
piece over the mantle of the fireplace that is extremely unique.

"Hey, Grandma say I am gonna be the ring bearer at your
wedding, Nila."

"Is that so, Mr. Camiko?" I reply as I turn away from the
mantle. "Looks like you got a pretty important job there."

The child nods while pulling from behind his back a small
orange pillow that he places what's left of an already eaten ring
pop on.

"You goin' show me your skills, huh?"

Instead of answering, the kid walks to the front door; stands
facing me with both feet together and perfect posture, proceeds to
march toward me like a soldier fresh out of boot camp. Head held
high, chin up, the kid is confident in his stride. When he stops and
stands before me arms at his side, pillow extended I set my wine
down on the marble, pick up the ring pop and put it on my finger.
Two magic words drip from my lips at the boy standing in front of
me "I do." I giggle as I kiss the cutie on his cheek. His face turns
almost as red as his grandmother's couch.

"You bettah watch out there, Miko; that's a almost married
women you pushing up on." Lady Reese calls out. The three

women in the room start to howl, the child in the genius is smart enough to escape the tomfoolery as he scurries off down the hall towards his room.

"Dang! Reese's Pieces, you done run off my backup husband!"

"Backup? If you wanted a backup husband, you can have that handsome tenderoni when Miss Clarice get through with him."

"Tenderoni?" Mommy Nomie perks up.

"Oh yeah. Nomie! She had this fiiiiiiiiiine young thang stop by the office today; that smile hmmph! Made me almost call the fire department, 'cus I about burn up in my chair that man was so hot to trot." She starts to fan the flames wafting her non-wine hand back and forth.

"He was that handsome huh?"

"I swear before a grand jury, my sweet Jesus and the congregation of First Church Nothin' But Da Truth that he was! He was a tall sip of tea, fine like Billy Dee in his Colt 45 days."

"Ooooooohweeee!"

One of the women lets out a real live squeal; until today I thought only pigs did that. Then again with the way they are carrying on, I can't tell the difference.

"Now lookie here, you ain't even married yet and you got yo' mistress coming down to yo' office, hmmph hmmm hmmm." Mommy shakes her head in slow motion.

"Iight, you." Pointing at Clarice. "And you." Pointing at Mommy Nomie "Let me be clear, I don't have a mistress, because that would make me lezzbun and I don't have a man on the side either. The man Lady Reese was referring to is an old friend of me and my fiancé." After laying down the law, I take a long sip of Asti, emptying the glass.

"Uh huh." Comes from Clarice

"Old friend." Mommy chips in. I ignore the both of them and head to Reese's Pieces fridge for some more of this delicious Asti Spumante. Returning to the living room, I see the two women divided between the couch and the love seat. Wanting a little more room, I join Reese's Pieces on the couch. My mind and mouth decide it's time for a question.

"Lady Reese is that you in that painting on the mantle?"

She slaps my knee as she says "No, no honey that is my Mama, I had this picture of her from when she was a little girl that I took to a painter I knew and he turned her into the work of art I always knew she was."

Clarice is right the portrait is breathtaking as it depicts a chocolate skinned woman wearing a white gown, in moonlight holding onto what looks like a glowing, mound of fire. Inside the mound is the earth. The woman has her whole world in her hands.

Mommy studies the picture. "Is she still living?"

"No, she done gone home to live with Jesus and watch over me." Her words make all of us take a sip from our glass.

"Matter fact it's 'cause of her I am her I am here, well her and my grandbaby that just ran away. When she died some years back, I was livin' in Shreveport, Louisiana while her and the rest of my family lived in Dallas. One June morning I got a call from my brother Tavis telling me Mama wasn't doin' too good and I should come see her. I didn't pay Tavis no mind 'cus he was always makin' things worse out then they really was and me and her wasn't on the best of terms anyhow. Later on that week, she died of cancer. When I finally made it back to Dallas for the funeral, Tavis gimmie this letter he say she wrote on her deathbed and I remembah it said, don't be like me, forgive your daughter and make peace. I cried like a rat eatin' a raw onion when I read that letter an' I promised myself I would try to make things right with my only child. I seen my baby girl at the wake an' I pull her to the side and tole her how sorry I was for doin' her wrong and she said she was sorry too. We cried and hugged and cried som'mo."

She takes a deep breath. "Then I moved back to Dallas to be closer to my family and my daughter; things were good after that. Got me a good job, got closer with my baby and even found out I had a grandchild. I was the happiest I had been in a long time. Then one weekend my daughter asked me to babysit Miko 'cus she wanted to go to some music festival with some guy she met. I agreed because Miko was a sweet, well behaved child and I loved him."

She draws a deep breath at the memory; her left knee is trembling slightly. On the exhale, she soldiers on with the story. "When the time came for her to come get him, she never showed. I called in to work that day and went around lookin' for her, couldn't find no trace. I called her, no answer. I called everyone I knew that she was friends or close with, no answer. After calling her for the third straight day from work, I filed a missing persons report. As of today, she still missing. I know in my heart and in my spirit she's not dead, but I don't know where my only daughter is. An' Miko ask 'bout her all the time and I tell him Mama be here soon baby. But he smart, he kno' bettah."

As the tears start to leak, Mommy puts her glass down and wipes Clarice's face with her hands. The gesture makes the former Waffle House waitress cry even harder as she collapses into Mommy Nomie's arms. Not wanting to drown in the river of tears I get up and head to the dining area which is about ten feet away from the couch. On the table is my purse, which I dig through looking for the pack of tissues I keep in there. After extracting the paper cloth in plastic wrapping I walk over and put a couple sheets in Clarice's hands.

"Heaven knows I didn't want ya'll to see me crying like this." She pulls herself from Mommy's arms.

"You all right, Clarice. Them tears is just life letting you know that you are alive and living, instead of just existing. You have a pain that I can't even begin to imagine. And when that love and that hurt you carrying start to overcrowd each other, love is the one that starts to flow freely because love isn't bound my any structure and you can't confine it. When you embrace the fact that love can set you free, you will realize that you can hurt. But you won't hurt forever cause you get so used to that pain, that after awhile it don't hurt no more; and that's when the healing start."

Mommy's words act as a balm, trying to heal pieces of a heart that shattered long ago.

Squeezing Mommy Nomie's hand in a gesture of gratitude, Lady Reese starts back up. An "Ah." escapes her before she starts to dab at her eyes. "After I couldn't find her, I made the decision to get me a fresh start. I remembered I have an aunt and a few cousins that live out here, and I figured this place was as far from Texas as I was willing to go. I came to stay with my aunt 'til I could decide if me and Miko was goin' to move here for good. After being here a few months, I started to like it here and then one day a little lady came into my job at the Waffle House and changed my life. Through the redness of tears her eyes manage to smile at me.

"God is good." Mommy testifies

"Amen." Clarice seconds the notion.

"Hallelujah! Now Lady Reese can we get some more communion up in here." The lady in the house hops off the couch to grab the three of us some more libations. Waiting for her return I decide to text Drian and see about him, in the few minutes it's taking her to return, Drian hasn't responded; I assume he is still upset. Letting alcohol be the grand distraction, I sip and laugh through the night as the seconds, minutes, hours tick away.

One of the Golden Girls speaks up."Oh, Lord it's after ten o'clock. Ooh it is past my bedtime."

Just like Pavlov's dog the other one says. "Me too."

The three of us prepare for two of us to leave. The two of them find it's hard to say goodbye as they stand holding hands, whispering inebriated words of encouragement to each other. While it's hard to say goodbye, it's easy to drop the mic and walk off stage. I grab my purse and head out to my car; outside in the dark of night the stars are shining brightly. In contrast, I am tipsy and full of dread about going home and having to deal with on the rag Drian and the chaos that has underlined our day. Maybe I should suck him off, make him forget about those other 99 problems. Feeling freaky like Adina, I call my fiancé deciding to be a dick tease. No answer, I call again, still no answer. Before I can call a third time I see Mommy Nomie standing outside the passenger door. I flush out the door handle so she can get in. Slightly off balance, she gets in, and starts feeling around the edges of her seat aimlessly before dozing off. I remain silent in the night as I drive toward my childhood home for the second time today.

As I drift into her driveway I gently nudge the sleeping beauty. "We home, Mommy."

Without a word, she unlatches her seatbelt, sits up straight, leans in and puts her wet lips on my cheek for a loud smacking kiss.

"Be safe, baby." She exits the Tesla. I watch her frump to the door and damn near fall in the house. I throw the Tesla in reverse, turn on 105.1 to hear some throwback jams and burn rubber down Mommy's block. I'm out of her neighborhood rolling up Chambers when Mr. DJ starts playing "No Scrubs"- the right song at the right time. I turn the volume up and let the windows down, *"Hangin' out the passenger side of his best friend's ride tryna holla at meeeeeeee!"* Hitting high notes like T-Boz and Chilli is not in my arsenal, but sweet baby Jesus knows I'm trying as I sing towards the heavens. I serenade to the soul of old school music until I pull into my driveway. Once in the house I see that it is dark and devoid of sound. I call out for my fiancé, no response. I fumble through the darkness to the bedroom, muscle memory leading the way. I cut on the light and see nakedness sprawled over the mattress. A laugh escapes me as I see that Drian forgot to put the sheets back on our bed. I slide on to the bare bed, letting the pillow top rub against my skin. After rolling around for a few seconds, I find comfort lying on my back with both hands interlocked behind my head. The house is quiet and peaceful, I wallow in both, as I feel sleep start to catch me.

CHAPTER 9

"**A**ll right, all right gents, if I may have your attention please." Says a giant man in a white suit. The gathering of men continue to chatter aimlessly, joking and taking swigs from a handle of Black Velvet whiskey that is being passed around. Noting his proclamation is being ignored the large man in the white suit slams both fists on a green felted hexagonal table. Poker chips, scatter and fall off the table, some of the chips hit concrete and make an echoing sound in this basement like dungeon. The commotion in the room ceases almost instantly. Every man at the table turns his attention to the Hercules donned in angel white. When the room is as silent as it's going to get the man-bear growls.

"Iight Mothefuckahs! Listen up Goddammit! Dis here ain't no bootleg, poot butt ass spot, dis' here is a classy after hours joint."

"If it's so classy why don't the bathroom have a do', nigga?" A man named Jasper yells out.

"Cause ya'll niggahs steal, especially you niggah." The giant says while pointing at Jasper. "Niggahs would take the white off rice, if ya'll could get away with it."

The raucous laughter circulates around the basement once more, at the truthful giant's observation. There are twelve of us so-called "niggahs" in this basement, well fifteen actually if you count the giant dressed in white, the bartender and suspect looking security guard.

"Is it possible to steal the white off brown rice?" A high yellow man named Ernie asks.

The man mountain lights a cigar. "Fuck you, niggah!"

"Speaking of taking off, hey tell yo' wife to take some of that hair off her pussy, so next time it don't get caught in my throat!" Caldwell Cornelius shouts to the giant.

In unison the twelve of us "niggahs" howl out. "Oooooh! Got 'emmmmmm!" The roar of amusement we fall into after is loud enough to drown out the king of the jungle's growl. The gargantuan man in white takes a drag from his cigar, exhales the smoke from nostrils resembling a furious Schlitz bull. His bottom lip has an upward turn as he lets out a grunt, which sounds like a chuckle.

"All right." The giant dressed in white says with authority. "Looka here, the ladies is ready and waitin' but I gots to lay down some rules fo' you niggahs. Don't try and fuck, suck or tuck on any of my dancers. You niggahs too ugly for any of my lovelies to give ya'll the time of day. And you niggahs who don't think they ugly, you still too broke to buy a used tampon from anyone of my ladies. We clear?"

"Yeah, yeah, yeah motherfucka enough with the chit chat, goin' head and bring out the kit kats." Caldwell demands while tapping on his wristwatch for emphasis. In lieu of answering the big man snaps his finger and the security guard and bartender pull from both sides of a circular door behind the giant. As the door opens more light enters the poorly lit basement. The abundance of new light starts to hurt my eyes slightly. Avoiding the potency of the light my eyes dart to a ceiling lined with metal plumbing pipes. One of the pipes is beginning to leak a droplet of water. Its slow descent makes it look like a lonely teardrop falling from a sky that is gray. Once the droplet hits the floor a flash of light transfers the twelve of us to the other side of the circular door. Standing in the room, what was once a blinding luminescence has transformed into a feverish tranquility. A lustrous glow radiates from a floor tiled with black marble and specks of diamond dust. The glow from the floor is balanced by the shade of peach they elected to paint the room with, the color conjures visions of an orchard overflowing with the ripe and delicious fruit. Sounds of anguish or excitement circulate from one side of the room where people are gambling at either craps, blackjack or roulette. More people are sitting at a bar on the other side of the room, imbibing spirits, grown on God's green earth, then manipulated and manufactured by man for profit.

"Ayo, you ready son?" Caldwell asks my left ear.

"Ready for what?"

"Deez bitches! Man I promise you I'm cuttin' something in here tonight. And when I'm cuttin' that hoe up with my samurai sword, I'ma dedicate each stroke to you. Ol' gettin' married tomorrow ass nigga."

"Thank you for being so unselfish CeeCee."

"You know I do what I can."

"Hey cuties, can I get you gentleman something to drink?" A woman with skin the color of red clay asks Caldwell and I.

"Yes you can, I'll take a vodka tonic with lime, please." If I hadn't known him all my life, I would think Caldwell Cornelius was an extremely polite man based on that exchange.

"And for you, handsome?"

"Do you have any Crown Black back there?"

"Yes we do."

"Okay, let me get a Crown Black and Coke then."

"Got it!" The server responds before bouncing away. As she prances away I notice that she is wearing a pair of neon pink boy briefs with white trim. The white elastic band around her waist has the word "Juicy" written in black lettering all around. Covering her breasts is a tube top bra that matches her undies. She is overdressed compared to the other women in the room, all of whom are naked and as thick as cake mix. A loud bell rings through the room and all the lights turn red. A baritone voice comes from a loudspeaker and says,

"Hey hey hey! I know all ya'll fellas came out here to see these girls shake they booty cheeks and show that monkey meat!"

The room erupts with catcalls, whistling and some men barking. The voice lets the banter die down before he continues. "Well goin' head and get ya umbrella and raincoat because Thundastormm is coming to the main stage, right noooooooooowwwwwww!" A spotlight shoots to the back of the room where an alluring caramel colored chick is standing on a mirrored stage draped in a black and gold boxer's robe. Most men in the room have swarmed the stage like termites on a log cabin. Their hoots and howls become deafening as the temptress starts to sway from left to right. With a snap of her fingers, the DJ drops the needle and "Mama Said Knock You Out" by LL Cool J starts to vibrate the room.

"Your drink, sir."

I shift to my left and see the red clay waitress standing before me. I peer around her for CeeCee, but I see no sign of him. Grabbing the beverage from the server with my left hand I use the right to pat down my pockets for my wallet. "How much I owe you?"

"Not a damn thing, drinks are on the house for you bachelor." The waitress responds while licking her lips.

"Well you have to let me tip you at least."

She grabs my manhood as she says. "Just the tip? Or can I have the whole thing?" Before I can answer she yanks my dick into a backroom behind the bar. The small space is filled with dark blue, almost purple lighting. Lining the walls are the kind of booths that you'd sit in at a restaurant, except the sides are about two feet taller and there is no table to separate the occupants. Keeping her stronghold on my manhood, red clay makes me follow her to one of the booths. No words are exchanged as she shoves me into one of the plush booth seats and snuggles up beside me; her body heat makes me take a sip of my cold beverage.

"You have some beautiful eyes daddy. That's why I grabbed you, 'cause I got a soft spot," she pauses to caress her crotch over her pink panties. "For some pretty eyes, hmmmm." She moans softly as she keeps on petting her cat. Struggling with my native English due to my brain experiencing temporary blood loss I jumble noises together that are so incoherent that the red clay woman starts to laugh at me, uncontrollably.

"Ooooh, daddy am I making you nervous?" She asks once she is laughed out.

"A little."

"Why?"

I take another hefty dose of liquid courage before I answer. 'Well it's not every day I get dragged by my dick into a blue lit backroom." I look directly in her eyes after my last word.

My gaze makes the server sit up straight and turn her analytic skills on me. "What's your name daddy?"

"Adrian."

She extends the hand that was just on my package and exclaims. "It's nice to meet you Adrian, my name is Nila."

"Nila?"

CHAPTER 10

"Nila!"

I feel a sharp nudge in my ribcage, after I turn my ears on.

"Nila! Get up, Robert is on the phone for you."

"What?" My eyes are still closed.

"Your attorney is on the phone and would like to speak with you."

Drian's words come at me slowly. Without moving any other body part, I hold out my right arm, and Drian drops the phone into the hand attached to the arm.

"Hello." I say once the phone makes it to my ear.

"Good morning to you too, Robert." I sound perkier than I feel. "No I have no clue what it is that you're looking at right now." I flirt with a yawn, while trying to digest most of what Robert is rambling about.

"Uh huh, as I knew you would; you are too good." I toss a compliment to him so I can catch a few more seconds of sleep while his ego deflates.

"Yes, I'm still here." I yawn, must've let the seconds turn into a minute. "Yeah, that sounds perfect. You and Maurice wanna come get me at around nine—Ahhh, nine thirtyish."

"Yep, car trouble. Okay, bye." I drift back to slumber with the phone still attached to my ear.

I feel heat nuzzling on the right side of my face and neck; initially I thought it was the cell phone I fell asleep with. When I feel the prickly stubble of an unshaved face and lips on my ear, I know my MisterLoverMane is near.

"Hey baby, I see you trying to get some of that early morning lovin', Mr. Yancy."

"Morning? Nila it's twelve thirty in the afternoon."

Gail Devers never leapt as high as I did after hearing Drian's words. I land flat on both feet, but gravity heaves me back to the bed. My equilibrium reminds me what dizziness feels like as I sit on the edge of the bed; palms flat on the mattress. I take three deep breaths and prepare to propel myself back into the rest of this day. On the fourth deep breath, I press my calves against the side of the mattress and use my palms to help push off the bed. Standing upright I feel a tingle run over my scalp and a ringing in my ears. I take a tentative step and wobble like a bowlegged duckling. After a few more unsteady steps, I hear childish giggling floating through the room.

"What are you laughing at?" I try to turn my body in my fiancé's direction. My legs are still a bit stiff, but I manage to do an about face and see Drian hunched over hands on his knees, laughing like he's front row at the Kings of Comedy.

"What is so damn funny, Adrian?"

The question does nothing more than add fuel to a raucous fire of laughter. Tears are starting to well in Drian's Bambi eyes. Every one of his snickers pulls at me like a pair of cheap tweezers. He makes it to a semi upright position before he tries to speak.

"Oh oh-kaaaay. Muhahaha!" Is all he can sputter out before I see his eyes dart to my night table. I shift my glance to get a better view of what amuses my fiancé so much and I see that the time on the clock is 8:02 a.m.

"Drian, you are such an asshole sometimes!"

"Nila get all out of your feelings, you know I had to get you was slippin'"

"I'm 'bout to slip my foot off in yo' ass."

"I don't know how you gonna do that while I slip deez nuts off in yo' mouf!"

I try to think of a comeback but the laughter overpowers both of us. I stroll to the other side of the bed; my tippies bring me to Drian's lips. He bends down to kiss me; even with morning breath my baby has some sweet lips. I work my way through his mouth like I am a dentist, while he tries to examine my tonsils simultaneously. The room temperature is starting to rise, causing warmth to grow between my thighs. Electing not to start a fire we can't put out right now, we separate like a wrapper from a piece of candy. I feel his fingers on the backside of my flesh as I scurry into our master bath to take a shower. Stepping into our bathroom (that's really mine) I feel a chill under my feet from the ivory colored floor tiles. I let my footsteps drag as I head to the octagon shaped shower/tub. I hop up the two steps that lead to the raised tub and cut on the hot water.

As the bathroom starts to steam, I look at the sparkle of the gold in the swirls that cover the walls in the bathroom. From a distance, the swirls look like a pattern of 6's and 9's flipped upside down in a bowl of alphabet soup. The flecks of gold in the paint start to shimmer as steam starts to mist over the lacquered varnish finish I put on top of the gold swirls. Naturally my eyes drift to an elongated oval shaped mirror that sits above a set of Florence sinks made from polished brass. There is a small spot in the middle of the mirror that has not yet been touched by the steam from the shower. I stare at myself in that spot, tunneling through my eyes to peer at my soul and see if anything is amiss in my spirit. I don't make it past the bags underneath my eyes before the water vapor blurs the entire mirror. Peeling off my sleep shirt, I take inventory of my flesh and remind myself that a mani-pedi and waxing have been added to the pre-wedding list of things to do. Unable to resist the lure of water any longer, I step into the octagon shaped shower and let the water wash down over me.

Showered and semi refreshed I slip a hot pink tank dress over a nude bra and panty set. I twist and contort in the mirror that sits over the dresser in my bedroom, making sure every curve is in just the right place. Out of the mirror and into my shoes, four chimes sound off in the house, Drian shouts that he'll get the door and I soon hear two baritone voices greeting one another. After one more glance in the mirror, I open the bedroom door to go and join the two men in the living room.

"Good morning Ms. Montgomery." Robert says with regality in his tone.

"Robert, bonjure." I reply with both hands outstretched towards my attorney. He takes up my grasp and I pull him close, planting a soft kiss on his left cheek, while he does the same thing to my right. We repeat the routine on the opposite cheeks before we relinquish our embrace.

"Adrian tells me you've been a bit under the weather still. Are you all right?" He looks at Drian lounge on our leather couch.

"Nothing I can't handle." I stare the legal professional directly in the eyes.

Robert blinks and then nods, content not to push the issue. I let an agreeable smile develop over my lips before I turn my attention to my fiancé.

"Drian baby, where are my keys and purse?"

My baby gets up off the couch and heads towards the kitchen. My eyes follow the man of reality as he grabs my purse from the table and brings it back to me. I wrap my hands around the hands that are holding my bag and I arch up to kiss the lips that belong to the hands. Mindful that Robert is watching and waiting, I don't let the oral interaction get too far out of hand. A cleared throat reminds me that the business of the day still needs to be tended to.

Robert waits a few seconds after clearing the imaginary particles from his throat. "Ready?"

I see Drian's eyes get angry and calm down in the time that it takes to blink. Extracting the purse from my lover's hands, I pivot in my Steve Madden wedges.

"Ready."

"Make sure you eat something." Drian's final words hit my ears as Robert and I head out the door. I shout back in agreement as I pull the door closed behind me. Looking forward I see Maurice, Robert's chauffeur standing curbside near the rear passenger door of Robert's maroon chariot. When we are within ten feet of the Tahoe, Maurice opens the rear passenger door for us. Inside the vehicle, I see that the rear seats are opposite-facing and covered in snakeskin dyed beige and burgundy. I settle in with my back turned to the driver. Robert elects to sit across from me, back to the rear window. Once our door is closed I hear the engine turn over and the sound of soft horns streaming around the SUV.

"You want to get some breakfast before we head over there?" Robert hands me water from a mini refrigerator installed under his feet.

"No, I want to get this out of the way as soon as possible."

"As you wish. Let's go Maurice."

I feel a shiver come over me as the automobile accelerates and pulls away from my home.

***

As I step out of the Tahoe, I see that a fog has descended over the summer sky and hovers especially low over the apartment complex that the Tahoe pulled up in front of. A firm touch on my right elbow starts my legs moving forward on the concrete path that leads to a building that has B-24 in large silver lettering. With my eyes still straight ahead, I hear Robert's dress shoes as they make their rhythmic click-clack against the pavement. Within seconds a hand pulls the black handle on the dingy forest green door of building B-24.

We enter the unit and my nose is assaulted by the stench of moldy mildew and what I assume is cat pee. The aroma is exacerbated by the fact that the hallway is sweltering. There is dark green carpet running the length of the corridor with doors on either side of the fabric; it's gray and worn down in the center from years of wear. Unaware of where I am going, I stop and usher Robert in front of me. I tread lightly behind the esquire and breathe through my mouth to avoid the odor.

Robert stops at the third door on the left side of the hallway, I position myself with my back to the left side wall, as to remain out of sight of the occupant. Robert looks at me and nods with his hand suspended over door 26. I nod back and Robert lets his knuckles slam down on the wood. Seconds pass, with no audible movement on the other side of the door, Robert knocks again, slower this time. Before his knuckles come off the wood, the door is yanked open to the length of the security chain.

"What the hell you want, mister?" An old hoarse voice asks from the other side of the door.

"I am looking for a Ms. Hortense Dewart." Robert replies with the charm of a seasoned litigator.

"What you want with her?"

Robert reaches into his jacket pocket and produces a card

that he gives to the person on the other side of the door. He waits for them to take it before he responds.

"My name is Robert Bland; I am an attorney, here to speak with Ms. Dewart on behalf of one of my clients."

Whatever Robert said was the right answer as the voice unhooks the security chain asks Robert to step inside. As Robert heads into the apartment, I follow his footsteps. The voice is a half foot ahead of us both, using a cane for stability to lead the way. An abrupt right turn leads us into a small kitchen, where the voice stops, and manages to see me for the first time this morning.

"Oh, no! Not this damn nigger-bitch in my house!" She points the wooden cane at me as Robert stands between us.

"Look here you old George Washington lookin' ass skank. I don't have the patience for your bullshit this morning, so sit the hell down, and shut the hell up."

"Fuck you, bitch! I'll be good and goddammed if I'm gonna let some ol' cotton pickin ' swamp nigrah talk to me like this in my goddammed house."

"Ms. Dewart if you would please be so kind as to let us explain why we are here." Robert attempts to calm the crotchety hag down.

"You, uh mister, uh, mister, uh, Bland you are welcome to stay, but I don't allow circus animals in my house, so that monkey has to go!" She steadies herself with the cane and uses her free hand to point at the door we just entered through.

"Robert..." Sometimes one word is all it takes to get your point across.

"I won't stay without her, Ms. Dewart." My attorney advises.

"Then you both can leave. Any further questions you may have can be asked to my lawyer."

"As you wish."

Robert turns quickly and touches the small of my back signaling for me to start walking towards the door. The wrinkled woman continues to ramble as my counsel and I go back from whence we came.

My right hand is on the knob when Robert fires off a teaser. "So I guess you don't want to know what became of Spade, then?"

"What that's you said?"

"You heard me crystal clear, Ms. Dewart."

"What you know about my boy?"

"May we sit down?"

Curiosity has captured the stray alley cat and she leads us through the kitchen to a small dining room with a square golden oak table in the middle of the room. The table is surrounded by four wooden chairs, ranging from light to dark, none of them matching the golden oak table. The woman with the dishrag face and I sit at opposite ends of the dinette, habitually Robert sits in the middle—hoping to bridge the gap. He unbuttons the final two of his three button French blue blazer before he makes his opening statement.

"The Denver Post called it the 'April Fools Annihilation.' April 1st, 1982 is a day that will forever live in infamy, in the recesses of your mind, won't it Hortense?"

A look of horror floods the ghoulish senior citizen's face after Robert's introduction. He straightens the clip on his tie before he continues.

"Before the twenty-fourth hour struck on that first day of April, you had lost the all of the family you worked so hard to cultivate. By 10:00 a.m. of that horrible Thursday, your only daughter, Stella Haggerty, hung herself at the age of sixteen. The police report states that you were just getting off work at that time. You were working as a phone operator at Bell South at the time, which means you couldn't have been the first one to discover her lifeless body dangling from the ceiling fan in the living room."

Hortense turns even paler after Robert's opening statement. Something I didn't think that was possible. "The report is unclear whether Spade or your husband Carl found the body and called the police. Investigators always assumed it was Spade who found her, cut her down from the fan and covered her with a blanket, making it appear that she was peacefully sleeping for the last time. By all reports, Spade loved and adored his baby sister Stella. It had to have destroyed him when Stella confided in him that your husband- their father- was raping her, and had been for many years before she took her own life. Finding her cold corpse strung up like a side of beef at a slaughterhouse was the straw and camel moment for the eighteen-year old Spade. In a rage, he was determined to murder the person he believed was responsible for killing the one person he loved most in this world."

Her sobs are soft and childlike; the tears have a hard time making it through a face full of wrinkles, and consequently her face resembles a semi-wet dish towel. Robert pulls an embroidered handkerchief from his suit pocket and hands it to the skag before he continues.

"The detectives discovered a letter written by Stella chronicling the graphic details of a father sexually abusing his daughter. Before they could question Mr. Haggerty, your husband was found savagely murdered at approximately 4:00 p.m. in an alley not too far from here. I read that he was stabbed eighty-seven times, his head was severed from his body, and that his penis was cut off and left in his mouth. All in broad daylight."

The silent sobs, have turned to loud exclamations as the attorney excavates decades-old pain

"Damn, now I see why you are the pathetic old turnip face wench that you are. Your life is worse than the World Trade Center on September 12, 2001." I revel in pouring rock salt in her wound.

She blows her nose in the handkerchief. "Shut up, bitch."

Robert clears his throat to restore some semblance of order. "By 8:00 p.m., a missing person's report was filled for Spade Haggerty, and a citywide search commenced the next day. Despite all efforts, no one has seen your only begotten son since that spring day in 1982. You've spent more than three decades trying to find your boy, which is why we're here."

For as wrinkled and crumpled as life has rendered her over the years, the childless mother sits strikingly upright at Robert's words; they offer the kind of hope that she has been dying for since 1982. Using professional compassion as his guide, he wraps his right hand in both of hers and whispers something only the two of them will ever know. Parting from their thirty second powwow, I see sentimentality in Robert Bland that I have never witnessed in all the time we've known each other.

"That's why we're here." Robert clears his throat for real this time around. "We want to offer you an opportunity to regain what was taken away from you all those years ago; the one member of your family who didn't die on April 1st, 1982."

"I'm the only member of my family that didn't die on that cold Thursday in April, God left me here to suffer for not protecting my children. Spade been gone so long I assume or pretend he's dead, so I can make it through each day with only an excruciating amount of pain."

"I have it on good authority that Spade Jeremiah Haggerty

is still alive."

The words whip the witch's neck closer to Robert almost as if she is trying to dive inside him. Her body language pleads for Robert to continue.

"If you agree to dismiss your suit against Ms. Montgomery, we will agree to reunite you with your only son."

"Don't be bullshitting me mister."

"Lady I could choke a bull with what I shit." Robert uses the last word to ascend from the golden oak table. He buttons his blazer and stands over Hortense like a priest would a lost soul. "You have my card Ms. Dewart. This offer will expire in seven days. If I have not heard from you or your legal representation in that time, I will assume that you would like to pursue the matter through the judicial system."

He turns to me and asks ever so politely. "Are you ready to leave, Ms. Montgomery?"

I nod and make my way through the small kitchen, with Robert preceding me to the front door. When my heels are inches off the linoleum, I turn back to look at the desperate widow, and think that I would have sympathy for her if she wasn't such a bitch.

Back on the street in front of the frayed apartment building, I can see that the fog has risen from the sky and dropped the sun in its place. The day is starting to feel more like July as I stare at the maroon Tahoe parked at the end of the concrete path. As soon as Maurice sees Robert and me trek towards the chariot, he opens the rear passenger door. The cool air conditioning from the vehicle blows strongly in contrast to the scorch of Denver in July.

"Where to, Ms. Montgomery?" Maurice rings out in a soft voice.

I look his employer in those sky blue eyes. "So, we gonna have breakfast or what?"

CHAPTER 11

"Thank you. Thank you. (Pause for applause) Ladies and Gentlemen, thank you for staying with us and for those of you that are just joining us we are here with Yenila Montgomery, drama survivor. In the past twenty-four hours Ms. Montgomery has had her fiancé arrested and thrown in jail. And just a few short hours ago she had to inform a grieving mother that her long-lost son may not be lost after all. Yenila, these past twenty-four hours have been filled with more ups and downs than a Becky giving brains in the turning lane. How have you managed to remain strong throughout it all?"

Curious sticks the half empty Dasani bottle that he is using for a microphone near my mouth.

"Boy, bye!" I playfully dismiss as I swat the bottle of away from my face.

"Okay so now you wanna play me huh? Iight, gurl watch when I get my daytime/late night talk show/webcast thingy. You gonna be begging me to interview you then!"

"Kiss my ass, Curious!"

"Right or left cheek?"

Head hung down and shaking slowly I try to use the motion to stave off the chuckles brewing in my belly, but my baby brother is having no part of it. He nudges me twice with his elbow.

"Give it up, chile! You know yo' lips too damn big to hide a smile!"

Curious is right, the dam restraining my amusement bursts

and the laughter starts to flow from me. Always comical and mostly carefree, Curious never fails to bring out the immature kid in me. And at a time where the winds of chaos are swirling, I need all the amusement I can get. Curious has been, and continues to be consistently good at reading my emotions and navigating through the me that the rest of the world pays to see. The world currently outside my eyes is centered on a large trapezoid shaped conveyor that is rotating clockwise. Periodically an alarm goes off, a red light flashes and bags start to appear on the spinning nickel plated conveyor. People remain huddled around the structure until they retrieve their luggage and depart from the baggage claim at Denver International Airport. Watching the individuals from a distance reminds me of pigeons looking for crumbs in the park. Just like the pigeons, people wonder around seemingly aimless until they can pluck the imperceptible morsel and waddle away in accomplished delight. Watching the birds scurry to and fro my eyes are captivated by a dazzling creature. I am drawn to features that stand out like peafowl plumage. There is a saunter in her strut as she makes her way through the flock towards the luggage merry-go-round.

"You see her?" Curious whispers in my ear.

"You know I do."

The woman is a little over five feet and the color of dark cocoa, like the type found on the Ivory Coast, her complexion lush and smooth. The mound of cocoa is wrapped in a white strapless dress that ruffles at the hem. Around her waist is a six-inch-wide houndstooth print belt with a silver buckle that is shape of a capital A. She wears a gold Michael Kors watch on her left wrist that the family chipped in and bought her for her birthday. She waits at the luggage merry-go-round, oblivious to the hawk eyes that Curious and I are giving her.

Curious decides to stop staring and get her attention. "DREEEEEEEEEEEEAAAAAAAA!"

I slap Curious on the wrist. "Damn, boy! Do you have to be so loud and so ratchet all the damn time?"

"You hit me one mo'gin and I'ma show you what ratchet really is Nila." Curious squares up his posture in my direction like he intends to do me bodily harm.

"Now, now, children. Lest we not forget, we are in a public place."

Curious and I turn to look at the source of the words we believe are being spoken to us. Two shakes of her tailfeather has brought the cocoa queen before my baby brother and me.

"Shut yo' ass the hell up!" Curious and I screech at her in unison.

She grabs her imaginary pearls before she declares. "Why, I never!"

I wait a beat before I retort. "And heffa you never will!"

She laughs as she extends her arms in my direction a precursor to our sisterly embrace. As she holds onto me, I smell a simple vanilla musk on her skin, a fragrance she has worn since before her period got regular. When her enthusiasm is curbed she lets me out of her embrace. She keeps both of my hands clenched tightly inside of hers as she leans back slightly to get a better look at her only sister.

"Ms. Andrea Tamika Montgomery, look at you and yo' dark chocolate self, I bet them boys down in Tuscaloosa be melting for you."

I marvel at the woman beautiful enough to be a Caribbean Queen.

"Well..." She lets go of my hands and starts to twirl in a

circle. "You know I do iight down in the 'Loosa."

"Iight is an understatement, I know somebody been hitting it right down there because you looking thick than a batch of cake mix, Drea." I tease my older sister.

If she wasn't the color of cocoa, I might have seen her blush at my remark. Trying to maneuver out of my airport inquisition, her gaze drifts over my left shoulder to the youngest of the Montgomery children.

"Curious, are you not going to come show your sister some love?" Andrea asks, to divert attention from her sex life. Seconds pass without Curious saying a word. Feeling something is amiss I turn around in less than an eye blink to see Curious slumped in a plastic chair, arms folded, bottom lip to the floor.

"Awwww, Georgy." Andrea coos as she walks toward our baby brother, "Please tell me you not still mad at me."

Curious George slumps further down in his chair and jerks his head to the left to avoid Andrea's eyes. Sister takes a seat in the empty chair on Curious' left side; reactively Curious shifts his posture to the empty chair on his right. Andrea grabs Curious by the hair on his chin and brings his face close to hers. The two stare at each other for what develops into an uncomfortable amount of time until I intervene.

"Hey!" I snap my fingers at them. "Five seconds ago you was all turnt up, Curious, yelling and acting a fool for Drea. Now you wanna sit here and pout? I'm done. You two either kiss and make up or pack this beef up like a to-go box, 'cause we got a schedule to keep."

I bark out the last few words to remind them (and myself) that we have a long weekend ahead. Before they can respond, I start walking in the direction of the sliding doors that lead to the parking lot. The sound of heeled shoes and luggage rolling against the asphalt is not far behind.

I hear Curious start whining behind me. "You coulda at least tweeted out about my show, Drea!"

"Really? Curious, seriously? You mad at me for not tweeting about your play?"

"Drea, please. This wasn't just ANY play, this was me in the LEAD role!"

While I can't see him, I can picture Curious behind me arms raised towards the sky vibrantly reaching, and shaking his hands for dramatic effect. The showman in him is always on. Abruptly the heels and wheels on the luggage stop, and Andrea's mouth starts to move.

"Georgy Porgy, I am sorry you know I'm not that great at all that social media stuff. Until Russell showed me otherwise, I thought Twitter and Facebook, was the same thing."

"Russell?" Both Curious and I are puzzled. An about face allows me to look at my sister with my third eye, the one that never lies.

"Who is Russell?" Curious and I ask.

"My boyfriend." The least shy woman I know suddenly acts demure.

"Wait, wait, wait. You got a boyfriend, now?" I stammer disbelief. "I don't think you've ever claimed anyone in all the years I've known you."

"Ummm hmmm." Curious seconds my emotion.

I'd never seen dark chocolate turn white before that moment. Andrea stands before us looking almost as pale as the dress she has on.

A twitch in my third eye activities the investigator in me.

"Okay so what is your boo thang like? What does he do? Where'd ya'll meet?"

Curious nods in assent. "Ummm hmmm, come on with the tea, child."

Never one to be rushed or forced into anything, Andrea takes a deep breath before deciding to speak. "Okay, we are in a parking lot at DIA, so if I answered your questions I would be literally putting my business out in the street. And ya'll know I'm not that kind of lady. Nila let's find your car and I'll tell you two everything as we ride to wherever it is we goin' after we leave here."

***

Foot on the gas, clear road ahead and the blue skies of Colorado set the backdrop for the story that starts to flow from Drea's lips. "I'm by myself at this burger joint down in the 'Loosa called T-Burger. And he walks in with a group of his friends..."

An up-tempo congo driven beat interrupts sister in the middle of her story.

An excited Curious leans from the backseat into the space between the driver and passenger seats. "Oooh! Oooh, is that him tryna FaceTime you right now?!?"

I give her my most commanding voice. "Answer it, Drea."

"Hey baby." A smile beams over Andrea as her boo appears on her phone screen.

"Aye, chocolate Mami! What you doing?" I notice Drea's

bae has a little Spanish-Latin accent.

"Uh I'm here getting interrogated about you, Papi! Say hi to my brother Curious!" Sister pans her iPhone to spotlight our brother.

"Hola." Russell says with cool and calm.

"Heeeeeeeeeey!" Through my rearview I can see Curious wave using only four of the five fingers on his left hand.

"You gotta congratulate the bride!" Andrea brings the phone to my face.

"Hola! Felicitaciones, Senorita." Russell keeps the cool in his tone.

I turn to look at the screen briefly, not wanting to keep my eyes off the road too long. "Well Feliz Navidad, to you too!" I say before turning back to the road.

My remark causes Russell to erupt in laughter, then Andrea, then Curious.

"What ya'll laughing at?"

"Mahahaha. You, you, you'juss Muhahaha!"

Andrea can't muster a complete sentence over laughter getting the best of her.

Picking up where Andrea tried to start, Curious wipes tears from his eyes. "You just told that man Merry Christmas in Spanish." Laughter resumes.

"Ahahahaha," I taunt mockingly, "all ya'll can just shut the hell up. I'll admit my Spanish is a little rusty. I can understand it, but I can't speak it."

Curious keeps laughing. "Yeah, yo' ass is rusty all right."

"Say one mo' thing about my ass Curious, and you goin' be on the side of the road trying to figure out how to get my foot out of yours."

"You bet—"

"Now, now children. We have a guest" Andrea cuts in to interrupt our verbal affection for the second time this afternoon.

Curious barely lets the verbal chaos calm before he's back at it. "Are you gonna finish your story or nah, Drea?"

A smile starts off Andrea's recollection. "Okay so Russell walks in with his friends and they all look clean cut with their uniforms on and whatnot."

"Uniforms?" Curious interjects.

"Oh yeah, Russell is in the Air Force. Top flight! "

Drea and her boo complete the last two words in harmony, before she soldiers on. "So like I was saying, in walks Russell and after about thirty seconds I feel eyes on me. I pull my phone from my purse and pretend to check it but I'm really looking for the eyes that are looking at me. I scan the whole restaurant and I don't see anybody looking, but I still feel eyes on me. As a last resort, I turn on the selfie cam on my iPhone and pan up like I about to take a picture, and bam! Right there in the background is Russell, with all eyes on me like I was 'Pac. Since I know he's watching, I decide to give him a little show. I flip my Poetic Justice braids like White girls do with their hair, then I get up and walk real slow and easy like to the soda fountain. I stand there for a minute or two, let 'em get a good look at what I'm working with. And I had on these baby blue tights that kept riding up my butt, so I know he was getting a real nice preview that day. By the time I turned from the soda machine, I knew I had him. I held my head high and looked right in his direction. He tried to play me off by looking away, but he too late- he was caught in this chocolate trap"

Curious pretends to reel in a fish with his hands. "Ooooohhhhhh! Got 'em!"   Soft chuckles float around the automobile; Drea's boo is the one voice conspicuously absent.

"Russell? We ain't scare you off yet?" I ask Andrea's military man.

"No, no, not at all. I just find it interesting how Ms. Chocolate Trap over there retells our first meeting."

Curious perks up again. "Oooh, is she being stingy with the tea?" I prepare to get off on Mississippi and I-225 and head deep into the A.

"No, she's not being stingy, just one sided." Mr. Air Force responds voice still cool and calm.

"Well hell, who else side I'ma tell it from, Russell? I can only fully speak for Andrea Tamika Montgomery."

"Speaking of speaking, Mami would you like to tell your brother and sister what you have me saved in your phone as?"

"What chu mean?"

"Don't play Mami, you know what you have me saved as."

I turn my eyes from the road and see Drea squirming in her seat, writhing under the spotlight that her new boo has shined upon her. I twirl my right index finger in a circular motion, a non-verbal signal to my sister that she needs to come on with the come on. She squirms a bit more before she makes a sound that I think should be a word, but I'm not entirely sure.

"What?" Curious and I jump on her together.

"I said, Butter Ri-Can!" Andrea responds through clenched teeth. Curious and I remain silent, squelching our chuckles so we can fully hear the explanation behind the name.

"Ah, now Mami tell 'em why you call me that." Captain Cool keeps the heat on her.

"Because you so smooth, Papi." She purrs in a way that tells me that she has forgotten Curious and I are even here.

"So while you may have pulled me into your chocolate trap, I've been smooth enough to keep you around."

Andrea shows all her teeth. "Like a dog chasing its tail."

Sister ends the conversation as we pull into the strip mall, where the nail salon is located.

***

The hot air of summer feels foreign on my flesh after stepping out of the perfectly air conditioned salon.

"Whew, I needed that. Now my hands and feet is on fleek!" Curious rejoices as the three of us exit the nail salon, locked arm and arm.

"Me too." Andrea seconds.

"Me three." I take a deep breath and let the hot summer air fill my lungs. After an hour of smelling nothing but chemicals in that salon, my lungs need new oxygen. "Thank you Drea for paying for my manicure, and thank you Curious for paying for my pedicure."

"Shit girl, with them hooves you got I thought they was gonna charge me extra." My baby brother jabs.

"Hooves my ass, Curious! Yo' feet look like you done walked from Selma to Montgomery and back!"

"Shut up!"

"No, you shut the hell up!"

Drea who is in the middle of our arm entanglement looks to her left and her right before she asks. "What is wrong with you two, ya'll been nipping at each other all day."

"Curious only nips at me like that 'cause he miss me, we interact like this all the time, sister."

"Ummm hmmm, I love me some Nila. That's why I talk crazy to her, because I care."

"This is not the Nila and Curious I remember." Andrea unhooks her arms from ours. The three of us stop walk about five feet away from my Tesla. Andrea stands motionless, looking straight ahead, while Curious and I stand on either side of her, our eyes glued to her ears.

Looking at her ears, reminds me that we all have two ears and one month, so that means I have her full attention. "In all realness, I'm surprised you remember my name. You graduated high school, then ran off to Alabama for college. You're not around for Christmas, Thanksgiving etc. You wouldn't have seen the changes and development of me and our baby brother, because you ain't never around. Matter fact I didn't even think you were gonna come to my wedding. I'm happy you're here, but I'm shocked at the same time."

Arms folded across her chest, Drea continues to stare straight ahead at a blue sky, without a trace of cloud.

"She right, Drea. I don't want you to think we ganging up on you- even though we kinda are. But we coming from a loving place. The four of us were so close growing up, but when you left for school, we just haven't had that same bond. And like Nila was getting at, is we a lil' hurt at the fact we don't see and interact with your as much as we'd like to. And it wouldn't a killed you to retweet a certain brother's play."

Still staring at the clouds, Drea shakes her head and lets her arms sag down to her thighs. "Man, I'ont know why ya'll coming at me like this, I just graduated with honors from 'Bama and then to get accepted into their law school. That took a lot of work. Some people don't understand that hard work is the only hustle, which makes the accomplishment a beautiful struggle."

I position myself in front of Andrea. I look into her eyes with a love that only a sister would know and hold her face in both of my hands before letting my words flow.

"Sister, neither one of us is coming at you any kind of way. We know you graduated from the University of Alabama with honors because we were there in the stands cheering and getting turnt up when you pranced across that stage. This family is proud of you and what you are accomplishing; and in your desire to conquer everything between heaven and hell remember that we've had your back long before the struggle and we will continue to have your back until the day you struggle no more. Because that's what it means to be family. The energy, the love you feel flowing from me and Curious is real love, you know why it's real?"

"Why?" The word forms on Andrea's lips, but no sound comes out.

Pulling her cocoa face closer to mine I can feel a tremor pulsate through us. "It's real because we are willing to say what needs to be said at a time when you need to hear it the most. All the materialistic things, the social media displays of affection, don't mean shit- eventually they will fade. Love is the only thing guaranteed to last forever."

"Deeeeeeeeep." Curious snaps his fingers in a rapid motion, as though he is at a poetry reading. Drea rolls her eyes and I laugh as I take my hands from sister's face.

"You stupid, Curious. I swear."

"Come on bring it in, family hug" Andrea stands next to Curious and I with open arms. The power of the family powwow is interrupted by the melody of "Fancy" by a rapper from Canada.

"Hi Mommy. Yes, they are standing in front of me right now. We just got our nails did."

"Wait, I thought rehearsal wasn't until 4." I pull the phone from my ear to look at the time. And put it back to my ear to hear Mommy tell me what I already know. "Yes Mommy, I know it's 3:30. We're on our way to the church right now."

CHAPTER 12

A funky vibration rattles the latch that leads into Friendship Baptist Church. The rattle gives my limbs pause, but the sonic vibrations are too magnetic for my hand to resist. As I pull the latch and open the passageway, the sensation amplifies. Once I step inside the church, a contagious groove pulls me and my siblings into the sanctuary. There are twenty or so people in there, all of them friends, family or members of Friendship Baptist. It's surprising (but not really) to see Clarice up in the pulpit playing the organ. Behind her is a tall Asian man with sunglasses playing a bass guitar. Various other people are clapping their hands, shaking tambourines and swaying with the entrancing melody of "Shout" by The Isley Brothers. The sides and the roof of the sanctuary were constructed in such a manner that together they form a triangle, making the room appear larger than it actually is. Which makes the musical performance feel like it's surround sound.

Vance and Duane Bingham (brothers who perform under the name Instant Klazique) stand at the apex of the triangle in the center of the pulpit in front of a gold cross suspended from cherry hardwood. I'm not surprised to see them here- Drian recently agreed to be their manager. They lead the congregation in song; Sanctified and filled with the Holy Ghost my ears tune in and hear Vance scream out,

"Hey-Hey-A-Hey!"

The other twenty or so people and I shout back, "Hey-Hey-A-Hey!" As Vance sticks the mic out towards the crowd. Before I can draw breath to respond to the next round of call and response, I feel energy on my left side, I shift my gaze and my fiancé is standing before me like he was dropped down the heavens.

"Hey baby!" I exclaim as I wrap him up in a hug and kiss combo. But Drian's embrace is stiff and the touch from his lips is off beat. I pull him back close and ask him what's wrong.

"Nothing, everything is good." His voice is confident as he whispers in my ear, but his aura is still off center.

"Hey, this is the weddin' rehearsal, not the honeymoon! Ya'll two separate so I can hug up on Nila 'fore she officially yo' wife, Ayo."

I'd recognize Caldwell Cornelius' voice if I was deaf in both ears. I slide out of my fiancés arms, look him in the eyes and decide not to press the issues I see behind them. Instead, I choose to greet the man standing behind him- one of his oldest friends.

"Mr. Cornelius, it is good to see you again."

I put my arms out to embrace a hostage who became a friend last Fourth of July. When the hug gets too cozy for Drian's comfort, he yanks me from Caldwell's grasp. His show of territorial aggression sends a shiver up and through my pussy.

"Look here, CeeCee," Drian's hand is still on my bicep "this here is my woman, so you betta get ya own wife to hug up on."

I can't tell if Drian is kidding with Mr. Cornelius or not.

"Man, fu--," I smile as at Caldwell as he remembers that his wayward mouth is in the house of the Lord. "All I'm sayin' is I'ma be single for life, I ain't never havin' no wife."

"Hmmp!" The sound falls over my left shoulder. "You coulda fooled me with the way you was hugged up with that old broad the last time I seent you."

The objection from Curious makes Caldwell eyes shift and sweat form on the top of his bald head.

My eyes ask the question Caldwell Cornelius loathes to answer.

"Ahem." Caldwell is saved temporarily by a clear of the throat. Rotating to the presence behind my right shoulder, I let Drea into the semicircle that Drian, Caldwell, Curious and I had formed.

"Caldwell Cornelius, allow me to introduce you to my sister Andrea."

Using her right elbow to nudge me the side, Drea needs no further introduction as she extends a chocolate paw in Mr. Cornelius direction. Mr. Cornelius uses both hands to ensnare Drea's paw; he brings the appendage to his lips and kisses it lightly. The display makes Andrea glimmer like she's standing under a halo.

"You say this mocha chocolate tastin' P. Y. T. here is your sister?"

Caldwell turns his head and neck towards me, but never takes his hands off my sibling. "Shoot, I'da guess she was ya niece, or ya daughter."

"Thraummmm..."

Andrea makes a sound never before heard by human ears, translated into an indistinguishable language. But I understand perfectly well that she looks ready to melt in Caldwell's mouth and maybe his hands too, if he can survive her chocolate trap.

"Ahhhhhhhyyyyyeeeeeeeeaaaahhh! Whoooooooooo!"

The five of us turn toward the pulpit at the commanding

yelps of Vance Bingham. The vocal distraction serves as an alarm, pulling Andrea from the lothario's spell. Her hand slithers from Caldwell's grasp, as she, like the rest of us put our two hands together rapidly to applaud the singing duo. Acquiescing to age and beauty, the brothers Bingham step out of the pulpit as Clarice rises from behind the organ and to the microphone.

"Amen, ya'll!"

We all respond back to Clarice with the same one word declaration of affirmation.

"Good Lawd that boy can sang! He keep on like that, Nila and Drian may not be the only ones gettin' married this weekend."

A mischievous wink follows Clarice's words. Laughter peppers the auditorium, Clarice allows the noise to calm down before she continues. "But to be all the way real with ya'll, I am more than happy for the beautiful couple. They got that strong Black love that White folks tell us we can't even dream about."

"Amen!" Several voices in the room call out.

"Ummm hmmm, Black and beautiful love and we're going to help them tie that knot. Ain't that right ya'll?"

The people in the room who don't scream out words of confirmation at Clarice's remarks. Innately begin to turn around and look at where Drian and I are standing in the back of the sanctuary. As their eyes begin to focus on us, their hands clap furiously, rooting for Black and beautiful love. It is in these twenty or so faces that are cheering us on that I see a possible candidate for the dourness in Drian's mood standing next to Vivian.

"I didn't know Kian was coming."

After I finish my sentence I remember that it is a lie. Vivian told me Kian wanted to be a bridesmaid.

"Me either." Mr. Yancy responds with folded arms across his chest.

"Well she is your sister."

"Half-sister."

"Well then can you be halfway civil to her please?"

"We shall see."

***

As the sun descends in the city 5,280 feet above sea level, the moon rises to take its place. Caught in the exchange, the Colorado skyline looks like a Bob Ross painting as I drive north from Friendship Baptist with brother and sister in tow. The dusk before night is rippled with the color of a blood orange interspersed with a glow the hue of butterscotch candy, all spattered on an indigo canvas. Ingesting the majesty reminds me that there is a God somewhere, because creating something this illustrious is beyond mortal capabilities.

"Where is my little buddy, Nila?"

Even though I already I know who Curious is inquiring about I ask anyway. "Who?"

His eyes call bullshit on me from the rearview mirror, but his lips play my game. "Where is Princess Adrianne, Nila?"

"Ask her bitch ass mama."

Drea perks up in the passenger seat. "Who is Princess Adrianne?"

"Drian's daughter." Curious and I answer.

"Now, Yenila tell me where my little buddy is please."

His words are borderline polite, but his tone is deadly serious. Curious developed a lifelong bond with Drian's only child after the two spent part of the last Fourth of July together as hostages of a deranged drug addict.

"I don't know for sure, but I assume she is somewhere with her mama, since she done put a restraining order against Drian to keep him from seeing his own child. I told you that's why he got put in jail."

"Yeah but I didn't think the bitch would be so petty as to not let the girl be in her daddy's wedding."

"Never underestimate a hood rat's desire to be petty." Andrea pops in with a pearl of wisdom.

"Preach! Andrea, preach! Now what we should do is pull a Rambo on that bitch, pull out the jammy and flat blast her ass! That way Drian will be her only living guardian and she'll have to be with him."

I side-eye Curious. "There's one small problem with your theory, Curious."

"What?"

"We'd all be going to prison for murder."

"Naw, we won't. All we gotta do is plead insanity. It worked for Samuel Jackson in that one movie."

"Ask Nathan Dunlap how that worked out in real life." Drea drops her second barb in less than sixty seconds.

Puzzlement riddles Curious' eyes. "Who?"

"Damn Drea, you cold" I ignore Curious' query

"Truth is true every hour of the day."

I let the significance of Andrea's words dissipate through the Tesla as I go back to staring at the sky. Night has washed over and the array of colors are gone; only the blue of midnight remains with a dash of crescent shaped white.

***

The Brazilian steakhouse, constructed in America, has an oriental decor. The walls are splashed with a vibrant red a few shades lighter than the prop kind they use in gory Hollywood movies. Intermittently, the walls are framed with paintings of what I assume are Chinese symbols in gold lettering. Statues of Japanese warriors holding swords in various battle poses adorn both sides of the concierge desk in the lobby. The desk appears to be made from a single piece of ebony wood four feet in both height and width. Four ivory limbs hold the desk erect. I rest my forearms on the black tempered glass top, preparing to talk to the youthful, Hispanic hostess perched behind her ebony post.

"I am here fo--,"

A Spanish sounding voice calls from my left. "Senora Montgomery, right this way please."

My siblings and I turn to look at the voice belonging to a man of Latin decent. The gentleman is tall, and the color of gingerbread. His eyes are the lightest shade of green before it fades into blue. He shaved this morning but the stubble grew back before he had a chance to put on after shave. The man is dressed in a black suit, shirt and tie with shoes the same color as the rest of his ensemble. The three of us follow the Latin gentleman through a panel of double doors constructed of white frosted glass and ebony wood. The doors lead into a medium sized room that decorated like the main section of the restaurant. The room is furnished with four rectangular tables that are fitted to form a square. The tables are topped with white cloth, white plates, white silverware and glasses. Looking at the white tableware reminds me I need to get my teeth whitened before the wedding. Fifteen feet from the square of tables stand two Mexican men dressed in white server's jackets that are buttoned up to the neck. Each man has his hand on a brass handle attached to a pair of cream colored doors. Both doors have a vertical oval cut into them, fitted with pink stained glass.

With a nod from the Latin in black, the Mexicans pull the doors open to a space one could only describe as resplendent. The room is a full three hundred and sixty degrees trimmed at the floor and ceiling with a dark marbled walnut. Sandwiched between the walnut trim are walls textured in the gemstone topaz, the gemstone is back-lit giving the room a warm, golden glow. Centered in the circle of a room is a gargantuan O shaped dinner table made from the same marbled walnut wood as the molding on the ceiling and floor. The top of the marbled walnut table is petrified and there are places set for at least fifty people. At the top of the O on the opposite side of the room sit my bosses Mr. Weldon Taylor and John Tyson to their far right is Robert Bland and next to him is Drian. The four men are all smoking cigars and laughing from words uttered before we entered the room. Noting our arrival, the four men stand and wait for the Latin in black to bring us over.

"Didn't expect you to beat me here, sweet thing." I call to my fiancé when I'm three quarters of the way to him

Drian shrugs, puts his cigar down into a crystal ashtray and holds his arms out to me. A giddy feeling wafts over me as I patter over to my husband-to-be. His grip is stout as he picks me up off my feet. Midair I lock my lips onto his and taste cigar and saliva in his kiss. As he places me level with the ground, my intuition reminds me that there is something he is still being coy about. Smart enough to realize the environment I'm in, I decide to queue the inquest until I have the time and resources to give my suspicion the third degree.

"Robert, Mr. Taylor, Mr. Tyson. How are you gentleman this evening?"

The three old, wise men all take a drag of their cigar and laugh as a cloud of smoke almost obscures their faces from view. If you didn't know them, you would think their laughter amidst the cigar smoke was just them being crotchety old men. But after many nights working late for two of the three men, I know that kind of laughter means that they are far enough from sobriety to be buzzed, but not quite drunk yet.

Mr. Tyson answers for the group. "We are like the hourglass that sits atop the highest tree in the North Pole."

I put my right index finger and thumb on my chin. "Nonexistent?"

Laughter and smoke is the only response that emerges from the venerable men.

Curious looks at me as I turn away from their billowing smoke. "Who they is?"

"Three wise fools." I respond with a sly grin.

"Tapas?"

One of the Mexicans in the white coat offers us toothpicked meat from a sterling silver tray that he supports with his left wrist and palm. I grab a morsel of food from the tray and Curious follows suit. Sinking into the hors d'oeuvre is an ambrosial experience. The meat is a cut of tender steak, marinated in a blend of spices and wrapped in a tomato chutney and Cojitia cheese. My stomach has been dormant since breakfast with Robert and Maurice chis morning; the bite revives it. As I grab another tapa to feed the fire in my belly, I feel a familiar arm drape over my shoulder.

"Man, these look good!" Drian reaches over my shoulder and grabs two tapas- he devours them before the toothpick touches his teeth. Like Drian did to me Drea slithers up on Curious' shoulder and picks food off the tray. Silence settles over the two of them as their taste buds do the talking.

Noticing a pause in the action the Mexican server nods at the four of us and heads towards the three wise fools before the four of us demolish the entire platter. At the back of his departure the doors with the pink stained glass separate and a fury of familial faces come wading through lead by the Latin in black. My parents, Drian's mother and sister and Clarice begin to trek towards the top of the O shaped table. Still hungry I look behind me for the man with the tapas but I don't see him; by the time I get my head back around, the room is swarming with people who were at Friendship Baptist for the wedding rehearsal earlier. I interlock Drian by the right arm together we traverse the area, greeting friends and family like a preacher and first lady at church on Easter Sunday. In the nave of our rounds, a panel opens in the wall, revealing a full bar. The Latin in black stands in front of the bar and clanks a glass with a salad fork until he has the room's undivided attention.

"Good evening ladies and gentlemen- welcome to Texas De Brazil. My name is Manuel and I will be your host for this evening. I want to congratulate the lovely couple on their upcoming nuptials."

The room explodes with applause at the Latin's last two words. I feel all the eyes in the room on Drian and I as the jubilation continues for close to a minute. As the acclaim simmers, the Latin in black resumes his speech.

"We're here to celebrate the happy couple. My staff and I, are at your command throughout the night; the food will start coming out shortly and the bar is open- drinks are on the house."

The room erupts in another round of cheers. Instead of waiting for the sound to subside the Latin in black takes a bow and steps away from the bar before he gets trampled. About eighty percent of the folks in the room bum rush the bar like thirsty shoppers on midnight of a Black Friday sale. Watching the people flurry to the watering hole is both sad and amusing to me; broke people can be manipulated to lose all class and dignity when free shit is on table.

"Look at them ovah there, actin' like scavengers. Ovah some free liqu'a." Clarice scoffs in front of me and my fiancé. Amidst the commotion, I didn't even see her come up on us

Mommy nods in agreement next to her. "Ummm hmmm."

"Ummm hmmm, girl I's just goin' stand here and wait for them to serve me."

"I know that's right Reese!" The ladies high five one another using both hands. I stand still and shake my head at the women.

"Drian baby, where is Ms. V?" Mommy asks.

"She flocked to the bar with my sister over there."

Clarice chuckles. "She must have that summertime thirst."

"Yeah, I think she real thirsty." Hopefully I'm the only one that picked up the disgust in Drian's response. Black mothers don't look too kindly on men bashing one of their own.

"Tapas?" A different Mexican appears this time with a tray of shrimp wrapped in bacon, drizzled in a red sauce. The four of us take one and then another of the seafood covered in swine. Just like the first Mexican, this gentleman waits for the pause in our grazing and departs with the sterling silver tray. Popping into the space vacated by the Mexican is the Latin in black, with a question in his eyes that makes it to his lips.

"Mr. and Mrs., may I get you two something from the bar?" The daughter in me signals for Mommy to order first

"I would like a Long Island please."

"Make that two." Clarice holds up her index and middle finger.

Manuel's eyes turn to Drian. "For you sir?"

"I'll take a Crown and Coke."

"And for the bride?"

"A glass of white Zinfandel please."

"Excellent choices, I'll be right back with your drinks."

As he turns from us the Latin in black vanishes into the room instead of heading for the bar. As I lose visual acuity on the Latin, the sound from the speakers' increases and the needle drops on "Get Down On It" by Kool and The Gang. Clarice grabs my man by the hand and the two start to step the beat.

I yell after them as they sashay into the room. "You betta watch whose man you dancing with. You know I'll cut a..."

"Don't worry Nila; I'll always be here for you." I hear the assuring words, but I can't see a source. I look from left to right for the source of the words, and remain confused. The three taps on my outer left thigh solve the mystery.

"Camiko! Hey boy!" I plant a wet kiss on the left cheek of Clarice's grandson. "You are a sugar lump I swear, at least I know I won't be lonely as long as you're alive."

I grab his hand and Mommy's too and the three of us dance to the vicinity of my fiancé and mother figure. Shaking the moneymaker my mama gave me, I get lost in the eighties groove and let the music move me around. Camiko and my mommy aren't too far behind as they bend their bodies to the beat. By the end of the record, the group multiplied to include Andrea, Curious, Vivian and Kian. The nine of us evolve into a Soul Train line semicircle percolating and gyrating to the rhythm like it's the only thing we know how to do. As the final chants of "get down on it" close out the five-minute musical odyssey, I dab at my brow and look for the host that has my wine. Unable to visually locate him, I head toward the Ark of a table with my boo's hand wrapped in mine.

"Daddy!" Drea sprints in heels no less to the man standing behind me. I turn and watch her leap into the arms of the man who gave us life, Tuskegee D. Montgomery, Sr. Our father is a tall burly man, with shoulders as wide as the rectangular tables in the other room. He's as black as charcoal at midnight and strong as a buffalo. His beard and hair are vivid silver, like a quarter that has just entered circulation. He has a large nose and thick lips; features archeologists would classify as Negroid. I think my father looks like what the Great Sphinx of Giza would look like if he took on a purely human form to grace the earth. Seeing her cling to him reminds me I haven't shown him love since he's been in the room.

"Let go of my daddy!" I drop Drian's hand and hustle to our father.

"Hey Daddy!" I nuzzle into the right side of his heavyset frame.

"Hey Yenila." He opens his right arm wider to accommodate both daughters hugging at his torso.

"Hey son, ain't you goin' come speak to ya daddy?"

Both Andrea and I turn our heads in the direction that Tuskegee is calling out to. We both see Curious, standing with hesitant posture about five feet from us. Curious begins a slow, deliberate walk towards our father. Looking at Curious invokes memories of John Coffey walking down the Green Mile. While Curious is taller than Daddy, he cowers in his presence. Andrea and I slink under daddy's armpits as he opens his arms to a man that is his sometime prodigal son.

The Latin in black finally reappears. "Your wine, Senora."

I thank him in Spanish and he smiles at me like he thinks I'm an idiot and turns to ask sister if she'd like a drink. Before she can answer, bells start to chime in the room. The double doors give way to a group of belly dancers who precede numerous men carrying meat on large skewers. Upon their arrival, everyone in the room scrambles back to the table big enough to fill up an airplane hangar, this time I'm part of the scurry. I see Drian is already seated and the chair on his left that I was sitting in is now occupied by Ms. Vivian. Robert, who is seated on his right, observes my circumstance and relinquishes his seat. The esquire moves a few seats down and sits in the vacant chair next to Mr. Taylor.

"Ms. Nila how are you girl?" Ms. V leans with her elbows on the table. There is a tumbler of dark liquid in front of her, and I can smell rum in between the words of her question.

"Busy as can be." I keep my answer vague; from experience I know that talking to an intoxicated Vivian can be as productive as telling time on a broken clock.

"Who you telling?! This wedding has me working hard than a lumberjack with a broken ax." She laughs loudly, picks up the tumbler and downs what is left in the glass.

"Ohhhh. Nila did you see my baby walk down that aisle? My little honey Kian is a cutie, ain't she?"

She turns her head to look a few chairs down at her only daughter Kian who is sitting next to the perennial playboy Caldwell Cornelius. Vivian is accurate when she said Kian is a cutie. Kian is eye catching with her light skin and long brown hair.

Her eyes and nose are on the slender side and a loose fitting halter top showcases a six pack that could belong to a fitness model. In the heyday of music video vixens, Kian could have reigned supreme, based on her looks. In the few times we've spoken, I get the vibe that she doesn't have much outside of her physical attractiveness. To compensate, she invests a lot of time, energy and resources into the only thing that she can make money from. She'll soon find out that through the maturation of life, beauty fades and so too does ugly; age is the ultimate equalizer. A sizzling heat next to my ear wrests me from the thought.

"Would 'chu like some lamb?"

A Mexican man in a white server's jacket stands before me with a delicious looking and smelling meat on a steel skewer. I nod at my plate and the server cuts off a few chops. Like his coworkers, he waits for my pause, bows and then departs to serve the next guests. The routine keeps up like that throughout dinner- the servers bring out slaughtered and cooked animals on sticks and serve until we say stop. They also bring out some decadent garlic mashed potatoes and a portable salad bar that matches the one in the main dining hall. There is a fellowship that develops over the food. Everyone is eating or drinking and involved in conversation; things are tranquil around the gargantuan dinner table. Looking at everybody I realize that this is what peace is, and that we often miss it because we we're too busy to tune into what is blossoming right before our spirit.

"I love you." A force of energy whispers in my ear. I tilt backward and gaze upward to see the fiancé I know is there.

"I love you, too" I purr before I let his lips touch mine.

We could have been kissing for minutes or seconds I lost track of time in his lips, the catcalls bring me back to the reality of the room.

"Don't be tryna go half on a baby up in here!" Someone

yells out, and the room starts to shake with laughter. Amongst the laughter, I see Caldwell look at Drian and motion for him to come down to where he is sitting. Drian must have agreed, because moments later I see him weaving through servers and dinner guests to get to Mr. Cornelius. When Drian is hallway there, I see Mr. Cornelius and Kian get up from the table and head toward the double doors with the stained glass. The gentleman in Caldwell holds one of the doors open for Drian's baby sister and once she passes through the threshold Caldwell follows right behind her. Seconds later Drian also wanders out of the same door. The intuition in me sends goose bumps up my spine. I am convinced that whatever has been bothering Drian just walked out one side of those double doors.

"Nila! Hey Nila! Where are you running off to?" I feel Andrea's arm interlock with mine as we both head for the stained-glass doors

"What?" I was unaware that I was no longer sitting in my seat.

"Girl, with as fast as you was walking, I figured you had to go to the bathroom."

"Uh huh, yeah." I agree just to keep forward momentum toward the doors.

"Good, then you can le—"

I assume Andrea would have finished her sentence if the stained-glass doors hadn't catapulted open like they were never attached to the hinges. One of the white-coated Mexicans flies through the air at the end of Caldwell's fist like a surfer thrown from the ocean by an angry riptide. An enraged current in the form of Drian overtakes Caldwell and begins to kick the server like he was a practice ball at FIFA; it doesn't take Mr. Cornelius long to join in on the practice as well. As the two men unleash their feet of fury, I see a tidal wave forming in the space between their movements.

"PICK 'EM UP!" Kian roars like lioness trying to scare off a predator.

Drian and Caldwell pick up the man they've been pummeling by his arms and hold him upright. The battered Mexican wobbles and moans like a drunk in the middle of a field sobriety test. His head is swaying in every direction like a slinky in a see-through dryer. Captivated by the defiance of gravity, I failed to see Kian pick up a sterling silver serving tray. Before I can blink, Kian uses her two short, violence filled arms to try and behead the Mexican. While she fails at decapitation, she succeeds in ensuring that he will need dentures the rest of his life. The sound of blood and teeth hitting the floor turns the room into frenzy. I can feel people moving around me rapidly. Instinctively, I pull Andrea with me as I rush to Drian. By the time I make it to him, he and Caldwell have dropped the Mexican into a heap. I shove the two of them towards the hole in the wall they left and yell obscenities at them, which I don't even understand. I don't stop pushing and yelling until we're outside of the restaurant and Caldwell and Drian are headed to their impromptu getaway cars.

"Nila?" Sister calls.

"What?!"

"Stop yellin', they gone."

Andrea grabs my forearms, "I said, they are gone." She speaks slowly, as if instructing a child. "They drove off like you told them to. Now get yourself together before we head back inside."

I don't know if it's her words, touch or tone, but calm washes over me after she finishes speaking. Sister grabs me by the hand and we stroll back to the crime scene. Unconcerned with movement, my mind focuses on the events at hand and how things went from happy to violent faster than a commercial break. That and who has the shit job of having to pick up that Mexican man's teeth.

Andrea pulls me from my focus. "I still gotta pee. Where is that bathroom at?"

A male voice answers her before I can. "Straight back down that hallway at the end of those tables."

I turn my eyes to the voice, recognizing the face perched in front of the hostess podium. "Mr. Wiggins."

"Ms. Montgomery, it is a delightful surprise running into you here this evening."

My newfound client produces his right hand for me to shake. After accepting the offer, I turn to introduce Sister as well, but she is long gone.

"Yeah I thought I have some dinner and see a show in the midst of all this chaos."

The bearded man nods and laughs at my entendrë response. "Weddings can be quite the circus.

"Never a dull moment."

"The waitress will seat you now, sir." The Hispanic hostess speaks from behind the ebony podium.

"Well I guess that's me. Enjoy your dinner, Ms. Montgomery."

"Thank you, I will. Enjoy your dinner too, Mr. Wiggins." We shake hands once more before Mr. Wiggins follows the hostess into the main dining area.

***

The hidden dining room is mostly empty by the time I make it back there. The door has been put back on its hinges and the room is being cleaned by two women who have been tasked with removing the evidence of violence that was spilled on the floor. The three wise men, Kian Vivian, Mommy, Daddy and Curious all sit in a horseshoe-shaped arrangement of chairs in the middle of the room. The eight of them are silent, waiting for me to speak. I decide to ask the most logical question first.

"Where is everybody?"

Mr. Taylor answers in the left end of the horseshoe. "We thought it be a good idea if they adjourned for the evening to give us a chance to talk."

"In that case, there is only one thing I want to know." I pace the semicircle until I am standing directly over Kian. "What the hell happened?"

Charged by the adrenaline still flowing through her veins, Kian explodes from her chair, knocking it over in the process. I can see her chest heave up and down as her lungs contract and expand with each furious breath. "That mothafucka stuck his hands up my skirt and tried to act like he my goddamn gynecologist! Fuckin' beaner goin try and finger fuck me like I'm some hoe off the 'fax. I had to let his ass know I don't play that."

She turns away from me after her words. I can feel the heat from the rage that still burns inside of her from being violated. Any agitation I had about the situation dissolved after her admission. Part of me wishes she actually severed the Mexican man's head from his body, but the teeth she knocked out of him will have to be justice enough. Done with Kian, I turn to the wise men for my next inquiry "Where do we go from here?"

The three men laugh like they don't have a care in the

room. Once the chuckles cease, Mr. Tyson clears his throat. "All of you will go home, get some rest and get ready for the impending wedding. Mr. Taylor, Mr. Bland and I will take care of everything here."

A grin cracks my lips as it dawns on me who owns this restaurant. I look at the biological family I have in the room and I tilt my head to the double doors where Andrea is now standing. As I stroll to the exit I feel like I am flying solo, I turn back and look at the horseshoe and see Mommy, Daddy and Curious sitting as still as statutes on a monument.

"Montgomery's!" I charge, "Let's go

CHAPTER 13

The roads of life are the long, meandering sort. The hypnotic allure of the terrain allows you to cruise without a care in sight. Until you hit a pothole, or skid on patch of black ice, or get blindsided by a drunk driver who runs a red light. Your temporary serenity is shattered by an inconvenient reality. The illusion of calm was just distracting enough for you to careen into a calamity that was there the whole time. That melee at the restaurant was my wreck and wake up call. I have been on cruise control during the majority of the wedding festivities. Common sense tells me that there are too many moving parts for me to control everything. But If I don't take back control of the wheel this whole thing will turn into a series of unfortunate events- that I'll somehow be at fault for.

"Nila?" Curious calls out from the backseat.

I make a left turn onto my block. "Yes."

"Is you just not goin' answer my question?"

"I'm sorry Curious, I didn't hear you ask me anything."

"Uh oh." Curious stutters as I pull into my driveway, "If you apologizin' oooooh there must be something serious going on."

Andrea whips her head around. "What you talking, Curious?"

Curious sucks his teeth like he's trying to remove excess food before he speaks. "Look here, if the word unapologetic had a picture next to it, Nila face would be right smack dab in Webster's.

I've known this bish my whole life and she don't apologize for shit!"

I laugh at his truth as I pop the latch on my door and exit my Tesla. Outside of the air- conditioned car, I am confronted by a murky, humid heat, unusual for a Colorado night. The air smells of rain on the horizon and a gaze up towards the sky reveals dark clouds forming above my head. The muscles in my neck rotate my head clockwise, in an attempt to relieve some of the stress festering inside me. As my neck is on the downturn, I catch a glimpse of a small orange light that appears to be levitating on my porch. The orange light grows brighter and dims down every few seconds or so. Watching the orange glow dim and brighten sends a tremor down my tailbone.

"Nila why you ju–,"

I jerk my head rapidly to the left and bring my right index finger to my lips to silence Drea's would be question. When I turn back to the porch the orange glow has been extinguished. I signal with my middle and index finger for my two siblings to come close and follow behind me. My right hand fills with the cold steel that my kitten ear shaped knuckles are made from. Secure in grip, me and my siblings head with rapid caution to the porch from whence the orange glow came. As our pace quickens, I detect the chemical stench of cigarettes coming from my porch. Three feet from my porch steps, a motion sensor trips and white light illuminates the stranger sitting on my property.

"Who the FUCK are you!?"

"Nila, you sure have grown since the last time I seent you."

The stranger responds as he rises from one of the two coral colored chairs that decorate my porch. I notice ten or so cigarette butts surround his feet. The man is darker than night and aging badly. He is tall as a shrub and dressed in dark clothes; his shoes are made of patent leather they shine under the florescent lights.

I bring my kitten knucks eye level before I ask a second time. "Man, who the hell are you and why are you on my porch, leaving all these gotdamn cigarette butts all over the place?"

I can feel my arms trembling with rage, as I restrain the urge to attack the man trespassing on my property. The trespasser snarls at the three of us, revealing a top set of teeth that appear to be capped in gold. He is of medium build, unassuming at first glance. But his energy is one of violence; his posture is that of a man that is constantly ready to battle. The trespasser pulls a pack of Newports from his front pocket, retrieves one of the cancer sticks and places it in his mouth

I warn him before he can find a light. "Don't smoke another cigarette on my property." The three of us take the stairs as the nicotine fiend pulls a Zippo from one of his pockets and flips the top on the lighter, challenging me non-verbally to see if I'm going to do anything to back up my warning. Before either of us can blink, Curious strikes out with a limb as long as a cherry picker and knocks the lighter from the violent stranger's hand.

"I do believe my sister told you not to smoke on her property." Curious snaps in a voice that would scare me if I didn't know him.

The stranger laughs in a rasp as he reaches down to pick up his Zippo. He elects to put the lighter in his pocket before speaking.

"You know George I'm ashamed that you would treat your daddy like this. You too, Nila. Ya'll treat me like I'm some damn Jehovah Witness or something."

Andrea glares him down. "You up here standing before the threshold like a damn Jehovah Witness."

Curious raises up. "Wait, did this Negro just say he was my daddy? And call me by my government name in the process?"

I pause for a moment and let the recognition of the stranger's admission sink down in my brain.

"I am your father George; yours too Yenila. I'm Allgood Washington; it is a pleasure to meet you."

The trespasser extends a hand for anyone to shake but the three back up an inch or two and leave him hanging like the skin from an uncircumcised penis. Aware that we see him for the dick he is Allgood wipes his hand on his slacks, before putting it in his pocket for safe keeping.

"Okay this shit is just too crazy for words. Let me make sure I understand what is going on here. Mr. Washington, you were lurking on my sister's porch, smoking Niggaport after Niggaport until we show up to confront you, and the best story you can come up with is that you're our father. What I want to know is do you have any receipts to back up your claims mister Allgood Washington?" Andrea laces her words together like the ropes that tie up a pair of Chuck Taylor's.

Curious and I chime in like background singers. "Yeah!"

"Our?" Allgood pauses to use two of the fingers on his left hand to take the Newport out of his mouth. He looks directly at Andrea before continuing. "Well young lady I'd love to take responsibility for your creation, but I'm not your daddy. Only them two is my seeds." He points the fingers holding the cigarette at me and Curious.

"Like my sister said, do you have any proof of this, Allgood?"

Digging into the same pocket that his cigarettes are in,

Allgood Washington pulls out a photograph of three people sitting on an extremely ugly couch and hands it to me. It was taken with an old Polaroid camera, the kind that ejected the photo for the user to shake until it was developed. I recognize the woman in the middle as my mother in her younger days. The young man to her right is my father Tuskegee, and the trespasser on her left is the third man. Even in his youth, he looks centuries older than my parents. Studying the picture, I feel brother and sister flanking me on my right and left I'm interested to know their interpretations on the photograph, but my interest will have to wait until later. After looking at the photo, I am certain Allgood Washington has been a liar since he uttered his first words. It's possible he could be our daddy, but I need more than photographic evidence to prove it. I hand him back the Polaroid and shrug my shoulders, letting him know he has yet to provide sufficient evidence. Trespasser Washington puts the Polaroid back in his pocket, runs his right hand over his mouth in lieu of smoking another cigarette and inhales deeply before he elects to speak.

"Yeah me, Tuskegee and your momma used to be real tight back in the day. But just like in that picture, she managed to come between me and my brother."

Andrea snaps her head around. "Brother?"

"Yeah, Tuskegee is my half-brother. Same daddy, different momma. Getting down to the nub, Tuskegee and I had a falling out after he found out that me and Naw-mee had a thing going on."

Even though Allgood has buried himself with his own words, I elect to ask one final question that will cement his tomb. "If all of this is true, then why are you just now appearing, Allgood?"

The trespasser's nose and cheeks crumple up on his face; he knew the question would come, but he stews in the answer. Two more deep breaths through his nose and Allgood is ready to share. "Well shit it's not like my only daughter gets married every day, I came back because I thought you would like to have yo ' daddy walkin' you down the aisle."

"He will. I don't know what you plan to do on the day of my wedding because if I catch you anywhere in the vicinity, it will be a wedding and a funeral."

"Nila come on now; don't treat your father like this, honey." Allgood places his hand on my left forearm at the end of his sentence. That was a foolish mistake on his part, because my right arm is my dominant one. The hand attached to that arm slaps him with enough force that it sounds like a pang of thunder. The kitten ear knucks only partially scrape him, leaving two small gashes about a half inch apart on his left cheek. The speed of the assault is slow to process in the trespasser's mind; it takes him about four seconds to realize that he has been hit, and subsequently release his grasp of my forearm. When his synapses register the sensation of being struck, a magnificent emotion floods his eyes. Most people would call it shock. There is something closer to an invitation in Allgood's eyes.

He touches the gash on his cheek. "You goin' regret this, bitch."

I smile at his threat. "Allgood Washington, if you ever touch me again I won't be so gentle with you the next time. Now I don't know who you are, who you're working for, or whose daddy you actually are. And frankly, I don't give a shit. Listen carefully because I'm only giving you one warning. If I catch you around me and my family or on my property again, I'll cut off everything between your legs, puree that shit in my Ninja, then come back and feed it to you. Now get the fuck off my porch."

I point toward the stairs, while Andrea and Curious separate to create a path for the trespassing man. Allgood takes two lateral steps and turns back to me.

"You a mighty tough talkin' cunt when you got the booty bandit and some burnt Black bitch backing you up. But we ain't got to wait until later- we can set it of—AAAAAAhhhhhhhhhhh!AAAAAAAhhhhhhhhhhh! This fuckin' bitchdonesprayedme!"

After Andrea maces him Allgood can't figure out which to do first- cough, cry or walk away as the corrosive chemicals decimate his ear, nose and throat area. He stumbles like a blind man down a back alley until Curious snatches him up by his collar.

Andrea gets her digs in while Curious "helps" Algood down my porch steps. "Who you callin' a Black bitch, punk?"

As the two approach the curb, Curious grabs the back of the trespasser's slacks, picks him up and heaves him into the street like Uncle Phil used to do Jazz on the Fresh Prince of Bel-Air. I am astounded at my baby brother's strength as I watch that pitiful excuse for a human being fly through the night air. Unaware that he was about to take a flight, Allgood doesn't prepare for the landing; good thing his face is there to break his fall. His screams grow louder as he flounders in the painful after effects of the concrete kiss. Curious makes a big show of wiping off both of his hands like he's just "taken out the trash" as he walks back toward my house. Behind him Allgood crawls on the concrete like a baby who has yet to learn to walk. Headlights appear suddenly in the darkness and an engine accelerates at the same time. A dark sedan races up the right side of my block, stopping inches from hitting the grown man crawling in the street.

Curious turns around at the commotion and I start to step off the porch. Andrea is somewhat frozen between the two of us. My mind races back to the last time a dark sedan came speeding up on Curious in the middle of the street- the thought sends my feet sprinting to my baby brother until we're side by side on the sidewalk. The sedan remains still in the middle of the street, until both rear doors open and a man and woman exit the vehicle. The pair picks up the man-baby off the concrete and rushes him into the backseat of the sedan. Neither of them says a word, nor do they take their eyes off me and my siblings. Before the doors on the dark sedan close, it speeds off down the block. Curious and I stand motionless under the light of the moon, unsure if drama is over for the night or if it's just taking an intermission.

Andrea speaks up after the sedan is long gone. "I need something to calm my nerves."

Her words pull me and Curious out of our trance and the two of us turn to face her. "Crown or Ciroc?"

"Both!" Her and Curious answer, as the three of us head into my home.

CHAPTER 14

O nce my siblings and I are comfortably inside my abode, I make sure the front door is padlocked and the security system engaged. Then I dial a number I know by heart, but my Smartphone has programmed as 'Bambi Eyes'

"Hey baby, uh huh."

"Yeah I called to see when you are coming home."

"Because there is water under the bridge."

"Yep, sure is. Okay see you soon. Love you too."

Andrea looks at me as I break the connection with Drian. "Water under the bridge, what's that, some secret code?"

I glare at the nosy chocolate chip. "Ugh. Heffa you need to stay out of my mouth- my dentist don't be all up in my grill as much as you is right now!"

"I bet you Drian's dick be up in there on da regula though!" Curious tries to come to Andrea's defense.

"Oooooooooooohhh! Got 'em!" Andrea catcalls through cupped hands.

I step away from my front door and walk around Andrea so I can get right up in Curious' face. "Look here, trick! Don't you be worried 'bout where Drian's dick is! That ain't none of yo' damn bizness!"

I use the last word to mush my baby brother in his face. Curious lets his head snap all the way back and come full forward before he launches into his tantrum.

"Oh! No she did NOT put her hand in my face! Heffa, you know I blemish easily!"

I spread my arms like an eagle about to take flight and hop right in Curious' face. "Well what you wanna do about? Cry two tears in a bucket nigga, fuck it! Let's see if you really 'bout dat life."

"Chile! 'Bout dat life? Really I'm about to give you life and snatch it back like my name is Jesus!"

"Negro please! More like yo' name is Hey-zeus."

"Andrea, hold my gum, I'm 'bout to set it off up in here!"

Before Curious gets his chance to set it off, the mechanical sound of chains grinding spreads throughout the house, which means the garage door is being opened. I damn near knock Curious over to get to the door that leads to the garage so I can see my baby. Door open and looking into the garage, I see Drian behind the wheel of his new silver Durango, with company in the passenger seat. It dawns on me that it would be in my best interest to bring my car in the garage as well in case Allgood wants revenge tonight.

"Hey, can one of ya'll grab my keys out my purse and bring them here please?" I keep my eyes focused on my lover, until I feel a nudge in my back. I turn to see Curious standing before me, keys in hand.

"Thank you."

"Yea, whatever." Curious spits before he scurries into the kitchen for God knows what.

Turning my attention back towards the garage, I see Caldwell Cornelius coming towards me with a duffle bag in his left hand. The potent aroma of marijuana confronts my nostrils as he climbs the stairs that lead from garage to house. He greets me with a nod as I move from the threshold to allow him entry. As Caldwell passes me, Drian is just getting out of his SUV. I whistle at my lover and toss my keys at him.

"Hey valet! Can you park my Tesla in the garage please?"

Drian snatches the keys out of midair and smiles his response as he heads to get my Tesla. I keep two eyes focused on my baby because intuition is telling me that danger is still abound; and I don't want to get caught slipping. As Drian pulls my automobile into our garage and cuts the engine off. My ears detect grumblings from three adults that are either hungry or thirsty as they rummage through my kitchen to try and fulfill their needs.

As Drian gets out of my driver's seat I let the garage door down and engage the reinforced titanium steel gate we had installed behind the door—in case of emergency. As my fiancé nears the entryway of our home a set of outstretched arms are waiting for him. Before I can wrap him in mine, he envelopes me with biceps that are stronger than magnesium alloy. The power in his embrace frightens me a bit, because it reminds me of the impossible dream that life can sometimes be. One moment you're wrapped tightly in an embrace. The next you damn near break both arms trying to hold onto a feeling that evaporated before it ever touched the surface. In the moment that is now, I put flesh to flesh as I wet my man's lips with a kiss of uncertainty and he returns the notion.

"We hoped this day would never come." I declare in his left ear, after our lips part.

"Good thing we planned anyway."

"You wanna tell me what that shit at the restaurant was all

about?"

The strength that once enveloped me has now dissipated as my lover releases me from his grasp. As we separate, he stares at me, his Bambi eyes piercing me, attempting to expunge the banks of memory stored in the vault of my mind. I stare back at him intently intense, refusing to vacate the mental space my inquiry created. With both my physical and third eye locked on Drian, I clamp down on my desire to know the truth about the assault that happened earlier. Like the candidate who realizes he's lost the Electoral College, Drian concedes with the blink of his eyes. The blink is followed by a slow head shake and him mumbling what sounds like "I'll tell you later."

I follow my lover into the house we've made into a home, to put into action a contingency we planned for about a year ago. Feet over the threshold, he heads down to the basement and I go inspect all the rooms on the main level. With the domicile safe, sound and secure, Drian and I meet back in the kitchen, sit down at the dining room table and join three adults chatting and sipping on alcoholic beverages.

As Drian and I descend on the room, the chatting between the three stops abruptly. The three of them all take a synchronized sip from their glasses and stare straight ahead, as they slouch down in the padded leather chairs that surround our kitchen table. There are six chairs that outfit our dining room table. Two on both sides of the African Blackwood and one chair on each end of the rectangular table. As Drian takes a seat at the head of the table, I reach in the cabinet and grab two small tumbler glasses made from Waterford crystal. I fill them both with ice from the freezer, then hand one to my lover. I open the refrigerator and reach into the very back for the bottle of Ketel One I keep stored for special occasions. Except right now, I am tipping the glass in the case of an emergency. I pour myself a heavy shot and put the bottle back in its reserved space.

Vodka in hand I take a seat at the other end of the table, opposite Drian. From a crystal decanter that came with the Waterford tumblers, Caldwell pours an amber colored liquid into the ice filled glass I gave Drian earlier. Just as I do with Ketel One, Drian only drinks from the crystal decanter on special occasions. But the way he guzzles the liquor and sets the empty glass in front of Caldwell lets me know his mood is anything but festive. Caldwell pours him another drink; Drian finishes the second one faster than Usain Bolt does the 40-yard dash, and sets the glass before Caldwell once more. Sensing a pattern, I decide to interrupt the routine.

"Drian, baby can you hand me the grapefruit juice from the fridge please?"

He gives me a "Bitch, you know you could have gotten this shit yourself" look as he gets up from the chair to complete my request. I smile at my man for being smart enough to not say what's on his mind as he hands me the Ruby Red juice. He wrestles down back in his padded chair before he laments,

"Iight woman, come on with the floodgates."

I stare him straight in the eyes and take a long sip of my alcoholic beverage. I let the spirit burn in my chest and all the way down to my stomach before I even consider answering, then I take another swig. After a third sip, I lay out everything that happened with Allgood earlier. The only movement Drian makes while I'm speaking is a head nod once I near the end of my retelling. When I finish, aside from the sound of liquid flowing between lips, the table is silent.

Caldwell breaks the silence. "So you pepper sprayed this nigga, and tossed him in the middle of the street, like Uncle Phil off the Fresh Prince?"

The five of us start to laugh at Caldwell's simple but accurate assessment.

"Shit, had that fake ass Five Heartbeat reject not threatened the life of me and my siblings, he might've walked away under his own power." I cut in through the laughter.

The rest of the group nods in agreement.

Caldwell looks at Drian. "In some way shape or form, Tyrrell is behind this, Ayo."

"And most of my gut feels the way you do, CeeCee. But what I can't figure out who Allgood Washington is or the timing of his appearance."

"He is a damn liar, that's who he is!" The liquor in me blurts out "That sorry bastard snitched on himself when he called Mommy Nomie, Naw-mee! With the exception of Caldwell, we all know that she goes to great lengths to emphasize that her name is No-mie,—"

"Like you know you KNOW ME!" Curious and Drea repeat a line we've heard our mother say a thousand times.

"Exactly!" I point at my siblings. "If he really did 'know her', like that he never would have called her 'Naw-mee' because she hates that shit."

Drian is deadly calm before slowly stating. "Yeah, but mispronouncing your mama's name doesn't explain why he would pick this time to show up."

I am the opposite of calm. "Fuck all the who's, what, where, and why! All I need to know is the 'how.' Like how am I goin' get my shoe back after I break my foot off in Allgood's ass! That's all I'm worried about."

Caldwell nods. "Niggas is goin' be niggas Ayo, so it's pointless for us to try and figure out what we know we don't know."

Curious pours himself more Ciroc. "From where I sit the Allgood/Tyrrell drama comes down to two things. One, is revenge. It's as clear as Crystal Pepsi that Tyrrell and his people want payback for last Fourth of July."

Drian adds cranberry juice to Curious' vodka. "And the other reason?"

"The other reason?" Curious pauses to take a test sip of his beverage, measuring its potency. Once he is satisfied he begins again. "The other reason is money, which has been a powerful motivator since the days of the Roman Empire and Before Christ."

"Curious I don't know if it's because you been drinking or because I've been drinking, but you sound halfway smart after a couple drinks." I slur.

Curious shakes his head in slow motion. "Heffa, I swear you got 'bout four more times to say something crazy to me."

"Or else what?"

"I'm snatchin' them brows!"

"Snatch deez, nicca!"

"HEY!" Drian slams his hand on the table. "Both of ya'll shut up, please. I swear to God you two act just like Thelma and JJ when ya'll get together."

"Who you tellin' to shut up!?" Curious and I shout at Drian in unison, then fall into a fit of laughter at our sibling synchronicity.

Through tears of laughter I watch Drian get up from the table, dump what's left of his melted ice in the sink and put fresh ice in his glass. He returns to the padded chair and sets the glass in front of Caldwell, who pours him another drink from the crystal decanter. Drian doesn't chug it; this time around, he sips it slowly and puts the tumbler on the table.

"Now if it's all right with Thelma and JJ, I'd like to get back on track." Hearing no objections from the table, Drian marches on. "Mr. Allgood Washington."

Drea shudders. "That man is some kinda evilness, I can feel it in my spirit."

"Agreed. Which brings us to the here and now ya'll. Because of the danger on the outside, we want everyone inside safe. Nila and I have put the house on lockdown. No one leaves until we all leave. More importantly no one gets in either. The alarms have been set and all the locks have been engaged, and with all the pistols and pepper spray, I think everybody in here is well armed."

No one at the table says a word after Drian lays out the circumstances at hand. We all nod in silence, thinking about the danger on the other side of the front door. A shiver of fright wafts over me as I think about the lengths me and my family might have to go to keep the danger from coming into my home. There is a very realistic chance that someone could end up dead before all that's done is said.

"Nila?"

"Huh, what?" I mumble what I think sound like words.

Drian has my attention now. "What do you want to do about the sleeping arrangements?"

I breathe in through my nose and out through my shoulders before I sigh, "Curious can take the room in the basement.

Caldwell there is a couch down there too, unless you want to sleep with Curious."

Caldwell's head and neck don't move an inch but his eyes cut at me like a Hattori Hanzo sword after my last remark.

Drea looks my way. "And where is I goin' sleep?"

"Welp, since Adrianne is not here you can sleep in her room." I proclaim before a yawn catches me.

"Ooooohhhhhh where her room at, because I am getting super sleepy."

"Right over there." I stand up and point at the door to Adrianne's room, and sit back down because the liquor has made its way to my legs. In the time it takes for my butt to touch the seat, I see Drian has almost completely wiped the traces of anguish off his face, almost.

Drian leans back in his seat "I can see everyone eye's drooping, so I guess this family meeting is over."

I can't resist messing with him. "Wait, wait, wait. I know I just finished a vodka and grapefruit, but I am still waiting for the tea, honey."

"I told you I'd tell you later." Drian's tone awakens everyone at the table, and all eyes are on him.

"And later is now, baby." My response shifts all eyes to me.

With no easy way out, Drian sits straight up in his chair and turns his attention to Caldwell. Picking up the decanter, Drian pours a snort in a crystal tumbler with no ice or melted water in it. He sets the glass in front of Caldwell Cornelius. "CeeCee since it was you and Kian's mess that spilled over into the restaurant earlier, why don't you tell Nila what that shit was all about?"

Caffeine and drama must operate on the same neurotransmitters in the same part of the brain. Five seconds ago, I was ready to snuggle with the Sandman, but now that the tea is about to be served, I am alert, awake and anxious for Caldwell to pour. And just like the Queen of England at high noon, Caldwell is taking his sweet time deciding when to serve. He picks up the snort Drian poured him and downs it in one swallow. He lets the burn of the amber colored cognac settle in his chest before unleashing a loud, wet belch.

"Phentermine." He liberates another burp. "It's like a miracle drug for fat people, or celebrities who wanna lose weight fast and still be lazy at the same time. Because it suppresses yo' appetite and gives you energy like crazy."

Drea looks at him crazy. "Hold up, you say this drug makes you not hungry and gives you energy to the max? That sounds like cocaine to me."

"It does, don't it." Caldwell responds through a mischievous grin. "'Cept this drug is one hundred percent legal as long as you have a prescription for it. Now about three months ago I ran into Kian at Daytona Beach we both happen to be there for spring break. We got to talking, catching up on old times an' shit like that and about midway through the conversation she says she has a propo'sition for me. I'm thinking and hoping she goin' ask for some D. 'Cus she was looking mighty good in her bathing suit and I been wanting to give it to her somethin' serious since for a long time."

Drian glares at him. "CeeCee."

"Iight, damn. I'm just saying yo' sister is fine though. But anyway, she ended up asking me if I wanted to invest in a business she was starting up. She said she was goin' be selling Phentermine, vitamins, protein bars and a bunch of other health shit to gyms, health clubs and to the people she made contacts with the industry she is in.

Curious perks up. "Industry?"

"Yeah, she a video vixen. Slash model, slash actress, slash personal trainer. Blah, blah, blah. Essentially, she one of them use what you got to get what you want type chicks. When she asked me to "invest" in her latest entrenpo'nigga opportunity, I had my suspicions. I asked her what my return on investment would be and she said I could double my money. That's when I knew she was up to some shady shit. But I was too busy thinking with my dick to let common sense win out and I agreed to back her, if she would let me sample the product. I don't know where she could have hid the pills in that lil' ass bathing suit she had on, but I blinked and she gave me five of them Phentermine joints. I popped one right then and stayed up for twenty-four hours after that. My heart was beating all fast an' shit and I couldn't stop sweating. And I didn't even think about food, my stomach didn't even growl or nothin-' it was crazy. Popped another one the next day, exact same thing happened. That's when I decided to be a part of her hustle.

Caldwell takes another sip his drink. "An' sho'nuff I put in two hundred and fifty dollars in and a month later she gave me back five. I re-upped and put the five in and she gave me a rack back. Everything was lovely until I started to have a Nigga's Ambition. I wanted to start to know more about the hustle; how it worked, in's and out's and most importantly, I wanted to know who her connection was. I told her I would offer her more money for a percentage of her operation. And that instead of me 'investing' she would pay me monthly for various services I would provide her, such as introductions, distribution and protection. Life was good and my pockets were plump, but just like anything that is shady and goin' good eventually everything turns to shit and 'bout a month ago that's exactly what happened.

Caldwell takes a deep breath before continuing. "Kian called me in the middle of the night rambling about the shipment being late and she needed to go pick up the product like yesterday and she wanted me to meet her so we could go pick it up, 'cus she ain't wanna go by herself. She asked me to meet her at the

Montview and when I get up in there, she's fighting with some chick and her dude about some bullshit. And I didn't have the patience for that shit so I snatched her up and told her to get her shit together, and calm the fuck down. She looked at me like she wanted to try me, but the longer she looked the more she realized that was not the moment for games. Seeing that I was serious as death at a funeral parlor she switched her demeanor up an' started acting more ladylike. "

Another deep breath. "From the Montview we went over to this little after hours spot over on 22nd and Dayton. We chilled and talked for a little bit, but then she got a call and we dipped outta there and went down the street and met up with these Mexicans. It was two dudes and one lady that looked older but not old. The three of them kept they eyes on me the whole transaction. I guess they were suspicious I might try something. The drop went off smooth- she gave them the money, they gave her the product. Kian tells me she has one more stop to make and I follow her to Green Valley. Now mind you by this time it's like four in the morning. I am tired, frustrated and seriously considering getting out of business with Kian."

He takes another sip from his drink. "I follow her to an address off 51st kinda next to Omar D. Blair. We come up on the house and some ol' extra hood ass nigga answer the door wearing a fuckin' bulletproof vest! Man, I swear if she didn't owe me money still, I would have bailed out right then. The nigga with the bulletproof vest allows us entry to the home, but he said he had to frisk me before I went any further an' I told him that I wouldn't be the only one gettin' frisked if he put his hands on me. Kian steps to ol' boy in the vest and whispers in his ear- he laughs and me and Kian turn from him and head down to the basement. At the bottom of the steps is a metal security door- when we about six inches from the door, a slot in the middle of it opens. Kian puts some of the package from the Mexicans in the slot and it closes again immediately. The two of us stand in silence for thirty seconds before the slot opens again and out comes a bundle of money wrapped in orange cellophane with a brown paper underneath. Kian grabs the cash, puts in the brown bag and we head back up the stairs. The vested nigga is waiting for us at the top. Kian kisses his cheek and he opens the door so we can leave. I walk back to my ride without looking back and before I can get in and leave, Kian asks me to follow her. I tail her to the King Soopers nearby; she parks, gets into my car and hands me an' envelope with cash in it. I start to ask her about the trap house we just came from, but she put her lips on mine and kissed me so long and deep that I lost my sight temporarily. When my vision returned, I was sitting in my car still parked at the King Soopers with an envelope and my dick in my hand-- Kian was long gone. We kept up this routine for a couple more weeks until she called me and told me that both Mexican dudes got arrested and possibly deported and that the older Mexican lady was getting out of the game. At that point, Kian said fuck it and made her mind up to fuck them Mexicans over. She never paid the rest of what she owed them for her last shipment."

"So, she ran off on tha plug twice?" Curious barges in, unable to contain his pettiness.

"No! We ran off on tha plug twice because they knew my face, and since I was her most visible partner in this thing, her dirt is my dirt. After she realized she got fucked over, the older Mexican lady started making threats against Kian. And Kian tells the lady to eat a dick and then leaves town. Since them threats came down, me and my. 22 have been inseparable. Fast forward to tonight at the restaurant; that waiter we beat the brakes off of was one of the Mexicans we did business with."

"But I thought he had been arrested and deported." Drea drops in.

"So did I. But I recognized him instantly and vice versa, I signaled Kian and then I signaled Ayo too, because I knew I had to bring him up to speed in case something popped off. When I saw ol' Mexican boy dip in the back, the three of us got up to make our exit. As soon as we out the door, the Mexican comes in real quick from our left with a switchblade in his hand. His manly pride led him to make a foolish mistake; he brought a knife to a gun fight. Before I could get to my pistol, Ayo disarmed the dude and I knocked him back into the dining room. The rest ya'll seen with yo' own eyes."

I have a million questions I want to ask Caldwell, but my brain is overwhelmed with the fog that comes before sleep.

"Drian baby can you carry me to our bed?"

Drian says goodnight for the both of us as he picks me up out of the padded chair and carries me to the master bedroom. When my body lands on the mattress, I feel slumber before my heart has a chance to cycle through a full beat.

CHAPTER 15

The sound of seagulls squawking on the sea shore rouses me from my sleep. My body launches from horizontal to vertical in a moment of panic. Sitting upright, I look around in the darkness to make sure everything is all right. Three red numbers on a clock tell me it is 4:06 a.m. --- with my awareness gradually returning, I remember that I am in my own bed, in the house Drian and I have turned into a home. Operating of their own accord my feet hit the floor and my bladder leads me to the bathroom. While making water, I notice that my mouth is drier than a bowl of cereal soaked in sand. Bladder empty I head for the fridge for a bottle of Fiji. Popping the top, I guzzle the water like God handed it down to me from heaven. Thirst quenched, I head back to my bedroom. On the way there I feel a rapture develop in walls of my vagina. I don't know if Fiji is an aphrodisiac but it has my pussy feeling like a river runs through it. Horny and on the hunt for dick I open up my bedroom door and crawl into bed; preparing to check-in for my early morning dick appointment. Except the bed is empty, my dick doctor is gone. I ruffle through the sheets and blankets, expecting a grown man to be camouflaged within. Panic is percolating in my heart as I cut on some light, desperately searching for my fiancé. The sound of an engine being started and a reinforced steel door being opened, send me sprinting towards the garage. I get to garage door just in time to see Drian pulling out and racing down our block. The day is still new enough that the darkness hasn't turned to dawn. But I'm already hotter than sun in the Sahara. I reengage the reinforced titanium steel gate behind the garage door, and check to make sure the alarm system is on and working properly. Before I race back to my room, find my phone and dial up Bambi Eyes. No answer. The rage in me dials again, still no answer. As I prepare to call him a third time an unsettling feeling develops in my gut. My stomach is rumbling with anxiety at where my man ran off to at this time of morning. A soft rapt on my bedroom door, distracts me from the worry within.

"Come in."

The door swings inward and Andrea steps into my room. Motionless am I as my big sister takes a seat on my bed. "Hey." She says.

"Hey yourself." I respond, noticing that the sun is getting ready for its daily shift

She lets a few seconds pass before starting up again. "I heard the garage door open and doors slamming, I just wanted to check on you and make sure everything is cool."

I sit on the bed and bring my knees to my chest; then wrap my arms around my knees trying to find a physically comfortable place to speak from. "At this exact moment, I'm angry and worried with Drian. He just took off and didn't say a damn thing! I called him twice, no answer." I take a deep breath, letting the rage out of my lungs before continuing.

"Drian is the kind of dude that doesn't always disclose a lot while things are happening in real time. He'd rather wait and tell you everything after all is said and done. And that shit be pissin' me off! Plus I was trying to get me some of that early morning loving, but he fucked that all up."

"Thank God he did, because I didn't wanna hear you two gettin' ya'll swerve on. Especially since my man is halfway across the country."

"The way you was flirtin' with Mr. Cornelius yesterday I forgot you had a man." I unwrap myself from the upright fetal position.

"Girl hush! You know I was just being friendly."

"Uh huh, you was mighty friendly iight."

"Anyway," she stops to clear her throat. "Back to you and Drian, you know Mommy always used to say that you got to know your man better than he knows himself, because a sorry ass nigga is bad for your health."

My head starts to shake in slow motion. "First of all, I have never heard Nomie Montgomery say ANY of that. Secondly I'm pretty sure the last part of what you said is a lyric from an Ice Cube song."

"Oh, well maybe she only said it to me. Either way good advice is good advice."

"I can't disagree with that."

"You know what I wouldn't disagree with? Some breakfast. Because a sista is hungry right about now."

On cue my belly begins to rumble from Drea's suggestion. "I know that's right! What you cookin?"

"Me?" Drea pauses to clutch her pearls. "I am a guest here; I can't be expected to cook breakfast."

"Trick please! Idle hands don't get fed up in here. So if you wanna eat, then you betta at least help a sista out."

"Iight girl, damn I'll help. You lucky I like you." Drea responds as she makes her way off my mattress.

"Yeah, whateva."

Drea ducks just in time to keep from getting hit by the pillow I throw at her as she's walking out of my room.

***

I stand at the stairs that lead to the basement. "Curious! Caldwell! Come on now, breakfast is ready!" I hear one or both of them grunt, acknowledging that they heard my proclamation. I turn

146

from the stairs and step back into the kitchen. Drea has platters of eggs, French toast, biscuits, grits, pork bacon, turkey sausage, and assorted juices laid out on the kitchen table.

"Lookin' good, sis." I compliment Drea as I head to the cabinet to grab plates.

"Why thank you, and the food don't look too bad either!" Drea shoots back, never lacking confidence or conceitedness.

I just smile and shake my head in slow motion at her response as I start to set places at the table. As I am getting the glasses and silverware, Curious and Caldwell mosey on up from the basement.

"Damn!" Caldwell's eyes light up. "Ya'll got this shit hooked up! Everything on the table smells good. Wait, is that French toast? Awwww shhhhhiiittt! I know what I'm knocking down first."

"Morning ya'll." Curious greets as he sits down at the table.

"Morning Curious." I respond, while looking at Caldwell as he prepares to take a seat at my kitchen table wearing just a pair of boxers with Playboy bunnies on them.

"Uh, Mr. Cornelius I'ma need you to put on some pants, or shorts or somethin'."

"What?"

"You winking at me with your third eye."

It takes him a minute to register what I said. When he makes the connection, he looks down to check the slit in his boxers. "No, it's not."

"I know, but see how I got you slipping. Now go put on some shorts or something because the only dick I wanna see is my fiancé's."

Caldwell jets down to the basement to get something to cover up the Playboy bunnies. By the time he comes back to the kitchen, the three of us are seated and waiting for him to join us so we can pray before we devour the bountiful breakfast. Once Caldwell is seated the four of us join hands and I nod at Curious to lead us in prayer.

"Dear God, I want to thank you for the blood running warm in our veins. Thank you for the sound minds and the sanity that you give us, living among those that are insane. Bless the hands that prepared this feast, allow the food to be free of impurities and nourish our bodies. And as we embark on this day, a day that you have made. May the angels help us to lead the way. And please let your light shine upon our souls and help keep us safe. And I pray for all the one's we loved that done passed away, let them be there to greet us as we pass the gates. And when the time comes for us to be headed to the tunnel's light, I pray that it leads to eternal life. Aaaaaamen!"

"Negro did you just quote a Tupac song in a prayer?"

"Well actually since Tupac was an angel, all I did was quote from one of his hymns." Curious snaps.

"Shit he was one sexy ass angel then. Looking at him back in the day made me want to fall into sin." Andrea lusts.

Curious smiles and high fives her. "He sho' was, gurl!"

My siblings laugh while Caldwell and I pile our plates with food. Once brother and sister conclude their lustful reminiscence, they follow our lead. Gazing over the table, I see that I forgot to grab some Frank's Red Hot. My side eye also notices Caldwell sitting in front of his food, fork in hand but his food is untouched.

It's almost as if he is frozen in his chair.

I try to thaw him out. "Caldwell what's wrong?"

He shakes like a wet rat, then focuses his eyes on me before speaking. "Two things actually. Number one where is the syrup? Number two where is Ayo at?"

Without a word, I get up from the table and grab some Mrs. Butterworth's from the cabinet, since unlike Drian I know exactly where it is. I set the syrup in front of him before I respond. "Here's your syrup and I don't know where he is."

"Hey while you're up, can you grab the hot sauce please?" Drea chimes in.

"Sure, I didn't know I was cast in The Help part two but—,"

I stop my snappy comeback abruptly because I hear the front door shudder from someone trying to gain entry. My breakfast buddies hear what I hear and remain still in their seats. I put a finger to my lips indicating I want them to remain silent as I walk past them, taking cautious and soft steps to the master bedroom. Once in the bedroom I head straight for the night table Drian keeps his pistol in. With the firearm positioned in the palm of my right hand, I tepidly walk back to the front door. I look through the peephole and stop just short of taking the Lord's name in vain at what I see on the other side. I step back from the hole, unlatch the chain, disengage the deadbolt, and turn the knob to allow my fiancé entry.

"Damn baby I knew you were mad at me, but I didn't think you were angry enough to shoot me." Drian taunts when he sees the gun in my hand.

"Nila!" A little voice calls out before I can respond to my fiancé. Not even a second passes before I feel someone hugging at my thigh. After Drian takes his pistol from my grasp, I reach down with both hands and pick up his only child, Adrianne. Shock and surprise overwhelm my senses as I hold the little girl close to me. Just a few days ago Drian and I didn't know when or if we'd ever see his baby girl again.

"Hey cutie! How is my Bubble Belly?"

"I'm good, I misseded you."

The sweet song of her words almost brings tears to my eyes. I blink hard a couple of times and notice another unexpected presence creeping up my porch. I put the little angel back down on earth and whisper something in her ear. It doesn't take the blink of an eye for her to turn around and see Curious standing there.

"Un'kle Currius!" She holds both arms to the sky, indicating that she wants Curious to pick her up. My baby brother complies with her request and the two laugh and hug like the old friends that they are. This time last year, both of them had been kidnapped and held as leverage by a junkie turned small time criminal. During the time they spent in fear of their lives, they forged a bond words will never explain. Looking at the two of them I understand what joy means - at least for a moment.

"Curious why don't you take Adrianne in the kitchen and get her some breakfast, please?"

Instead of answering my baby brother starts to make noises like a train as he and Drian's daughter chug the few feet to the kitchen. Turning my attention from the precious pair I fix eyes on the other unexpected that appears on my porch this morning.

"Robert? Why isn't this a surprise?" I call out to my attorney as I close the front door and head to where he and Drian are standing. My skin instantly notices the change in climate coming from an air-conditioned house to the heat that is developing on this early July morning.

"Ms. Montgomery, a surprise indeed albeit a pleasant one on my end."

The esquire stands tall against the sun wearing a short sleeve white button up shirt with a spread collar. His dress pants are light gray with black pinstripes running through them. Even in "lounge" clothes, Robert is always dapper. This morning his shoes are what grab my attention the most. The shoes are pearl gray and made from the skin of an elephant. The tips of each shoe toe are accented with what I suspect is genuine ivory.

"Okay Robert enough with the charm, gimme the snake."

He smiles like he is about to close an argument before a grand jury. "Late last night I got a call from a very reliable source, that I also consider a dear friend. My friend told me that a warehouse in the Stapleton area had been raided based on a tip the police had received. One of the people arrested in the raid was a Ms. Angela Lamont. Now this friend that I consider very dear also holds a deep affinity for Mr. Yancy as well. This friend was also aware of the animosity between Mr. Yancy and Ms. Lamont. Since Ms. Lamont is currently in Denver County Jail for the foreseeable future, my friend asked me to step in as an advocate on Mr. Yancy's behalf to ensure that his only daughter did not end up in child protective services. I made a few calls to some people that owed me a few favors, and within a matter of hours I was able to reunite father and daughter."

"If I understand this correctly, someone snitched on a warehouse that Drian's baby mama worked at. She gets arrested and you and Drian swoop in like Batman and Robin to rescue Adrianne?"

Robert nods. "For the most part, yes."

"Uh huh and at this warehouse where they arrested Drian's baby mama, what crime was she changed with?"

"Selling stolen or counterfeit merchandise and possession of narcotics with intent to distribute." Robert replies calmly.

The look on my face must have betrayed the confusion coursing through my mind because Drian steps up to speak this time.

"Well for years it's been a well-known fact that Angela was slinging Fucci and Fouis Vuitton handbags on the low. What Robert hipped me to this morning is that some of those handbags came with a few "gifts" inside them."

"And what were these so-called gifts?" Curiously spilling out of me.

Robert steps back in to answer my question. "Well some of them were ecstasy pills. But they also found a large quantity of yet to be identified pills that are still being tested to determine what, or if any drugs they contain."

"Okay one last question gentlemen. What happened to the restraining order that Angela filed on Drian?"

The lawyer and the fiancé smile like a set of Doublemint twins that just made off with a Wrigley factory's worth of gum before Robert decides to answer. "Given the circumstances of Ms. Lamont's arrest, a judge decided it would be in Adrianne's best interest to be with her father. The judge issued a temporary injunction to the order of protection that was filed against Mr. Yancy."

Facing a rising sun, I put my left hand horizontally over my brow as a makeshift visor. With the movement, I've determined that I know all I need to know about Drian and Robert's early morning escapades. "Seems like you boys have had quite the morning; Robert why don't you go on in and get some breakfast. I need to talk to my fiancé for a jiffy."

Robert nods before smiling and heading into our abode.

I wait until Robert's all the way in the house before I go off. "Now you know that shit was fucked up! How the hell you just goin' take off without saying a word?"

Drian bats his eyes. "It all happened so fast. Robert called, you were sleeping peacefully and I didn't want to wake you."

"Well if that's the case why didn't you answer when you saw I called you, twice?!"

"What do you want me to say Nila? All I could think about was getting Adrianne, holding my baby girl in my arms, loving her like a father should."

I want to be mad at him, but I can't. My complaint feels petty compared to the expression of fatherhood I just witnessed. I stroke his face and bring his lips to mine; our kiss is long and sweet. When he pulls his lips from mine, he grabs my right hand, leading us inside our home. He's over the threshold and I'm halfway there when I hear a voice call out to me from the street. I turn around and see Juanita Dandy walking up our driveway.

"Heeeeeeeeyy Ms. Bride-to-be! Good morning!" The woman who sold us this house greets.

"Hey Juanita, good morning to you too! Come on in here and give me some love."

The beak nosed woman complies with my command and wraps both of her small arms around me. If she had on a pair of wedge sandals, she might come close to five feet—on a good day. Juanita is small in stature, petite, yet thick bottomed with well-developed hips and a big butt. Her upper-body is the opposite, a slim torso and breasts that might be a B cup depending on the bra. Her skin is the color of café con leche and she has a very large nose, like Toucan Sam. She looks like a woman who could pass for thirty, but she and I know she is closer to fifty. In addition to being a real estate agent, she is also my neighbor and president of the neighborhood watch. If anything happens on this block, you can bet Juanita Dandy knows all about it. She's also married to a very nice and sociable man named David, who unbeknownst to her, helped me and Drian out of a jam last Fourth of July.

"Huh?" I stammer as I feel the warmth of flesh on my left forearm.

"I said, you getting mighty close here huh? Coming down to that final twenty-four." Juanita repeats.

"You ain't never lied, I been as busy as a bumblebee building a beehive!"

"Ummm hmmm, I bet!"

The two of us burst out in laughter.

"Ooooohhhhhh girl is that coffee I smell brewing?"

Instead of answering, I grab Juanita by the hand and lead her to the kitchen where everyone else is congregating.

"Hey everyone. Look who decided to stop on by."

Juanita waves to the group and I hear someone clear their throat a signal that they would like a proper introduction.

"Excuse my manners. Juanita; I don't believe you've met my sister Andrea. We all call her Drea for short."

"Very nice to meet you Drea." Juanita bows.

"Pleased to make your acquaintance Juanita!" Drea waves with the hand that doesn't have her coffee cup in it.

"Oh, and this Caucasian that is standing near my sink is my

154

lawyer Robert Bland."

Robert extends his left hand to the petite beauty. "Very nice to meet you, Ms. Juanita."

She places her right hand in his left, and he brings the appendage to his lips and kisses it gently. Juanita shivers like a wet dog in frigid rain before she extracts her hand from Robert's grasp.

Juanita waits until she stops shivering to respond. "It is a pleasure meeting you as well, Mr. Bland."

Someone none too happy watching the interaction between the lawyer and the real estate agent lets out a throat clearing that could be mistaken for a baby lion's roar across the room. Juanita's neck jerks left towards the direction of the commotion. Once her eyes focus in, she sees the boy she seduced into manhood sitting ten feet away from her in my kitchen. Juanita and Caldwell look at each other for less than a fraction of a second, but in that moment, they knew no eternity.

"Adrian good morning, how is everything? I feel like I haven't seen you in forever." Juanita may be addressing my fiancé, but Caldwell knows who she's taking to.

"Everything has been going good, just ready to walk down that aisle and marry a beautiful bride." Drian replies, playing her game.

"Ayo," Caldwell rasps as he gets up from the table. "I know we got a lot of running around to do, so I'm about to go get dressed."

Before Drian can say a word in response, Caldwell is already halfway down the stairs that lead to the basement.

"Alas I think I am going to head out to ladies and gentlemen."

Robert announces abruptly

Drian moves with him. "I'll walk you out."

The mass exodus because of the awkwardness from Juanita and Caldwell, leaves only survivors in the kitchen, left to converse in the aftermath. I'm tempted to interrogate Juanita about the relationship she had with a teenage Caldwell Cornelius. I table the notion for now because I could see my inquiry doing more harm than good.

"Juanita have a seat, I'll get you some coffee." I instruct the neighborhood watch president.

"Well thank you. You know I came over here with a purpose too girl."

I set up the Keurig. "Oh yeah, and what is that?"

"I came to see what's up with the bachelorette party."

"Honey, you have come to the right place then," Curious cuts in. "Juanita, I know you got the Evite I sent out?"

"I did, but I want to know what's on the menu."

"One hundred percent grade A beef, honey! We got Mr. Di—, uhhhhh." Curious stops mid-sentence remembering that Adrianne is still in his lap. Catching his bearings, he starts up like a hot rod. "Okay so we have Mr. D-I-C-K In-Yo-Face on the menu, as well D-I-C-K Jamez, Marquis Manhood and Angina Williams, all scheduled to perform. We will have more meat than a slaughterhouse tonight, ya'll!"

"Oooooooohhhhhhhh!" Juanita makes a sound that I can only describe as a high-pitched squeak, after Curious finishes speaking. Hearing Juanita sound off, Adrianne attempts to replicate her sound, then Drea jumps in, and Curious too. Together they sound like a henhouse- if all the hens were tone deaf and high off acid.

"All right! Enough!" I cut them off for the sake of my eardrums.

I set a red mug filled with Colombian coffee in front of Juanita once the theatrics calm down. She asks for some cream and sugar and I comply with her request before taking a seat at the table.

"Okay girl so we know about tonight's activities, but what about tomorrow? You got your something old, something new, something borrowed and something blue?" My neighbor asks before she sips from her red mug.

"Yes I do! The something old / borrowed is the same thing. I am gonna be wearing the wedding dress my Great-grandmother, Grandmother and Mother all wore at their weddings."

"Ohhh! What does it look like?"

"You know what I have no idea, all I know is that it's cream colored, but my Mommy won't let me see it yet- she says that's bad luck. And let's see- the something new is this Fitbit."

I hold up my right wrist to show off the fitness bangle.

"I been wanting one of those myself- how much they hit foe?" Drea admires

"I don't know, Lady Reese got it for me."

"Lady Reese?" Drea and Juanita ask.

"Yes'm, Lady Reese is my Executive Assistant, except she don't do nothing but try and boss me around. She got me this because she didn't want me to get married and grow a front butt. I love that woman!" I let out a laugh at the generosity of the woman

I consider to be a second mother.

Curious nods. "And the something blue?"

"Ah! The something blue, well ladies only the hubby will get to see the powder blue thong I ordered special for him. It has clouds in the crotch area and the crotch is also detachable. So on our first night together as man and wife, I am going lay in the bed all seductive like, legs spread eagle wearing only that thong and I'm gonna let him get a good look as I part the clouds and say come to heaven!"

Drea makes a fist. "Grrrrrrr! Get 'em gurl!"

Drea's growl makes Juanita almost spit out her coffee, which makes me laugh and within a second the roar of laughter at the table rivals the crowd at Def Comedy Jam in its heyday.

Still wiping tears from his eyes Curious adds his two cents "So, since we're on the subject, have you tidied up your stairway to heaven, Miss thang?"

"Stairway to heaven?" I frown.

"Yes chile, have you taken the whiskers off that cootie cat of yours?"

"Oh, no I haven't actually. Thank you for reminding me, I'm gonna put that on my to-do list for today."

"Ummm hmmm girl, it is a necessity. Especially for you- got to have it lookin' shiny as a new penny for your new husband. Like this place I go to in Vegas, they wax errthang from ya elbow to ya booty hole!"

Drea's eyes widen. "You be getting yo' booty hole waxed, Curious?"

Looking at her face I can't tell whether she is shocked or surprised.

"Oh my sweet Jesus, yes! You can't have somebody down there grocery shopping and the aisles is messy!"

"So you be serving salads too?" Drea decides to double down.

"I sho' daggum do. Tossed, Caesar, Greek, Tabbouleh. When it comes to that, they call me Mr. All-you-can-eat!"

I throw my hands in the air. "Curious shut up! Right now, before I lose all my breakfast."

Drea shakes her head. "You nasty, Curious."

"You the one asked. So what that make you?"

"Curious."

"You wish, baby girl, I done already trademarked that."

I shake my head at the both of them and turn my attention to Juanita, "You see what I gotta deal with on this final twenty-four?"

"This one," she tips her head at Curious, "is a handful, I ain't even been over here five minutes and I don't know if I'll have any pearls left to clutch by the time I leave with as reckless as his mouth is."

I want to say something slick about what her mouth does, but thankfully the front door opens before I get a chance.

"Hey CeeCee! You ready yet!" Drian screams towards the basement, as he closes the front door and heads to our bedroom.

"Well let me get out of ya'll's way and back down to my own

house." Juanita proclaims suddenly as she rises from my kitchen table.

I think the possibility of having to see the child she raped into manhood two times in one day is just too much for the former substitute teacher to bear. The petty in me wants to create some reason for her to stay just so I can watch her squirm with the discomfort of her past. However, the adult in me wins out and I walk Juanita Dandy out.

"See you tonight girl!" Juanita waves at me from the sidewalk.

"I can't wait!" I respond with a wave of my own as I close and lock the front door.

As I turn from the door, Caldwell Cornelius is standing before me attired in blue jean shorts, a navy short sleeve polo and a pair of beige and blue boat shoes.

The instigator in me has to say something, "After all these years she still has the power to make you feel some kinda way, huh?"

"I guess so, I don't know how to explain it really, but it's like I'm under her spell or somethin'."

"Well she did rape you and get pregnant with a child that she claimed was yours."

Caldwell laughs. "You can't rape the willing."

"Yeah, yeah, yeah I know. But the facts is still the same; she took advantage of you at a young age and nobody around you said a word about it. If you had been a female and she a male, then we'd all call her a pedophile and send her to jail. Even now when the news comes on and we see a female teacher get arrested for sleeping with her students, first thing we say is: 'Dang she was that thirsty that she had to sleep with a teenage boy?"

"I don't look at it like it was rape though- I look at it as an old player teaching a young player the game."

"Uh huh, and even after all these years she's still playing you."

I can see in Caldwell's face that he wants to respond but the words never make it to his mouth. The two of us stand here for a few seconds as the truth comes tumbling down on Caldwell. Looking at him, I see the teenager that Juanita left behind; a boy trapped inside the fragments of the man that Caldwell has grown up to be.

"CeeCee!" Drian calls from our bedroom.

Caldwell doesn't say a word as he turns from me and heads to the place where Drian was calling him from. As Caldwell walks away, brother and sister come marching in the living room with Adrianne right behind them. The three of them sit on one of the black leather couches in my living room, while I take up residence in the cashmere zebra print chair I bought myself as a housewarming gift a few years back.

"Nila can I watch cartoons?" The pint-sized princess asks.

"Of course you can, Bubble Belly"

Needing no further instructions Adrianne picks up the remote and flips channels until she finds a cartoon that captures her interest. Once the toddler's needs are satisfied, the child-at-heart decides to speak.

"Okay sister, what's on the agenda for today?"

"For starters, I am gonna get my cootie and booty waxed so it can be shiny as a new penny," I smirk while looking dead at Curious. "Then I thought we could go to yoga,"

Drea jumps in. "Hmmm! You know I have never been to yoga but I always wanted to go. I am excited already!"

"Yeah, the lady I go to, Svetlana, she is the best! She has a way of getting you in touch with the you within. I can't explain it fully, but by the time we're through ya'll will know what I mean."

My siblings nod in anxious agreement.

"Then you know we have to do some retail therapy."

"Hmmmm yess, yess Lawd Jesus! I am here to tes-ta-fiy! That retail therapy is my addiction and I don't need no intervention, hallelujah!"

By the end of his proclamation, Curious is up on both feet flailing his arms to the sky like one of those inflatable tube men you see outside of a store that is having a sale. His shenanigans are contagious enough that within a blink, he and Adrianne are up flailing and shouting all over my living room.

"Ajae, what are you doing?" Daddy Drian asks, his presence in the living room appearing seemingly out of nowhere.

The toddler and the adult stand still like their feet are made of cement. Seconds pass.

"Uhhhhh playin' wit Unkle Currius." Adrianne answers when she remembers that her mouth still works.

"Uh huh, well go to your room and get your backpack and stuff. We've getting ready to leave soon."

"Okay Daddy." The pint-sized princess takes off running like that's all her legs do.

"Babe, ya'll bout to leave soon?" My fiancé asks after Adrianne zooms past him.

"Yes sir, me and the crew got a busy day ahead."

"Be safe out there tonight."

"See you tomorrow Mrs. Yancy." He says as he and Caldwell trample down into the basement.

CHAPTER 16

I pull up to the valet stand in the underground garage of the Ritz-Carlton. I get out of my Tesla. I leave the keys in the ignition, grab my purse and make eye contact with the young White kid working at the valet stand. When he comes over to me. I hand him a ten-dollar bill.

"Don't scratch my baby."

The youngster nods agreeably as Andrea and Curious get out of my automobile; they both have their hands full with shopping bags. As the young White boy pulls off in my Tesla, a golf cart pulls up in front of me and my siblings. Behind the wheel is a man my Grandmother Inez would call "high yellah" because of his complexion. His hair is black and cut short and his eyes have an epicanthic fold, making him look slightly Asian. He has no facial hair and a nose with a thin bridge and wide nostrils. Below the wide nostrils are a set of full lips that are a shade of pink that scientists spend years trying to replicate and sell to the public.

He steps out of the cart. "Good day, my name is Mr. Wale Nandi I'll will be your Concierge zis evening."

The man bows once he is done speaking. Appearance is a first impression and Mr. Nandi cuts no corners. He is spiffy in his three-piece navy blue suit. His dress shirt is white with baby blue windowpanes and he has on a bowtie with yellow with dark blue polka-dots on it. His shoes are the color of oxblood and there is a white and yellow daisy in his left lapel.

I can't quite place it, but there is a slight French accent in Mr. Nandi's speaking voice. His version of the language doesn't sound authentic to the country, but more so as if French is his second language.

"If zu wi'l hop in I'll 'ake you to your suite."

I take the seat next to Mr. Nandi and brother and sister bring up the rear.

"Ready?" The concierge asks.

"Ready." The Montgomery children answer in unison.

The concierge drives a short distance on a concrete path before steering left, stopping in front of a pair of steel doors. The gentleman taps on the horn and the mechanical doors open to a hallway with floors that are paved red underneath lights that have an orange glow. The concierge picks up speed until another set of mechanical doors begin to come into focus and he stops just short of these doors and steps out of the cart.

"Follow me, pl 'ease." As he walks through the second set of mechanical doors, holding the right side open for my siblings and I to pass through. Five feet ahead two brass elevator panels await us; the concierge glides the required distance and punches in a numeric code that allows the panels to open. Elevator music fills my ears as a man sings about the girl from Ipanema. My eyes ingest an elevator that is walled with purple velvet and trimmed in gold. Several crystal teardrops form a chandelier that hangs from the ceiling of the elevator. I remind myself to try and keep my mouth closed as I am entranced by the entire splendor. The elevator stops on a floor that has no number and we exit the vertical transportation device. Stepping off the elevator my feet touch a floor that is made from marble that is satin white in hue and has recently been polished. The walls of the corridor we're in pay homage to Michelangelo's work at the Sistine Chapel. The only visible break is a cream-colored door with a gold handle. The concierge walks straight to the door, taps a badge in the center of it and the door opens automatically.

"And 'ere we are, zee Ritz-Carlton suite."

The concierge holds his left arm bent at the elbow in the direction of the room, indicating that he'd like us to enter.

To this day, I have never seen a more decadent space than what sits before my eyes right now. The Ritz-Carlton suite is the size of a small airplane hangar. Grabbing my attention first are windows that showcase an eighteen by twenty-foot view of downtown Denver. The Rocky Mountains in the background bolster the aesthetic appeal of the skyscrapers that were constructed in front of them. The suite has a very modern design the flooring is made from dark brown walnut that helps offset the beige tone that the walls are covered in.

"An' if you'll follow me 'zis way I will show you to the master bedroom."

The four of us walk left from the main room and head down a hallway that has fish tanks on both sides. The tanks are filled with fish that look like the exotic kind that celebrities have on MTV Cribs.

"Here we are, ze master bedroom."

I hear the concierge keep talking, but my eyes are drawn to the bed. It is a king sized Victorian canopy style. Beautifully crafted from what might be an assortment of cherry, oak or pine woods all finished in a black varnish. The bed is cornered by four pillars each with intricate Spanish carvings on them. Yellow marble shaped like leaves adorn the top of each pillar. The bed is outfitted with black and gold pillows and a Versace blanket with its signature insignia in the middle of the cloth. At the foot of the bed sits a black and yellow Ottoman bench.

When I tune my ears back in, the concierge is still speaking. "...And ze bathtub is made from Italian marble. And zer is also an adjoining room on zee other zide of the room."

From the bedroom, he takes us back out into the main area that on the right side leads to a kitchen which includes a personal chef at our beck and call. There is also a media room with a large flat screen TV, Playstation and a pool table.

The tour ends where it began. "We also have a masseuse and an' esthetician on site. Anything zu wish is our command."

"Excuse me Mr. Nandi, where are you from?" I ask, curiosity eating away at me.

Wale Nandi smiles with just his lips before answering, "South Africa."

"Which part?"

"Johannesburg."

"Hmm, well that explains the accent I hear."

"I like his accent, I think it's cute." Curious thirsts in.

The South African gentleman begins to blush. Whether from awkwardness or flattery remains unknown. "Well then, I'll leave the three of zu be unless zu need anything else?" Wale asks to break up some of the tension.

"Yes Mr. Concierge- in about an hour can you send up the masseuse please?" Drea asks.

"Certainly."

The gentleman bows before us for the second time today and puts his hand on the golden handle, preparing to depart.

"I'll walk you out." Curious offers as Wale Nandi is halfway out the door. The Concierge doesn't say a word as my brother follows out behind him.

    With all the testosterone out of the room, I take a seat on one of the two couches in the main room of the suite and stare out at the skyscrapers and Rocky Mountains of Colorado.

    "Your brother is something else!"

    Drea cracks up. "Girl you ain't neva lied a day in yo' life!"

    We giggle like little girls and then the room gets quiet. I don't know what Drea is up to; all I care about is the breathtaking view from the Ritz that is bringing peace to my mind. Lost am I in the beauty of the sky.

                    ***

    Four knocks sound on the other side of the door of the master bedroom in the Ritz-Carlton suite. Squeezing into my candy apple red liquid leggings is more important to me than seeing who is at the door though.

    "Nila you ready?" Sister asks.

    "Not yet." I rise off the bed and pull the leggings out of my butt.

    "I'm coming in. You decent?"

    She opens the door before I even have a chance to answer.

    "What difference would it make if I wasn't? You just come barging in any damn way."

    "Heffa please! You ain't got nothing I ain't already seen."

    "Oh yeah, well what about this?" I flick two middle fingers at my older sister.

Coincidently, Sister uses her middle finger to scratch the bridge of her nose.

"Ooooohhhhhh that is a cute bra girl! Where you get it?"

"Uh, Frederick's I think. I like it because it has pockets on the side." I turn to the left to show Sister the secret pocket stitched into my black leopard print brassiere.

"That is tight! I like that. If I had bigger breastestes, I'd steal that from you."

"Klepto much?"

"You know I'd only steal from you because you my sister."

I shake my head in slow motion as I slip into my white tank top with a Mickey Mouse Gangsta design on the front and fix my hair into a ponytail.

"Anyway chick, I really came in here to tell you to hurry up. Folks out here waiting on you. Party is 'posed to start at eight."

I look at my Fitbit and see that it's almost nine, which means the party is on CP time. From the other room, I start to hear "Dance (A$$)" by Big Sean and Nicki Minaj playing. Of their own accord my hips just start to move to the beat.

"Sister who out there bumping the jams?!"

"Guess you'll have to bring yo' ass out chea and find out." Andrea turns a tailfeather and walks out of the room.

I slip into my white with black patent leather trim Air Jordan XI's and decide to take sister's advice and head out to the main room of the suite. Closing in on the room I see the couches have been moved against the wall closest to the front door, and chairs line the periphery of the room. A full bar has been setup on the left side of the room with a young Black dude behind it flirting with an individual I am indifferent about. In less than twenty-four hours she will be family. Tonight though, I will serve the broad a glass of Beyoncé style lemonade.

"Hey Ms. Kian, you look cute." Flattery is the sincerest form of manipulation.

"Hey future sister-in-law! Thank you, so do you!" She puts her hands in mine. Kian air kisses my right cheek and my left. I return the gesture.

"Where is Ms. Vivian at?" I try to figure out how much patience I am going to need for the night.

"Oh, she stayed home. Drian asked her to watch Adrianne."

Thank God for small miracles. Having all the info I need from Kian, I look around the room for a diplomatic way to drop the Tater Thot. Spotting the DJ booth, I've found my salvation. I tell Kian to enjoy herself as I excuse myself to go stop by the DJ booth. Mentally I take note to keep an eye on Kian in case she wants to chin check somebody else. Walking away from the bar, I veer towards the right side of the room where the DJ booth has been set up. My girl DJ SheaButta is live, spinning on the two's and few's. The middle of the room has been left wide open for the entertainment that has yet to arrive. I also smell food in the room, but see no traces of the edible nutrients. I wave at SheaButta and start to head in her direction, until a knock on the front door stops me. I don't even check the peephole before pulling the gold handle.

"Hey Ms. Bride-to-be!"

"Lady Reese!" I wrap her in a hug. "I should've known you'd be one of the first people to show up."

"Sweet thang, you bettah know it! You know the party don't start 'til Clarice sho' up and it sho' don't end until I shuts it down!"

We both laugh at her craziness.

"Clarice, I swear you are something else! I don't know what to do with you sometimes!"

"Shoot, I do! You can get me something to drink off up in here. Shiiiiiiiit, we at the Ritz-Carlton- I know they got all the good liq'ua up in here."

I don't even get a chance to point her in the direction of the bar before she spots it over my shoulder and starts heading that way. Deprived of libations myself, I decide to follow her.

"Hey cutie, can I get a Strong Island and…" Lady Reese turns to me for my order. I hold up two fingers indicating I'd like a Strong Island as well. "Okay two Strong Islands baby."

I notice that Kian is nowhere to be seen.

"I see you got on your Fitbit." Lady Reese says to me once the bartender leaves to fix our drinks.

"Yeah, you know I got to keep that front butt at bay. Plus, it matches my outfit." I hold up my wrist and do a half turn so she can get a good look at me.

"Ummm hmmm, I see you girl!" She puts her hand up for me to high five.

"Uh excuse me what is all this high fiving ya'll doin' over here?" Curious walks up on me and Lady Reese dressed like Eddie Murphy in Delirious.

"Say brother you need to high five 911, because you 'bout to have a heatstroke with all that leather you got on!"

"For your information hussy, this is breathable leather!"

Curious spins around as quickly as a cat and reveals that the ass has been cut out of his leather chaps. I'm thankful I haven't had food or drink yet because that sight brought sour to my stomach.

"Curious I swear we will fight tonight if I see yo' ass one more time!"

"Welp you might wanna get some sunglasses, Helen Keller! Boop!"

Before I can crackle and pop, another guest decides to knock on my door. Opening the door this time brings me a blast from my past

"Oh. My. God! LaTanya is that you?!" I ask in disbelief.

"Live and in the flesh girl! Congratulations!"

My old running partner dives at me with both arms open. I return her embrace and we hoot and laugh in one another's ear. I met LaTanya long ago when I used to run the streets of Park Hill looking for boys and trouble and she introduced me to both. We we're both young and down for whatever back then, until she decided to get married and start a family and we kind of lost touch.

"You look good girlfriend!"

"So do you, the years have been good to you!"

LaTanya looks like she's still in her thirties, lighter skinned and hair long, black and beautiful enough to be on a box of Dark and Lovely.

"So how is your husband and kids?" I ask as we head towards the bar

"Good, good. We just built a house out in Green Valley. You know I have been pleasantly occupied with that."

"I know that's right! You gotta have me over for your housewarming." I squeal.

"Nila I love you girl, but I don't know if my house is ready for you just yet... You remember what happened at the house I USED to have in Park Hill?!"

"No! Do NOT put that on me that was New-New!"

LaTanya rolls her eyes. "Uh huh..."

"Excuse me miss, may I get you something to drink?" The milk chocolate mixologist chimes in.

LaTanya laughs long and loud while shaking her head at me before she orders a Tequila Sunrise from the man behind the bar. We hear a banging coming from the other side of the door. As I take a step in that direction, Curious cuts off my path and dashes for the gold handle. Two men appear on the other side after Curious opens the door.

"Is them the strippaz?" Drea inquires appearing literally from out of nowhere.

LaTanya chimes in. "I guess you'd have to ask your brother now, huh?"

"LT! Is that you girl? Come hug ma neck!" Drea demands.

If LaTanya and I used to hang like a pair of eighty-year-old titties then Andrea and LaTanya were as close as butt cheeks.

They used to do everything together and their closeness made me feel some kinda way for a little bit. Three more knocks at the door bring more guests to the Ritz-Carlton suite. Seeing that Curious has disappeared with the two mystery men, I elect to resume my duties as doorwoman. This time around, the gold handle brings a double dose of trouble.

"Nina and Melvina! The wonder twins are in the house!"

The twin sisters step into the suite in a synchronized stride, right foot after left. They've been together so long I don't even think they know that they do it.

"Congratulations girl! We are soooooooo happy for you!" They even talk in unison.

"Thank you, ladies." I hug both twins at the same time and they almost suffocate me with they Tig-Ol-Biddies. Twins by nature, they're different in style. They're both sociable and fun as hell to be around, but their differences are subtle and only seen if you get to know both of them (which is rare). Nina is the older of the two (by ten minutes); she's the more laid back and quick to dismiss if she feels like you dissing her. Nina is more of a playa than her sister. More than a few times we got into a discussion about a man, or two, or three. Luckily for me they always chose her, which freed me up to marry my baby Drian. Sometimes in life the best choices are the ones you don't make. Melvina is the kind of woman that other women like. She is polite and personable, warm and inviting—on the surface. Underneath that surface she can be ruthless as Jerry Heller and Easy E, if you're dumb enough to try her. She's the type of chick that will smile in your face and watch your house burn down to the ground behind you if you get on her bad side. Whereas Nina is a playgirl, Melvina manages to be a serial monogamist, changing dudes once every time a Black President is elected.

Once I'm able to breathe again I resume my duties as hostess. "It's good to see you two, why don't you head to the bar—

," I don't get a chance to finish my sentence as the twins are already three quarters of the way there. Looking at them, I remember that I still haven't gotten my own drink.

I cup both hands around my mouth before I yell at Clarice to get her attention. When she looks at me, I make a drink to mouth motion with my right hand. She nods like she understands and I pull the gold handle with my left hand even though I didn't hear a knock. Standing in the hallway with her hand in midair is my friend Maria.

"Damn girl, how'd you know I was here?"

"Maria guuuuurl, you know I know everything!"

She tells me to shut up before she wraps me in a hug.

"Damn Maria you and yo' arms is so damn little I'm shocked you got them around me!" I tease the short Hispanic woman as I close the door behind us

"Well with as thick as you been gettin' I am shocked they fit around you too!" She snaps back.

I can't help but laugh. "Melvina! Come get yo' girl!"

Melvina waves with the hand that is free from an alcoholic beverage and Maria storms at her with all her might. I notice DJ SheaButta digs way back in the crates as "Just Got Paid" by Johnny Kemp starts bumping through the room. I see the ladies start to dance about the room and magically Curious has reappeared, shaking his man cakes in his Eddie Murphy/Prince inspired outfit. It looks like a good time is being had all around. The person on the other side of the door ensures music won't be the only thing bumping on this night as they bang on the suite door. A turn of the gold handle brings a face I saw earlier this morning.

"Juanita! Hey girl."

"Hey Ms. Bride-to-be! You look cute in that Mickey Mouse top!"

"You too girl I like those wedges you have on. Come on in and join us."

As Juanita enters the suite, I hear a glass shatter and feel cold liquid splatter near my ankles. As I turn to see the cause of the commotion, I hear the women behind me gasp,

"Mama!"

"Juanita?!"

Clarice is in a state of paralyzed shock. I've heard people say 'white as a ghost' to describe shock before, but with the way Clarice's complexion looks right now, a ghost would offer her a free makeup tutorial. Juanita is a mirror image of Clarice at this exact moment. I grab Juanita by the hand and we step over the broken glass that shattered between us and Clarice. Even with us coming toward her, Clarice is cemented in her spot in the Ritz-Carlton suite like she was built into the design. It's not until Juanita sidesteps me and puts both hands on Clarice's cheeks, that she moves a muscle. Her tear ducts collapse and send enough water pouring down her face to rival the Noachian flood. The music has literally stopped and the eyes of the room are on the three of us, on what is supposed to be a freaky fun filled night. Resolute on keeping the party going and unsure of exactly what I'm dealing with, I grab both ladies by the arm and the three of us head to the master bedroom. As I prepare to close the door behind us I see Curious staring at me from the main room I nod at him, and he knows what to do. Seconds later I hear music playing again and someone yelling about a broom. Not wanting the ladies to get too comfortable in my room I instruct them to take a left, into the adjoining suite attached to my room. The room is almost a carbon copy f mine except it has a queen-sized bed and a loveseat to the right of the bed. Clarice and Juanita both sit on the loveseat and I remain in an upright position. Seeing a box of tissues on the nightstand; next to the bed, I grab a couple and hand them to Clarice. The ageless beauty dabs at the corners of her eyes until the tears stop falling. Feeling as though I've waited a respectable amount of time, I let the interrogation commence.

"Can either of you please tell me what is going on?"

Silence has wrested control of the ladies' vocal chords, suffocating whatever words were on the verge of liberation. The sound of a deep, chest-ratting breath stirs the room before Clarice decides to speak.

"Why did you run away, Juanita?"

Juanita looks at me and then down at the floor and then back at me again. Her eyes tell me that she wants me to flee, but knows there is nowhere to hide. "Mama I didn't know what else to do I panicked." I thought I was gonna be brought up on charges." That boy was young and I was in love, and I didn't think I could take care of a child."

"But you couldn't call, write, reach out in some kinda way?! Here you up and vanish, leaving that boy without a mother and you know he be..." Clarice stops as the tears start up again.

"Mama I didn't have no one else to turn to, I just didn't know what to do! I'm sorry."

It's the two word apology that starts Juanita to bawling, crying just as hard as her mother. I am floored by the revelation and have a river of questions, but their heartache outweighs my inquisitive nature at the moment as the two sit and cry tears of anguish for longer than I can stand.

"It's more than clear you two need time to talk and express yourselves, so ya'll sit back here and take all the time you need."

I don't know if they hear me over the sounds of their agony, so I just leave the room and head back out to the party. Walking the corridor, I gaze at the fish swimming free and unburdened by life. I am envious of them.

"Everything good?"

I nod to my siblings. "With me? Yes. With them two? Not so much." The pair don't get to ask a follow-up question because Miss DJ decides to interject.

"HEY LADIES!" DJ SheaButta calls out over the microphone in her booth.

All the females in the room shout back at her in response.

"Let's give it up for our girl Nila who is getting married TO-MOR-ROW! Aww yeah!"

More hooting and hand clapping spills out from the ladies in the room as they turn all eyes on me. I put the four fingers on my right hand to my lips, pucker up and proceed to blow kisses at my friends.

"Okay all right, ladies I just got word that in five minutes the appetizers are gonna be served, if you know what I mean!"

The women go H.A.M. at the announcement, leaving the lettuce and tomato by the wayside. Miss DJ turns up the speaker volume and lets "Boss Ass Bitch" by PTAF rumble the room. It's fitting that there are those on the outside that want inside this room; the rhythmic knocks on the door serve as proof.

"Oooh I see ya'll got the turn up goin on up in here, Oh-Kay! Muhhaha!" My friend Margaret shrieks before I can get the door all the way open. Behind her are two more of my girlfriends Shantel and Kaliesha.

"Hey Shantel, hey Kaliesha how are you ladies?" I ask as I welcome all the ladies into the suite.

"We are good," both women reply. "But the question is, are you on your best behavior Ms. I'm-getting-married-tomorrow?" Kaliesha inquires like a news reporter as she has her Smartphone camera in my face.

"Kaliesha are you recording this?!" I ask.

"Yep! We LIVE streaming on Facebook right now!"

Before I can say another word Margaret jumps into the view of the camera with me. "Hi Facebook!" Margaret waves excitedly. "I wanna congratulate my girl Nila on her wedding tomorrow! I'm so proud of you! Muah!" Margaret blows a kiss to the camera and then puts one on my cheek. Shantel, I observe has managed to stay out of view of the camera by semi-hiding behind Kaliesha.

"Kaliesha you keep recording a little longer and it's 'bout to be Facebook XXX off up in here!" I warn the sophisticated woman of what's to come.

"Uh, in that case I think I'll stop the recording right here because we don't need no evidence of that life!" She cackles.

"Uh huh. Ladies the bar is over there and there is also food somewhere in here. If you follow your nose you'll find it." I instruct the partygoers, and they venture off to fulfill their needs.

I see Curious step to DJ SheaButta and say a few words before she hands him the microphone. Not long passes before the volume of the music goes down and the voice of Curious takes its place.

"LADIES!" He screams at the top of his vocal register.

Every woman in the room screams back at him.

He smiles brightly at the warm response. "Ladies if you would please I need all of ya'll to clear the floor because the show is about to begin."

Applause and catcalls.

"Yess, bishes, yess! I know ya'll came in here tonight to celebrate my sister and see some fine man meat and booty cheeks," Curious spins around to show the cutout area of his leather pants, causing a vast majority of the women to gasp or laugh in astonishment.

"Oh yeah ladies the turn up is real and we about to get LIT! I know everyone of ya'll bout to have a conniption fit, when you see the size of these grown man diiiiiiiicks! Ooooooh weeee! Without wasting anymore of your time, put yo' hands togetha and get yo' singles ready for Marquis Manhood and Mr. Dick-In-Yo-Face!"

The lights go out and a disco ball and strobe lights illuminate the room. A cloud of smoke blasts the center of the room. As the smoke dissipates, two tall men, one chocolate and one caramel come into view. The men are dressed in black and white striped jumpsuits like prisoners used to wear in the forties and fifties. Their wrists and feet are shackled together with chains. They pace around the room slowly and in rhythm, until the needle drops on "Down In The DM" by Yo Gotti. The two "convicts" shake their chains and start gyrating in front of various women. The women act like they have no shame as they grab at the men who are now shirtless, revealing six packs and chiseled pectoral muscles. As the song about thirsty direct messages fades out,

"Wait (The Whisper Song)" by The Ying Yang Twins fades in. The two exotic dancers flex their chest muscles to the beat of the song. Once the chorus hits, they rip their pants off and all hell breaks loose and dollars start to fly at the exotic dancers like fireflies at a fire fight. Both men have on thongs, but the undergarments barely contain their manhood. More than a few women seem anxious to take the men up on their offer of genital liberation, as they grab at the ball bouncing men. The strippers pull a woman from the crowd and begin simulating sex acts with her. The chocolate skinned brotha is behind her simulating doing it to her doggy style while Mr. Caramel colored has her head in his crotch pretending (at least for now) that the woman is giving him oral pleasure. The song starts to slow down to a slug like pace before the DJ blends it into "Bump n' Grind remix" by R. Kelly. The men start to slow grind in front of the women wearing only their thongs and Timberland boots. Each stripper pulls an individual woman from the crowd, the chocolate man grabs Kian and the caramel cutie grabs my college friend Leigh, who must have crept in while I was dealing with a reunited mother and daughter.

Curious comes on to the floor and hands the men two chairs which they position back to back. The strippers seat each woman in a chair, then blindfold them both. The strippers circle the women slowly, stalking them up close. Leigh and Kian reach out blindly trying to get a grip on the dancers, but the strippers playfully evade their grasp. The record makes a quick cut and "Anaconda" By Nicki Minaj starts to jam, in a flash the dancers stop in front of their prey and spread their legs open and proceed to slither their Anacondas all over the ladies and their private parts. As the record starts to thump so to do the strippers, slow stroking and smothering both women like funk on a skunk in an underground tree stump. The strippers are slick with sweat or baby oil, making me glad I am a safe distance from them because I'd be dammed if I'm paying to have stripper spooge cleaned from my clothes. In contrast to me the other ladies in the room are savoring the show, several of them asking for a turn in the chair.

In the middle of the song, the strippers back off of the chair bound chicks and start to work their way out of their underwear, and the room starts to rain dollars at the sight. The caramel dude has a dick so long and thick that he could stick it in your pussy and it could go all the way to your tonsils. Mr. Chocolate is also well endowed; his dick looks like it could cause a hysterectomy in a game of "just the tip." A plethora of women surround both men and after a few seconds it becomes impossible to tell who is dancing for whom, with all the hands and dollar bills flying. A loud explosion vibrates the sound system and then the lights come back on, indicating that the performance is over. The dancers pick up all the dollars off the hardwood while the women applaud tawdrily. Three knocks appear at the door, bringing more company to the party. Curious sprints to greet whoever is on the other side. I make a path towards the window, where I see an old friend standing.

"Muzzie!" My once upon a time hairstylist is looking out at the beautiful view of downtown Denver.

She turns around slow as a slug. "I was wondering how long it would take you to notice I was here."

"Me notice you? Hmmph, funny I thought this was my bachelorette party you supposed to come speak to me!"

"Why forgive me Nila, how are you doing?" Sarcasm drips from her every word.

"Well, I am doing just peachy Muzzie thank you for asking." I dish right back.

Muzzie looks at me like she has something else smart to say, but the notion is stifled once the sound of trumpets goes off in the room. The sound of horns is followed by four men dressed like ancient Egyptians and carrying an elaborate gold throne. The arms of the throne have lions carved into them; the seat is at least six feet tall, clothed with nacré velvet that is maroon in color. The centerpiece is the bejeweled crown ornamented on top. It appears to be made from a dazzling assortment of crystals, rubes and emeralds. By every measure the throne is fit for this Queen. The four Egyptian servants set the throne in the middle of the floor, while Curious takes up residence on the microphone, again.

"Ladies if I may have your attention please?" Curious asks as sweet as sugar.

A hush falls over the room.

"Thank you so much." Curious smirks. "Can we have the Queen for the evening come and take her place on her throne? Nila, come on over here, Sister."

As I start my strut to the throne, the room launches into cheers and applause so thunderous I look out of the window to make sure it isn't raining. Before I sit down, I make sure to bow to all my 'subjects' in the suite. Resting down onto the throne feels as comfortable as a pillow top mattress made in heaven. It is in this moment that I decide come hell or high water, this throne is coming home with me. Curious takes the bejeweled crown and places it on my head. He whistles using two fingers and the Egyptian servants push out a colossal three tier cake that is at least five feet tall and four feet wide. The cake has been designed to look like a giant Oreo cookie. The bottom tier resembles half of the chocolate cookie. The middle is cream and the top is the other half of the cookie with the Oreo logo on it. Each tier also has red, white and blue string lights that make the cake look like one big Oreo cookie firework. I can see many of the women in the room snapping pictures of the illustrious confection, reminding me that I don't know where my own phone is.

"Ladies, ladies, LADIES!!!! The moment that you have all been watin' and anticipatin' for is finally here!" Curious proclaims like a Court Jester.

The assembled groups of women start to howl like hyenas in heat, making Curious pause temporarily. I sit in the bride's throne, reveling in the energy.

Curious waits for the catcalls to subside.

"Allow me to introduce the man you've all come to see, this brotha is made from 100% USDA Grade A beef! He's got a footlong that women all over the world want to handle! Without further ado, I present to you King of the Sausage Slangers MISTER DICK JAMEZ!!!"

The ladies in the room all explode with excitement. Curious bangs on the fake cake three times and a surprise comes spilling out. Instead of a half-naked stripper, there is a man dressed in all black holding a semiautomatic rifle; Mr. Felix Williams.

He points the rifle at me. "Nice to see you again, dumb bitch."

I smile back at the onetime actor and brother of Tyrrell Ramirez-Williams, a junkie who turned small time criminal last 4th of July. On that day, Tyrrell and his crew kidnapped Curious and Adrianne and used the ill-gotten hostages as leverage to get Drian to commit a robbery. For reasons I can only speculate on, that same night Felix was assigned to tail me. When he thought the time was right, he tried to take me hostage too. In reward for his efforts, I left him bound and bullet riddled in an abandoned building about a year ago.

"EVERYBODY GET ON THE GROUND RIGHT FUCKIN' NOW!" Felix takes the rifle off me and points it at the other women and the few men in the room. While their eyes and ears work, their bodies aren't as willing and all the women in the room remain frozen. Felix fires a round into the ceiling.

"I said, BITCHES GET ON THE FUCKIN' GROUND NOW!" Felix repeats, trying to sound tougher than he actually is.

The women in the room regain the use of their senses and obey.

"You mothafuckas think you exempt?" Felix points the rifle at me and Curious. "Both ya'll get on the goddammed ground!"

I glance at Curious and he looks back at me. I get out of the bride's throne and we both lower to the ground as Felix climbs out of the prop cake. I assume a plank position on the Ritz floor and keep my eyes on him. When he puts his right foot on the ground, I pounce and knock the thespian on his back; the rifle falls a few feet from the two of us. I knee the sorry bastard in his groin, climb on top of him and wrap my hands around his throat. Felix' eyes start to bulge from his head as my stranglehold gets tighter. His hands reach for my face, in a defense from being choked to death, but I am determined to send him to the devil. Although the person who cocks the gun behind my left ear might have something to say about my determination.

"Get off him nice and slowly, cunt." The unrecognized voice instructs.

I relinquish the hold on Felix' neck and push myself up, using his bird chest for leverage.

"Put your hands up in the air and walk backwards towards my voice." The unfamiliar familiar voice says calmly.

Coughing and gasping for air, Felix finds his way off the floor and looks around for his rifle. A Mexican woman has possession of it, the same woman who came to scrape Allgood off my street. Felix reaches for the weapon, but the lady withholds it.

"Mijo ir a buscar esa otra perra!" The Mexican woman says to him.

He looks at her like he wants to argue but he bites his tongue before spitting in my direction. "Me and you goin' have us a nice time together, puta!"

"Felix move yo' ass you heard what she said!"

The voice tosses Felix a pistol. "And make sure you check all the rooms. I saw this twat take two bitches back there somewhere."

Felix nods before moving off to do what he has been told.

"I liked you better when you were behind the bar fixing drinks." I spit over my left shoulder to the voice I finally recognize.

"Move a muscle and I'll paralyze you, bitch." The bartender whispers in my ear.

Even though he can't see it, his words bring a smile to my lips.

"Okay, ladies and gentlemen, listen up because I'm only going to say this once. All of yous get up off the floor and get on the right side of the room." The Mexican woman barks.

She puts her finger on the trigger of the semiautomatic weapon for emphasis. The ladies, strippers and Egyptian servants do as they're told. Rapidly my worry quickly shifts to Clarice and Juanita. I pray that they are smart enough to hide in the adjoining room with the door locked. I know worry will get me killed- I push the emotion down and focus on my breathing as a distraction. I look around the room; terror is written on every single face.

The Mexican woman gestures with her rifle. "Ju got her?"

"Yeah I got her." Felix has a pistol in Kian's ribs.

"Good, now go sweep the other room and let's get the fuck up outta here." The bartender commands to Felix.

The faggot with the nice eyebrows shoves Kian next to me and the bartender with the gun before he heads towards the master bedroom of the Ritz-Carlton suite. My mind makes my eyes shift through the room for a way out. With a gun at my back and a semiautomatic rifle at my front, I don't see a way out- at least not one where the innocents are completely out of harm's way. I inhale through my nose and exhale through my mouth once more. After my fifth cycle of breath, Felix sprints back into the room.

"We all clear?" The bartender asks Felix.

"Yeah we all clear."

"You sure there is nobody back there? I know I saw this hoe take two chicks to the back room.

"Gotdamn niggah! What the fuck did I just say? And I know I didn't stutter, stammer or stop. I told yo' raggedy ass ain't nobody back there! You wanna be Luke Cage so fuckin' bad why don't you take yo' ass back there and check."

Since I can't see him, I can only imagine the stank eye the bartender is giving Felix right now.

"Felix! AJ! Cállate. Vamonos, rápido!" The nameless Mexican lady breaks up the bitch fight.

The angry bartender shoves his gun in my lower back. "Move bitch. Start walking towards the door."

"Look here you ol' California Raisin lookin' ass nigga, you ain't goin be—"

The rest of the words never leave my mouth as I feel a blunt object cause sharp pain at the base of my skull. It takes less than a synapse signal for me to forfeit my grasp on consciousness and succumb to the darkness

CHAPTER 17

The singe of a chemical burn ripping apart the membranes in my nose brings me back to a state of consciousness. The pungency of the chemical causes me to gag and try to gasp for fresh air. Involuntarily my body decides to circumvent the nose and use my mouth as the conduit for oxygen. The reroute is a dead-end as my mouth is blocked off by an adhesive scrim. Attempting to use my hands to pry away at the tape covering my mouth I realize that they are bound behind my back. A cold panic crawls up my spine as I realize I have no idea where I am or how I ended up restrained. Pain teeters panic as the chemical salt is put under my nose again. Forcing awareness to the agony at the base of my skull, where an excruciating throb lingers from the object that I was knocked unconscious with.

"Nila can you hear me?" A husky male voice asks.

While my ears process the sound, my eyes seek the source of the sound. Even though my eyes are wide open, everything in my line of sight is black. Through the tape, I mouth what sounds like yes.

"Good. Allgood."

At the voice's command, the sheath of darkness is snatched from my head. Adjusting to the reintroduction of light, my eyes squint and pick up the sight of Allgood Washington wearing a bomber jacket and snarling like a pit bull. I see a mass behind Allgood but before I figure out what it is, Allgood violently grabs my head and neck, forcing the extremities to the left.

The second face to appear in the light after dark is that of Kian. She is hanging from a metal rod constructed into the walls of this space. Her feet dangle about a foot from the ground, tethered with industrial strength zip ties. The zip ties also constrict her arms, which are fastened behind her back. There's a dog collar around her neck, looped to what looks like a meat hook. Helping to keep her suspended from gravity. There is also black adhesive tape covering her mouth.

Kian is my looking glass; I imagine I'm strung up just like her. My imagination doesn't get too far away from me, as the reality of death falls into my line of sight. To the left of Kian about two feet down is the carcass of what was once a live cow. The animal has been slaughtered, skinned and left to age next to several other cattle in the same state. From behind the bovine, the nameless Mexican lady from my party lurks up next to Kian. Up close, I see that the Latina has a face that looks a jack-o-lantern in the middle of decomposition. It is beginning to shrivel with age and is overwrought with wrinkles, pock marks and divets. The consequences of a lifetime of failing to tend to her skin. The senora has on a sea green trench coat with fur lining the collar and a smile carved in her face. She reaches into one of her coat pockets and produces an ivory handled straight razor, which she unfolds with her right hand.

"Usted piensa que sólo puede robar a mí y salirse con la suya, puta?" The Mexican woman says to Kian before slapping the shit out of her.

The clack of flesh hitting flesh sends a tremor through me, and kick-starts the rest of my senses. Regaining body awareness, I feel goose bumps forming on my flesh, most of which is uncovered. The fabric from my bra and panties is the only thing keeping me from being fully exposed to the subzero climate in this meat freezer. Languishing in the frigidity, my muscles begin to contract of their own free will, attempting to keep me warm as my body plummets below ninety-eight point six.

The sound of metal on metal sets my sight on Kian once again. The Mexican woman stands behind her with a handful of

Kian's Yaki wrapped around her left hand. With the straight razor, the senora saws through Kian's weave until it's no longer attached to her skull. Tears start to form in Kian's eyes as the Mexican woman repeats the process until Kian's scalp looks like a soccer ball, with black swatches in random places all over her head. Laughing like a clown high on nitrous oxide, the senora stands over a pile of natural and synthetic hair that was recently attached to Kian's scalp. Deciding that she's finished being a barber, the Mexican woman walks around the front of her unwilling client so she and Kian are face to face. The smallpox faced senora makes a sudden movement and grabs Kian's cheeks with her left hand, staring continuously into her tormented eyes. Bound with tape and zip ties Kian can do very little that's not at the Mexican woman's mercy.

"Oh, perra estúpida que quieres humillar, ¿eh? Bueno vamos a ver lo tonto que miras con un solo oído que nosotros?!" The Mexican menace cackles.

Feeling the heaviness of dread coming, I try to turn my head before the Mexican crumb cake face broad slices off Kian's right ear with the straight razor. But Allgood's hands hold my head and neck in view like a pair of vice grips.

The wretched, bottomless agony in Kian's cry makes me forget she has tape over her mouth. The tears that were too stubborn to leave during her impromptu haircut pour from her eyes and freeze before making their way down her cheeks. Unlike her tears, a tide of crimson gushes from the hole where her ear used to be. The red river spills down the right side of her face to her neck. Shock and panic at the makeshift maiming is causing Kian's heart to pump the mixture of cells, plasma and platelets at a faster rate than normal. It only takes a few more seconds before the blood of life covers her right shoulder and turns the strap on her pink bra into a deep maroon. Kian violently writhes and contorts herself on the metal hook, trying to will herself through space and time to find the kind of peace of mind that her body will never again know. If the model/drug dealer doesn't calm down soon, she may just bleed to death in this room designed for slaughter.

As Drian's sister struggles for freedom the Mexican maniac stands at arm's length in front of her. She dangles Kian's ear in her face with her left hand, and holds the bloody razor in her right, cackling like Wicked Witch of the Wes the whole time.

"Now who's fuckin' who, puta!?" The demented senora taunts in the ear no longer attached to Kian's body before she tosses it somewhere near a side of beef. The senora turns her attention to me with a twinkle of malice in her eye. The negative temperature in this freezer makes the Senora spew fumes of oxygen from her mouth and nose that resemble the exhalation of an angry dragon as she starts to walk towards me; heaving harder than a hoe over a hot plate.

The Mexican foot-face broad points at Kian with her razor. "That bitch over there was just the warming up. The fiesta is about to get started on yous."

"Ummm hmmm, Algood holds my head and neck and breathes funky breath in my ear. "I'm going take my time with you, bitch."

"Essie, Allgood. Let's not get too far ahead yet. There'll be plenty of time for games with Ms. Montgomery, but we need to have us a lil' chat first. Allgood you can let the lady go now." The faceless voice commands.

When the perpetrating thug releases me from his grasp, my head falls downward instantly. The rest of my body has a split reaction. The absence of Allgood's body heat reintroduces me to the polar climate of the freezer. A frost develops at the soles of my feet and turns into a shiver in my knees. By the time the frost reaches my shoulders, I'm convulsing vigorously. The spasms last for about fifteen or twenty seconds before my being comes to a stillness. I look up, and am dumbfounded at the sight that stands before me.

"Mr. Wiggins?"

My prospective client greets me with a smile. "Ms. Montgomery, what a pleasure it is for me to see you again."

Evander Wiggins stands before me outfitted in a heather gray pea coat with black buttons. Atop his head is a black Kangol style hat with a white racing stripe down the left-hand side. His beard is as black and lush as it was a few days ago when he came to my office, lying about wanting to organize a party for his employees. It seems like a decade has passed since then. Seeing him here and realizing there was no truth in what he told me, a genuine fear has ruptured in stomach. Allgood and the Mexican tramp have been lowdown and trifling from jump street; both of them are clear and present evil and I knew it from the door. Evander Wiggins is the proverbial snake in my grass, an Inland taipan, masquerading as a garden snake. As the arctic cold seeps into my bones, so too does the recognition that Evander Wiggins is the most malignant piece in this equation. Subterfuging his intentions since our initial meeting Evander poses a fatal danger, the danger of the unknown.

"Nila?"

"Yeah?" My mouth wants to say more but my mind can't deliver the words fast enough through the freeze.

"Good you're still with us; I was worried the chill had gotten the best of you." Evander removes the glove covered hands from his pockets and walks toward me before rekindling his spiel. "Ms. Montgomery, I wish we'd met under different circumstances. You are actually not that bad of a human being."

"Thank you, Mr. Wiggins. Your kind words are heartwarming at a time like this." My sarcasm hasn't frosted over yet.

The remark gets a slight chuckle from Evander. After adjusting his cap, he continues. "Ms. Montgomery, I must confess I've been less than forthcoming about my identity,"

"Why you don't say?"

There is no laughter for my wit this time around. Evander remains stoic and soldiers on like I never said a thing.

"Yes, it is true I am not the man I appear to be. Since I was a little boy I always liked to get into character and act, challenge myself you know? Coming up I participated in stage plays, musicals, even did a little stint off-Broadway. From coast to coast I've set the stage, and left it all behind. But I guess we're all actors to a degree, gallivanting around from day to day with life as our stage."

Abruptly Evander spreads his arms wider than eagles' wings and does a three-hundred-and-sixty-degree spin before shouting "Theater in the Round!"

Sensing that he's been pining for this stage since we met, I try to maintain an inkling of interest until he works his to crescendo. I fail at my attempt however as I let my eyes drift over Evander. Bore do I at what looks like a door behind him, presumably the only exit out of this Siberia.

"Oh yes Ms. Montgomery, acting is in my blood. It is embedded in my family DNA. Everyone in my family is a somewhat of a thespian, but none of us compare to my nephew Felix. That young man is truly gifted."

Felix? His nephew?

"Ms. Montgomery, just like with any character an actor portrays, eventually comes the time for the actor to step off the stage and back into the reality of life. I prepared for almost a year for this role and over the past few days I have delivered Oscar worthy performances with you and your secretary, your sister and even that cop who dropped by your office unannounced. I had all of you fooled and eating from my palm. I've been closer than your shadow, but you wouldn't have seen me with bionic vision. The wedding had you so preoccupied, it gave me the ideal opportunity to slip in and capsize your world. But alas the charade is over and it's time for my mask to come off. Before you today, I stand no longer in the guise of Evander Wiggins, but as the man that I am; Mister Ezekiel Williams. Those who know me well call me Zekie."

Concluding his monologue Evander Wiggins/Ezekiel Williams takes a bow in front of me. Before he can return to a vertical position, I have put his piece of the puzzle in place.

"Zekie huh? Uncle to Felix and the ever-trifling junkie Tyrrell Ramirez-Williams." I scoff.

The self-proclaimed thespian casts a scowl as his response.

Almost a year ago before he botched his attempt at kidnapping me, Felix dialed a number and advised the caller that I was in his possession. After the tables had turned on Felix and my bullets burned through his flesh, I asked him ever so politely who he called and he told that he had called his Uncle Zekie. Felix confided that at the very least, Uncle Zekie planned to torture me in an abandoned building. Deferred but not deterred one year later, insatiable revenge is the reason that Ezekiel "Zekie" Williams has me hemmed up like a slaughtered cow in this meat freezer.

"Since we both know you're thirsty for revenge—,"

"A dish best served cold, wouldn't you agree?" Ezekiel Williams is unable to resist the self-evident pun.

Annoyance lifts my right eyebrow a quarter of an inch; I let it remain arched for about thirty seconds before I begin again. "Your thirst brought us to this intersection of life. What is puzzling me now is why are those two here?" I tilt my head left at the Mexican hag and Allgood.

Ezekiel takes off his left leather glove and fishes through the right inside pocket of his coat. Pulling them like a fish out of water Ezekiel extracts a pack of Kool cigarettes. With the cigarettes occupying his left hand, Ezekiel pats himself down with his right, consistent with the movements of a man searching for a lighter. Patting himself down three times Ezekiel remains unsuccessful at locating a light. Noticing his predicament Allgood flips a red Bic lighter at Ezekiel. Thanking him with a nod, Ezekiel knocks a cancer stick from the pack of Kools and places it between his lips, he then hands the carcinogenic box to the other unrestrained individuals in the room. Within seconds, the trio lights up like a torch at the Olympic games. Ezekiel takes a long drag from his cigarette and blows the smoke out of his mouth. Looking at him puff on nicotine, it strikes me that Evander Wiggins didn't seem like the type of man who would smoke I wonder was if that was part of his character or did Ezekiel improvise that element out of his personality.

"Family." Ezekiel stops to take another pull from his cigarette. "Family is the cornerstone of life. Family is what turns a house into a home and keeps lonely from being alone. Family is the bone that keeps flesh from collapsing in on itself. Family is very important to me and very important to Allgood and Essie as well. That's why they're here- because you have tried to destroy our family!"

Lunging at me on the last syllable in the word family Ezekiel jabs his half smoked mini torch into the flesh of my left thigh. A compulsory reaction causes me to retract my thigh from the source of the burn. The G in me refuses to give Blackbeard the pleasure of hearing me cry out in despair. Matter of fact, the burn from the cigarette hurt very little. Consequence unintended Ezekiel's torture technique sent a positive charge through me. Responding to the shock of trauma my heart is pumping like it's trying to explode from my chest. The rapid cardiac cycles generate fresh blood that starts to run warm through my veins. Lips turned upward I fix eyes on Ezekiel, grinning like I have lost all grip on sanity. Gaze requited Ezekiel stares back at me with the same insane delight in his eye. For a scant moment in time, I peer into the eyes of someone who that in this moment is just as crazy as I am. Staring at each other for what could have been an ungodly amount of time or no more than a few seconds Ezekiel and I come to a mutual yet unspoken understanding; only one of us is making it out of this freezer alive.

Outcome decided, we elect to get back to the matters of the moment. Mindful that the stage still belongs to him Ezekiel lights up another cancer stick, inhales deeply, letting the nicotine cycle through his lungs. Once the mania has subsided, he turns his attention back to me.

"Family, Ms. Montgomery is the only thing that means everything to me. I hold you and your fiancé personally responsible for the imprisonment of my nephew Tyrrell."

"Oh really?!" I retort indignantly. If my hands weren't tied behind my back I'd be clutching pearls as well. "Because I'm the one to blame for your junkie ass nephew shoveling that shit in his body, then deciding it was a good idea to take innocent people hostage and use them as leverage in a sloppily planned robbery. It's funny you say that you hold me responsible for your nephew's incarceration, because with the way that pussy punk bitch acts, I'd swear you were talking about your niece."

Slap! The Mexican woman backhands me so quick I didn't even see her hand until it was already back on her hip.

"Don't chu insult my mijo like that, fuckin' pendeja!" She points her left index finger in my face.

I'm sure it was the comment about the niece that made the pumpkin faced Mexican broad backhand me. The assault leaves me with a stinging sensation on the left side of my mouth. Giving credit where it's merited, I felt genuine anger in her blow. With the crater faced Mexican's familial interest exposed, the only unanswered family tie is Allgood's, I'll get to him in due time though.

"I bet you hit harder than your junkie ass, soap droppin' mija!" I can't resist rubbing a wound I know is raw.

Crocodile Face veers toward me wanting to strike again but Allgood beats her, thumping me hard enough in the mouth to draw blood. I mix the iron metallic tasting substance with saliva and spit the concoction dead in Allgood's face, hitting him dead in his T-zone. His face is as stoic as stone on a statue, as though he's not standing in front of me with a face full of bloody spit.

The tar colored torturer looks for something to wipe his face. "You might wanna save your spit, bitch, because I like my blowjobs sloppy."

"I'll make sure to pass that along to them twinks you be messin' wit over at Midtowne." I quip.

Allgood tags my ribs with a one, two combination punch that could tenderize a two-dollar steak. Not completely unfazed by the barrage of brutally from the spooge of Satan, the G in me is defiant in outwardly showing any signs of the distress within. Antagonist awakened, I can't refrain from assailing the ugly, mini Sasquatch in front of me.

"Or better yet why don't you get Felix to blow you after you have your Viagra Colada? According to Curious, that punk gives some of his sloppiest performances from his knees."

I brace for impact, but contact is delayed as the scrapple faced bimbo grabs Allgood's arm like she wants to tag in. Either unwilling or unable, Allgood protests with just a turn of his shoulders. The senora persists and the pair argue without saying a word. Their dispute lasts long enough for a more composed component to intervene. Ezekiel steps in front of me blocking the savages from continuing to inflict their masochistic desires on me.

"Essie, AG calm down. That's enough for now. We got time. Let the little girl have her fun, because she is about to suffer for a lifetime." Ezekiel cautions the Mexican wench and the tar black brawler

His words have the desired effect and the duo retreats.

"Now Ms. Montgomery, where were we? Oh yes, we were discussing your attempted demolition of my family. Not only did your actions result in the revocation of Tyrrell's freedom, but you personally shot Felix twice and left him bloodied and butt naked to die in that abandoned building. In addition to that, you and your siblings maced and bludgeoned my dear friend Allgood over here."

"And?"

"And?" The deceptive actor has a look of offense on his face. "And this is not even accounting for the loss of revenue your family has robbed my family of."

"Loss of revenue?"

The uncle to a pair of losers takes a long pull from his cigarette before using the cancer stick to point in Kian's direction. "It's been brought to my attention that the little lady over there rudely refused to pay for a shipment of products that Essie cosigned to her."

He stops his sentence to take another pull from his cigarette and to blow the smoke in my face. "And in this family, playing with our money is playing with our emotions. And unfortunately, we're not heirs of Milton Bradley, so we don't make money from the games children play."

He drops the butt of the Kool on the diamond cut steel floor and stomps on it with the heel of his shoe. Unimpressed by his tough guy performance, I stifle the yawn forming in the back of my throat. Instinctually my eyes gaze over to the left, observing that Kian is also unmoved. She is no longer straining against her restraints nor moving a muscle whatsoever. Seeing a motionless Kian sends a prickling vibration down the bottom half of my spine. Noting the alarm in my visage, Ezekiel's eyes dart to Kian.

"Kian!" I call out of panic.

The mutilated model/drug dealer is as responsive as the cattle hanging a few feet away from her. Ezekiel stares at her for half a second more before turning away. Realizing that a supporting actress in his production has gone off-script, I see fear evolving in the character of Ezekiel Williams. The Theater in the Round is beginning to crumble under his feet. As the scene shifts to panic. Real life has decided to make a cameo. Life has chosen to improvise on him, throwing an unrehearsed element on stage. He recognizes that, if he doesn't act quickly, the curtains will close on a life and there will be no encore. The pictures in motion behind Ezekiel's retina bring into focus the possibility that his next role will be that of a prison inmate. If Kian's life wasn't hanging in the balance I'd be rolling in critical acclaim at his impending demise.

The unbalanced actor turns to the only unbound woman in the room. "Essie come here!"

Following his instructions, the Mexican woman with the corroded complexion moves in his direction. Once she's a step or two away from him, Ezekiel hurries over to Kian. Before the two of them reach her, the actor in charge turns to Allgood who is standing arm's length from me. "Hey Allgood, go get AJ please."

"Uh huh, okay." The ape in human form nods and makes an about face as he heads to the door.

In the fraction of a second it takes him to turn, I use

everything in me to propel my legs up towards the ceiling. Midway through the ascent, I tuck my legs into my chest and loop the arms tied behind my back over them. As gravity pulls the legs back down, I wrap them around Allgood's neck and retract him to me. I ensnare him in my thighs and use every fiber from every muscle in my body to catapult upwards off his shoulders like a kangaroo on a Pogo stick. Flying through the air like an arrow, I arch my neck forward to unlatch the meat hook from the dog collar around my neck. Off the hook, I begin my decent back to the arctic. Dropping faster than a hoe's drawers at a cut party, I tighten the human seatbelt I have around Allgood's neck and shoulders as we both collide with the carbon steel floor. Upon impact with the algid steel my bare flesh feels like I hit the iceberg that sunk the Titanic. Ignoring the frostbitten sensation temporarily, I unzip the hidden pocket on the side of my bra and extract the four-inch serrated pocket knife I stashed there. Between my hands being cold and still bound and the commotion between my legs, I fumble to get the blade open. I don't usually try to kill a man when I have him down there, but I guess there is an exception to every rule.

I ratchet my legs like octopus tentacles adhering tighter onto Allgood from the shoulders up. He ruts aggressively against the force of my thighs, struggling to free himself. In his struggle he flings his fists over his head, trying to land blows anywhere on the bottom half of my body. Try as he might his arms are too short to reach my lower limbs. The more he strains, the tighter I clamp down on him, trying to crush his neck and skull like a macadamia in a nutcracker. Feeling the burn in my hamstrings, I constrict like a boa around the woman-beater. Allgood keeps struggling for his life like a lion cub in the jaws of a starving adult alligator. Life, when reduced to a barbaric level factors into a simple equation: will outlasts want. Allgood wants to be free, but I will send him to hell before I let him out of my clutches. A piercing pain rips through my inner right leg, where the thigh transitions into the knee. as a result my right leg jerks outward about a quarter of an inch, but it might as well be a mile for Allgood, as the movement alleviates some of the pressure that was about to bust his windpipe.

The repugnant pug savors oxygen as he gasps for air. His laborious inhalations remind me of a pig's squeal. Finding space between my thighs, Allgood begins to turn his head, neck and shoulders in my direction, inching toward me. The knife I ram into his right jugular vein stops all momentum. I force all four inches of the blade into his neck and twist the handle like the key in a car's ignition. Instantly blood squirts everywhere like water from a sprinkler with a busted spigot. Allgood stretches his arms like the elastic on a fat man's waistband, fighting to get his hands on his neck and stop the bleeding. His efforts prove to be in vain as his own blood chokes the life out of him. Allgood wallows about just like the cows in this very room the moment someone brought a knife to their throat and left them to drown in their own blood. As the tide of crimson rises on Allgood a wet, gurgling sound emanates from his throat. The sound lasts for only a few seconds, giving way to a stillness that washes over the corpse of the evil Allgood Washington. May he be sodomized in hell.

"DROP YOUR WEAPON NOW! I SAID RIGHT NOW!" A voice booms from the light outside of an open freezer door.

Blinded and illuminated by the light, I try to look up in the direction of the booming voice, but my eyes are pulled to a more pressing concern. I can't see the person through the light, but I can see a smiling Ezekiel Williams standing at point blank range with a pistol pointed at my head. I'd like to say that at the moment I saw the pistol bearing down on me, time sped up, or slowed down, or that my whole life flashed before my eyes, or that I was frozen in time. Truth is, when you're staring your own mortality in the face; there are no feelings or thoughts. You just are.

For less than half of a fraction of a second after watching Ezekiel pull the trigger on his pistol, I make peace with the fact that the last earthly sound I will hear is the explosion of a bullet leaving its chamber. Before the fraction can make it to a whole second, I hear four rapid-fire firecracker-like explosions. Ezekiel falls like a redwood after being detonated with C-4 and lands on his back a few inches from me. There are four bullet sized holes in his pea coat and a pistol still in his hand.

"HEY YOU! PUT YOUR HANDS WHERE I CAN SEE THEM! AND GET DOWN ON YOUR STOMACH!" The voice booms again.

Looking to my right see the Mexican shrew lowering herself to the frigid floor, obeying the commands of Lieutenant Frank Nash-Cunningham, who is moving rapidly towards her. The lieutenant is flanked by two uniformed police officers. With his weapon pointed at the senora, Nash-Cunningham nudges his head in the direction of the gun in still in Ezekiel's hand. The officer on his left takes his handgun from its holster and quickly closes in on Ezekiel's body. The Caucasian officer is young and has hungry eyes. His eyes widen at the sight of me covered in an enormous amount of blood. Disguising his distress, the officer moves closer to Ezekiel until he is close enough to kick the pistol out of his hand. The hungry-eyed officer puts two fingers on the actor's neck; looking for a pulse, I assume.

"He's dead, Lieutenant." The young officer confirms what I already knew.

The lieutenant finishes putting some silver wrist jewelry on the Mexican skank before he looks up. "Call for backup and an ambulance too."

The young cop starts talking into a radio microphone that is attached to his left shoulder. I don't hear everything he says, but I do pick up on his request for an ambulance. With the two bodies at my feet, the officer should be calling the coroner too.

The female uniformed officer turns to me. "Are you all right, Miss?"

"Well let's see, there is a dead man between my legs, I'm freezing and covered in blood so… hell naw I'm not all right!"

The lady cop nods, pulls a pair of blue latex gloves from her pocket and puts them on before squatting down next to me. She pulls a utility knife from her front pocket and cuts through my wrist restraints.

"Can you stand up for me please?"

Hands free and at my sides, I try to push myself up, using the steel as leverage. The attempt is a little more than a notion since I can't feel the legs that are bound and tangled up in Allgood's dead body. Seeing my struggle the officer walks behind me and places her hands underneath my armpits, pulling me off the dead man and into a standing position. Thankfully my feet are still bound together; without that sense of security, I might have collapsed before I could stand. A snapping sound near my Achilles frees my legs from restraint. The officer that freed me from the zip ties interlocks her left arm with my right. Together we step over a corpse and walk towards the only exit in the freezer. Vulnerable because of my lack of lower body stability, I concentrate exclusively on putting one foot in front of the other. After taking the required number of steps, my exodus from the artificial Antarctic is completed. Feet firmly out of the freezer, the climate has shifted from North to South Pole. Twitches ping through various muscles, responding to the change in temperature. As my sensory receptors revive, they alert me to a crawling sensation on my legs. I look down and see Allgood's congealed, partially frozen blood thawing out and dripping downward, creating a puddle at my feet. My hands are also covered in red.

"There is a wash station over there." The female cop directs.

Not noticing what direction she pointed in or if she pointed at all, I scan the room. To my left at a ninety-degree angle is a fire truck red shower basin. Starting at the base of the basin, a copper pipe extends about six feet high with several handles affixed in different places. At the very top of the pipe is a rain shower head. The plumber contracted to build the station was tasked with emphasizing substance over style, using only what was necessary to complete the job. As a result, the contraption looks like a shower that suffers from anorexia.

"Did you want to get cleaned up, Miss?"

Seeing no reason to respond verbally I start moving towards the wash station. Three steps into my journey, I feel a presence behind me. I turn around and see the bartender turned kidnapper from my party. The open 20 x 20-foot freezer door obstructed him from my view, as he is hogtied and tucked behind it and the front left outer edge of the freezer. Looking at him hogtied reminds me of something.

Backtracking in blood, I rush over to the dark brown skinned kid, who looks no older than twenty-one. As I wind my right leg like a soccer player preparing for a penalty kick, a terror sprouts in his eyes. About a foot from him I start a slow trot; by the time I reach him, his eyes are closed and I have enough momentum in my right leg to plow my right foot into his face with devastating authority. I hit him hard enough to cause his left eye socket to cave in on itself. The adrenaline must be running high in me because I feel no pain at all in the lower half of my body. The kidnapper kid can't say the same. He howls in agony as I retract my foot from his face. His eye is swollen and turning purple, making it look like a baby Grimace is growing from his face.

"At least you saw me coming, BITCH!" I spit at the little bastard that knocked me unconscious earlier.

About faced and back in front of the lady in dark blue, I see her stifle a laugh and give me a woman to woman nod as I pass her on my way to the wash station. Feet inside the basin, I hit the red handled lever that I assume is the hot water control to the right of the water fountain. The water that rains down on me from the showerhead is almost as cold as the freezer. I lean left to avoid being directly under the cold water rain. After a few seconds, the water starts to transition from cold to warm to hot. I adjust the temperature so I don't scald to death. While fiddling around with the level, I feel a bottle attached to underside of the fountain. Snatching it off, I see that the label says antibacterial wash. I pop the cap and douse myself in the solution. Using my right hand as a washcloth, I scrub the tainted blood from my body. Peering up towards the ceiling like I usually do when I shower I see that the fluorescent lights above my head are a hue of orange and the ceiling is the same pistachio green as the walls. For some strange reason the color combination makes me crave rainbow sherbet. The pistachio green walls are in sharp contrast to the rest of the space I'm in. The color gray is all around me from the conveyors to various machines, there is even a gray Stainless Steel dividing fence that outlines the walls in this large industrial space.

"THOMAS!" Frank erupts.

The roar makes my head snap out of sightseeing and brings my attention back to the open freezer door where Nash-Cunningham is exiting with a lifeless Kian in his arms. The female officer runs the few feet to assist the lieutenant. Frank sets Kian on the floor a comfortable distance from the cold of the freezer door. Flat on her back, Kian starts to convulse and then abruptly stops.

Frank doesn't hesitate. "Barbosa, get on top of her!"

"Wha what?" The lady in dark blue stutters.

"She's going into shock from the cold and the blood loss. She's got a pulse but it's weak. Get on top of her and try to warm her up."

Finally comprehending the severity of the situation, the female officer takes off her gun belt and climbs on top of Kian.

"Thomas!"

The young officer runs from wherever he was and almost falls in front of the lieutenant.

"Where is the ambulance?" Frank grumbles.

The young officer looks scared. "The ETA is five minutes out."

"This woman may not have five minutes! Tell them to hurry the FUCK up!" The human in the lieutenant growls.

The green White boy starts chattering into his radio again as Frank takes off his tie and cream colored dress shirt. He hands them to the woman on top of Kian. Without a word, she wraps as much of the shirt as she can around Kian's lifeless body.

Frank puts two left fingers on her wrist. "Hey beautiful."

"Lieutenant I don't think she's breathing."

"Gotdamn! No! She will not die here," Frank stops just short of slamming a balled fist into the concrete. Regaining composure with the upswing of his fist, Frank looks to the female officer under his watch. "Barbosa, you do chest compressions while I do mouth to mouth."

Petrified, I stare at the officers of the law as they make good on their vow to protect and serve, I feel water continuing to rain down on me, washing away the blood of life beneath my feet. As the traces of life wash away, the police duo works frantically to save Kian's. With the element of oxygen in abundance Nash-Cunningham attempts to breathe life into the lifeless, while Barbosa pounds on her chest. Kian remains unresponsive after each round of cardiopulmonary resuscitation. The wings of my apprehension start to fly towards the sky; aggrieved, I wait for Kian to breathe again.

CHAPTER 18

Slipping fast I find myself back down memory lane trying to avoid replaying the events from a night that left two men dead. Instead I recline into a curved sectional sofa lined with suede beige colored cushions and pillows. The outer section of the sofa has been outfitted with leather dyed a toffee color. A matching circular ottoman sitting in front of the sofa keeps my feet from the floor. Images from the flat screen television mounted on the wall project before my eyes but I can't focus enough to ingest what they mean, or if they even have meaning at all.

Whoever put this together must know something about what some ancient Chinese philosophers would call Feng Shui. The room is fairly large and rectangular; the entrance and back wall are wider than they are long, while the parallel walls in the room are of equal length, running about ten feet inward. Backwards as it maybe, the walls set the foundation for the floor in this room. The flooring is patterned to replica a giant three dimensional Rubik's Cube; blending energetically with the four walls. Each partition has its own vibrant personality in the form of color, shifting from yellow to red to blue to green. A beautiful communal table occupies six feet of the room and fills some of the room's vastness. It's made from knotty pine, sanded down and stained with a varnish that recreates the color of raw honey. Two benches upholstered with leather the hue of cognac, reside underneath the three foot high table. About four feet from the entrance of the room is a kitchenette with a microwave, sink, and ice machine. Further down there are two refrigerators, lockers and three vending machines that line the red wall. As the color on the wall swashes from red to blue, there's a square window with security bars on the outside. Shrubs, decorative rocks and cigarette butts are the only thing visible under the night sky, but the view lets me know that there is still a world out there. Moonlight sneaking into the half-lit room casts a shadow on the green felt atop a pool table. Balls racked and ready for action, I grab a cue stick from the stand to the left of the table, preparing to occupy my mind with a game I used to be good at. Before stick hits ball, I hear the beep of a numeric code on the other side of the door. After a mechanical click, a woman who is maybe five feet tall walks in carrying a white plastic bag and a clipboard. Behind her is the lady cop from earlier. From opposite ends of the room, we each walk about a half mile to meet one another in the middle.

"Ms. Montgomery, I am Blessica Campos Senior Nurse here at Rose Medical Center." The short woman tucks her clipboard under her left armpit and extends her right arm and hand to me. I grasp the nurse's hand, shuddering morbidly as I recall the fate of the last person in my clutches. Possibly aware that she is in the hands of death, the nurse makes the handshake brief electing to get down to the business of why she is here.

"Officer Barbosa has informed me that you have been the victim of an assault. We'd like to photograph your injuries if that's all right with you?"

The smile she attaches to the end of her question informs me that I have no say in the matter. Her request for permission was a mere formality, like the bank teller who holds your cash hostage until you give them back the signed withdrawal slip. I shrug my shoulders in a conciliatory manner and the woman who looks like she was born in the Philippines nods.

"Wonderful, follow me please." She pulls on a handle embedded in the yellow wall and allows me to walk through first.

The room is dark and has a sterile chemical smell that reminds me of bleach. Nurse Campos flips a switch behind me and blinding white light fills the bathroom. In only a few short steps I've gone from penthouse to outhouse. The bathroom is a little more than half the size of the room we recently exited. It's tiled from floor to ceiling with what were once porcelain baby blue tiles. The blue was vibrant and fresh when they installed it maybe forty or fifty years ago, before me today the tile is drab and turning gray from age. The tile on the floor is cracked and chipped in no particular order, while the tile on the wall looks like it's holding on tighter than Precious' bra clasp. Straight ahead I see a set of three blueish-gray bathroom stalls, partitions separating each of them. By happenstance all three of the stall doors are open, revealing luxurious stainless steel toilets. Which by the way they look appear to be standard issue in most prisons. Keeping with the theme a slab of stainless steel is mounted to the wall three feet to the left of the door we entered through. Formed in the steel are three individual basins, most would consider a sink. A few inches above the steel sinks, sits a shelf made from the same material. Affixed to the steel shelf is a mirror that runs the length of the steel slab the basins were formed in. Giving whoever is unfortunate enough to have to use the sink an opportunity to see what life in a prison bathroom would be like. The entire setup was installed for uniform functionality

"Ms. Montgomery, are you ready?" The nurse holds a silver digital camera in her right hand.

I nod in the affirmative. Nurse Campos checks to make sure the camera is functional and points it at my face.

"Can you pull your bottom lip down for me please?"

I comply with the request from the nurse I assume is Filipina and pull the flesh away from my teeth, exposing the laceration that Allgood and the Mexican hag caused.

"Great." The nurse snaps two pictures with the silver digital camera.

"Okay can you remove your shirt and put your arms straight up in the air?" She stops speaking so she can demonstrate the movement she wants me to emulate.

I remove the navy blue POLICE shirt that I got from Officer Barbosa and toss it on the steel shelf. A chill runs through me as I stand before the nurse in a blood-stained bra and panty set. Mimicking her movements, I put my arms up towards the ceiling so she can photograph the bruises Allgood left on my ribs.

"Good, just like that." The chubby cheeked nurse encourages. "Okay you can put your arms down now. Stand up straight like you would normally."

She points the camera at my legs, photographing the cigarette burns and the newly discovered bite mark that Allgood sunk into my flesh as he tried in vain to free himself from the clutches of death.

"And can you turn around for me please?"

I turn towards the door and the camera continues to shutter. I hope this heffa is shooting me from the waist up; I don't want everyone in the Aurora Police Department looking at the junk in my trunk.

"What?" I snap over my left shoulder, past ready for this photo shoot to be over with.

"I said we'll get that stitched up for you after we're done here." Blessica repeats

"Stitch what up?"

I turn around to see the nurse's eyes jut a quarter inch from the socket before she answers. "You have a good-sized gash on the back of your skull."

Instinctually I run my right hand up the back of my neck until I get to the base of my skull and feel what she was gawking over. The gash is wide and feels like it has scabbed over, or my thick mane has acted as a man-made bandage. Feeling the wound makes me wish I would have inflicted more damage on that little bastard who hit me from behind.

"Have you taken all the pictures you need, Ms. Campos?"

The sentence was posed as a question, but as I stare into the nurses' oval shaped orbs, she knows I'm done being photographed. The medical professional is smart enough to understand the meaning behind my words and bows her head in acknowledgement. The nurse puts the camera into the lower right front pocket of her scrub jacket before opening the white plastic bag she brought into the room.

"All right Ms. Montgomery, Officer Barbosa advised me that you might need something to wear. I bought you these." She opens the bag to show me the plum colored scrubs inside. "Feel free to clean up and change in here."

After her last two words, I notice that there are two shower stalls in the room. Both are equal in size with a yellow shower curtain covering up each stall. Gentle pressure on my left forearm moves my focus back to the woman in front of me.

The nurse removes her hand from my forearm. "Officer Barbosa told me that you killed one of the men who did this to you."

"I did."

"I wish the world had more women like you."

Blessica Campos smiles in admiration before sidestepping me and heading out of the bathroom. Alone with my thoughts, I step over to the shower and turn the handle until the water starts to run warm. Turning back around, I look at myself in the mirror, trying to track all the changes that I've been through. Focused on the eyes looking back at me, I study them, trying to see what is in the space between. Stepping outside of myself, I transcend space; looking inside myself I engage time, begging the ever evaporating commodity to spin back the clock for me. I want to return to a time when my heart was solely mine and death didn't flow through my hands.

Living life has taught me that love is the only logic. Love is part of the reason I'm still alive, and part of the reason Allgood Washington and Ezekiel Williams are deceased. Before today, I could say that I'd never been the cause of another human being's death. Even as I stand here now, the fact that I had to kill someone has not set in. Post-traumatic stress has temporarily suspended my emotions, as numbness creeps over me. Ezekiel Williams was right when he said I was distracted, not by the wedding as he presumed but by laissez faire. I uncharacteristically deferred control of my life this weekend over to everyone else, and catastrophe engulfed all of us as a result. I have been absent in the presence of my own life for the past few days. I can try and fool myself and say I was focused on so many different things, moving in too many different directions. Fact of the matter is, I have not been at my best when the circumstances wouldn't allow for anything less. I was content with coasting through my wedding weekend like a bottle in water; going with the flow almost got me killed.

I recognize that life doesn't often give second chances; stripping out of my blood-stained undergarments I look at the threads that bonded together to make the fabric. I stare at the crimson splatter that transferred itself from Allgood's neck as his bond on life was severed, so that mine could continue. I look to the heavens and thank God for simple truth stitched into small miracles.

***

Showered, and freshly stitched up I sit at the communal table listening to Maze and Frankie Beverly sing about joy and pain from a speaker that is nowhere in sight. Eyes around the room

I observe that Officer Barbosa is also out of sight.

"Nurse Campos?" I call out with another inquiry in mind.

"You can just call me Blessica, Ms. Montgomery." The nurse says over my left shoulder.

"Well in that case call me Nila, Blessica." I turn halfway around on the bench and extend my hand to the new friend I just made.

"It's very nice to meet you Nila." Blessica takes my hand in hers. She holds my hand a few seconds longer than I expected, letting go after she sees the question still in my eyes.

"What is this space that I'm sitting in? I've been to many a hospital and never seen a room like this before."

The nurse pauses to let a sneeze pass by first.

"Bless you."

"Thank you, okay so to answer your questi–,"

The four heavy knocks on the door stop the nurse mid-sentence. She heads to the door and opens it. A lieutenant from the Aurora Police department enters, followed by a lawyer and Ms. Clarice. My brother and sister bring up the rear. Everyone but the officer of the law comes to slather me with affection and reassurance.

"Ahem! I will excuse myself and allow all of you your privacy." Blessica decrees once the kissing and hugging has subsided. After the door closes behind her the interrogation begins.

"Lieutenant Frank Nash-Cunningham. Care to give us a rundown of what you know so far?" I ask with urgency in my tone.

The lieutenant is the only person in the room standing. Clarice and my siblings are all sharing my bench, while Robert sits on the opposite bench, back turned to us so that he is facing Nash-Cunningham.

"Oh, I'm sorry I thought I was the one asking the questions around here. Forgive me for forgetting that my boss put you charge, Ms. Montgomery."

Mindful that Frank is an Alpha type who loves to exert his authority and feel like he is in control at all times. I decide to try a different route to get to the information.

"Frank?" I purr sweetly.

"Yeah," His hands are on his hips.

"Grab a Snickers, because you're not yourself when you're hungry."

Everyone in the room but Frank bursts into laughter after my quip. I can tell from the look in his eyes he is not amused by my remark. I glare back at him with frog in my gaze, challenging him to jump.

"Now lady and gentlemen, can we put our nuts back in the sack and get down to the business at hand?" The sage mediator, Robert Bland cuts into the tension between me and Nash-Cunningham.

"Frank how did you find me?" I elect to be the bigger man between the two of us.

Before Nash-Cunningham can open his mouth, Clarice steps in. "Sweet Thing I am SO grateful that you wore that Fitbit tonight because that's how we found you. When I found out that you'd been kidnapped, the first thing I thought of was that Fitbit because I got you one that got GPS in it. I linked it to my Fitbit so we could keep track of each other's progress, thank God for that because I was able to see where you were on my phone."

Clarice points at Nash-Cunningham, who is leaning against the red wall, arms folded across his chest. "He gimme his card that day he came to the office and said if you ever gave me any trouble, I could call him and he'd set you straight. Lord knows I wanted to call him for personal reasons, but not for the reason I had to call on him for tonight."

Clarice's comments get the lieutenant to show his top row of pearly whites.

"That Fitbit saved your life. When I saw you were moving, me and your brother and sister ran down to my SS and started tearing up asphalt to try and catch up with your kidnappers. I was on that highway doin' at least one twenty, weaving in and out of lanes with no regard for anything but your life. And as I'm zoomin' I see flashing lights behind me and I'm like ain't this a bitch! They hit the sirens like they want me to pull over, but they wasn't ready because I was not stoppin'. This was gonna be a high-speed chase until Curious stepped in and told me that the Fitbit had stopped moving at a meat packing plant. I told Curious to call Lieutenant Nash-Cunningham and tell him and the cops following us where you were.. And as soon as he hung up the phone, the police chase turned into an escort. By the time me and the cops arrived to the plant, the lieutenant was already there waiting in the dark of night with his bulletproof vest on, if I didn't have my headlights on I probably wouldn't have seen him. The lieutenant asked me if I was sure this was the place that the GPS stopped at and I told him yes. Then him and the cops that escorted me went into the building. My insides were goin' crazy just sitting out there in the dark, looking at nothing but darkness. Me and your siblings just started praying right there for your safe return. Sweet Jesus."

Andrea and Curious make a nonverbal sound that I interpret as them agreeing with Ms. Clarice.

"I agree, that Fitbit saved your life." When Clarice called me and told me that you had been kidnapped, I thought the worst until she told me about the GPS. We were able to track your location all the way to that meat processing plant in Denver. And obviously you know what happened after that. What I want to know from you Ms. Montgomery, is what happened in that freezer before I showed up?"

I recap everything that happened in the freezer to the best of my memory, sparing no detail. At several points in my story, I see people in the room cringe in disbelief. Looking at their reactions makes me wonder if I should turn the events into a screenplay. As I conclude my reiteration, I realize I need to know the outcome of a central character.

"Frank how is Kian?"

For the first time since we've been in this room Frank cringes at something I've said. His eyes tell me he doesn't want to answer my question; his mind knows he has no choice but to answer. Head tilted down to the Rubik's Cube, he uses the thumb and ring finger of his left hand to massage the tension in his temples.

"She is in a coma." He pulls his head upright. "Doctor says her brain was deprived of oxygen for quite a bit of time. He said that even if she comes out of the coma, she has a long road ahead."

After revisiting the bleak prognosis, Frank shakes his head slowly. Standing before us clad in black slacks and a black V-neck tee, (rags compared to his normal attire), the lieutenant looks vulnerable, almost remorseful that he couldn't have done more to save Kian's life. Replaying his words in my head, I pick up on a sorrow that I have never heard from him before. If I didn't know him to be an asshole by nature, I'd swear the Tin Man has a heart.

"Have you had a chance to interview the lone female

suspect yet" My lawyer asks the droopy faced lieutenant.

Frank smirks. "We have tried but magically she has forgotten how to speak English. I'll let her rot in Denver County Jail for a few days until I can find a translator."

"What about ol' boy that hit me from behind? You get anything from him?" I inquire.

"Oh you mean Pele?" Frank winks, letting me know the asshole in him has been revived. "According to his ID, he is Allgood Washington, Jr. son of the man you killed. A brief look at his rap sheet let me know that the twenty-four-year-old is shaping up to be quite the criminal. Identity theft, assault, robbery, domestic abuse, selling stolen goods- the kid's a concerted criminal."

"And what about his sperm donor?"

"Allgood Washington," two words bring out the Vanna White in Frank. "Over forty years ago, Mr. Allgood Washington, Sr. was convicted of attempted rape and assault with a deadly weapon. As the files read, Allgood was high off PCP and tried to rape the girlfriend of a man who he considered to be like family. The boyfriend found Allgood trying to violate his woman, a struggle ensued between the two men and Allgood stabbed the man in the chest just a few inches short of his aorta. Amidst the chaos Allgood escaped the scene, not completely unscathed, though. A couple of officers picked him up a few blocks from the scene with bullet wounds in both buttocks."

Imagination untethered, the six of us cackle at the thought of a man trying to hobble away with bullet riddled butt cheeks. Once the amusement fades, Frank begins again.

"Allgood was paroled in the nineties just long enough to make Junior before he got sent back. Apparently serving as getaway driver in a bank robbery violated his parole. He was released from prison two months ago. Ms. Montgomery, would you care to guess who his cellmate was for his last few months in prison?"

"Tyrrell?"

Frank looks insufferably smug. "Correct."

I have a question of my own. "Who shot Allgood?"

Frank Nash-Cunningham licks his lips. "The detectives investigating the crime were unable to conclusively prove who shot Allgood. Aside from the stabbing victim, there was no other blood found at the scene. The detectives also couldn't locate a gun on the premises either. Officially Allgood's shooter remains unidentified. But looking at the notes in the case file, the detectives believed that it was more probable than not that the girlfriend of the stabbing victim, Nomie Valentine pulled the trigger on Allgood. "

Frank Nash-Cunningham's words put Allgood's piece of the puzzle in place. Separating what I know from what has yet to be proven I decide to play coy with the lieutenant. "What did you just say?"

"You heard what I said. Your mother shot Allgood Washington for trying to rape her and kill your father; the investigators just couldn't prove it. Now I'm smart enough to realize that you are trying to play me, so if you don't start telling the truth, the whole truth and nothing but the truth, with God as my witness I will arrest you right here right now, for obstruction of justice, wedding be damned."

"Excuse me," Andrea steps in before I have a chance to respond. "If I may speak?"

Frank nods at her.

"A few nights ago, Mr. Washington trespassed on my sister's property spewing some fabrication about being my sister's real father. The three of us found his story to be less than credible and we politely asked him to vacate the premises. When he declined and became belligerent, we had to use force to remove him from my sister's property."

Andrea is going to make a very good lawyer someday with the way she is able to weave words together in an articulate manner. In the meantime, Robert stands up and prepares to address the court.

"Lieutenant, if I am to understand this accurately, I must recap the events. We have my client being stalked, harassed, kidnapped and beaten by two people who are now deceased, one of whom died from bullets that you fired, while Ezekiel Williams had his gun pointed at the head of my client. We have Allgood Washington sharing a cell with Ezekiel's nephew Tyrrell Ramirez-Williams, the man my client help put in prison a year ago. This is the same Allgood Washington who attempted to rape my client's mother and murder her father forty years ago. The way I see it is that for Allgood and Ezekiel, the motive was good old fashioned revenge. They had a mutual ax to grind. Now if you want to talk about truth, the truth is this: if you handle this the right way, this whole ordeal will net you a Medal of Valor and more than likely another promotion. Now if- - -."

Knocks against wood halt Robert's closing argument. Closest in proximity to the door, Robert is the one to open it. On the other side is a face I'd recognize if I was blind, crippled and crazy. Passion pulls me from the bench and momentum puts me in Drian's open arms. Our lips and tongues intertwine like knotted up shoelaces, neither of us knowing how to get the other untangled.

"Ahem!" Some hater in the room clears their throat loudly enough to interrupt the lust between me and my boo. The distraction works as Drian pulls his lips away from mine. I grab my fiancé's right hand and I lead him back to the bench I was sitting on. Seated and comfortable next to my man, I nod at Robert to continue.

Robert bows at me before turning to the lieutenant on his left. "Now Lieutenant Nash-Cunningham, as I was saying this case has epic greatness engraved all over it. But you got to get everything right. I's dotted and T's crossed. As you can see Ms. Montgomery is excited about becoming Mrs. Yancy in less than," Robert pauses to pull his watch into eyesight. "In less than fourteen hours. The soon to be married couple is leaving for their honeymoon on Thursday. I'll have her in down at the station on Tuesday to give a formal statement and answer any questions that you may have. How does that sound?"

"Tuesday." Frank Nash-Cunningham extends his left hand for Robert to shake.

I don't know how much I pay Robert exactly, but it's nowhere near what he's worth to me in sociopolitical equity alone. He has the kind of poise and maneuverability that allows him to swim with sharks while wearing sirloin swimming trunks. He always finds a way to emerge from the waters with more bravado than before.

"Adrian how is Kian?" Frank asks my fiancé.

I see a spark light up in Drian's eyes as he is preparing to answer. "She's awake and alert."

My baby keeps it short and sweet while responding to the lieutenant, but looking at Frank I can tell the abrupt words are sweet music to his ears.

"Frank did ya'll ever find her ear?" I inquire.

"Yes we did. Thankfully the two of you were in the freezer so that slowed the decomposition and the doctor said it was in good shape. He was waiting for her to stabilize before putting her through any surgery. Hearing that she is awake and alert makes me optimistic about her recovery. Adrian, is Vivian up there with your sister?"

"Yes."

"Well I better go speak." Frank runs both palms over his hair slicking down the sides.

"I think I'll go with you." Robert announces while adjusting the lapels on his suit jacket.

Prim enough to lure a corpse from a casket the lawyer and the lieutenant head for the door, before they can make it all the way out a shock surges through me.

"Frank?"

The lieutenant turns around, positioning his body in such a way that half of his body is already in the hallway. "Yes."

"Has Felix Williams been taken into custody yet?"

"No. We have an APB out on him but as I stand before you now he is still a fugitive from justice."

A disconcerted energy rattles through my bones with the knowledge that there is still someone out in the wilderness of the world, intent on returning me to the dust from which I came. I rotate my neck all the way to the right until it pops; I unfurl and repeat the motion to the left side. I want to make sure my neck is flexible enough to keep my eyes over my shoulder, until Felix is off the board. The past few days have reminded me that life is a game that is never to be played you either survive and advance or you expire. Since Thursday survival has been my struggle. As the days faded into night I have found myself traipsing through the valley. Harm has been a one-way street paved by the tyranny of evil men. Repeatedly death has emerged from the shadows, casting its reflection against the night. Fearless in the face of evil I know that the light of day is my salvation, but only if I can make it through another night.

"Huh?" I stammer still in the mental fog of night.

"Did you want to go up and see Kian before we leave?" Drian has his left hand on my right thigh, I don't know if he put it there before or after asking me that question.

I stare into his Bambi eyes for about three seconds before deciding that it's best to tell him the truth. "No, I want to baby but I can't. I've seen too much fucked up shit tonight to go visit her."

His eyes understand, so his mouth doesn't question.

"Okay so what is we goin' do now? Because I am not trying to sit up in this room all morning." Curious asks with exhaustion in his tone.

It dawns on me that until Curious mentioned it, I had no idea what time of day it is. Maybe because my body is focused on a more pressing need. "Man, I'm exhausted. Only thing I want to do is visit the Sandman." Fatigue speaks for me.

"Matter fact, where are we sleeping tonight, because I'm not going back to the Ritz-Carlton. Damn I never thought I'd say that." Drea says.

"Me neither." Curious seconds.

"Welp Montgomery chicklings, sometimes it's good to go back to the nest, so I say we sleep at Mommy and Daddy's house tonight."

Drea and Curious nod in agreement.

Lady Reese has her hand on the door handle "Iight then, let's get on up outta here. Oh Suggafoots, I got yo' purse in my trunk."

"Praise God! Thank you Reese's Pieces, you always looking out for me."

The four of us follow Lady Reese out of the room with the Rubik's Cube floor. Too tired to walk I hop on Drian's back and he carries me down a hallway with dim florescent lighting, out into the hospital parking lot. Outside, lungs full of fresh air, I exhale and inhale slowly through my nose and gaze up at the sky. Savoring the darkness of night, because it allows me to truly appreciate the stars. Two rapid high pitched beeps sound through the air, pulling me from stargazing.

"It's open." Drian calls to my siblings, who are standing next to his Durango.

Once he puts me back on hard earth I notice something. "You look tired baby."

"So do you."

"What did you and Mr. Cornelius get into last night."

"I don't know if I should tell all of CeeCee's business like that."

"Okay no problem, you can tell me in the car on the way to my parents house. Speaking of which where are you sleeping tonight?"

"More than likely I'm coming back to the hospital I told Moms I'd come back up there and keep her company."

"Seems like she has more than enough company to me."

I don't know if he responds or just opens his mouth to respond because Lady Reese decides to blow her horn at us at that moment. Pulling up in front of me, she rolls her window down and hands me my pink and baby blue Guess tote bag that I bought on a whim. I look inside to make sure everything is still in there, satisfied I look back up at the woman who saved my life.

"Thank you again Lady Reese."

"You know I take care of you girl, you're a daughter to me."

I noticed that Clarice didn't use the word "like" before daughter. She deliberately extracted the adjective because she views me as bonafied family, it is taking the resolve of a Tibetan monk not to bust out in tears at the overwhelming love I feel running warm though my veins and flooding my heart.

"Iight Suggafoots, I got to hit it, you know some of us have a wedding to go to tomorrow or should I say later today, aww hell you know what I mean."

Saving me from crying like Viola Davis in every movie she's ever in Lady Reese steps on the accelerator of her Black '98 Impala SS and burns rubber on me as she flees the parking lot of Rose Medical.

"Iight baby let me take you and your siblings home so ya'll can get some rest." Drian says to my back as I stand motionless watching Lady Reese's taillights until they disappear. After lingering for a few more seconds, I turn around to the most beautiful man in the world holding the passenger door of his silver Durango open. My feet glide until I climb into the SUV, and nestle into the seat. Safe and secured in the automobile my king closes the door to his chariot and before he can turn the engine over I am a sleeping beauty.

THE FINAL CHAPTER

As motion moves me forward, words come flowing through my mind. *"If you catch hell in the daytime,"* my Papa used to say *"Then you goin' catch double hell at night, 'cus that's when everybody go to sleep and them demons start doin' they dirty work."* These past few nights have given me enough hell to last several lifetimes. Like a leaf caught in an upwind, the mercy of nature has determined my direction for much of the last four days. It is in my introspective visage that a revelation assaults me. I have spent the past few days hiding behind the night, tiptoeing through the shadows trying to make it to daylight. Pulling into the parking lot at Friendship Baptist Church I realize there is nowhere left to run; nowhere left to hide–love awaits me. In a synapse snap I experience an awakened current convulsing through my body. My eyes veer up towards the sun and icy tingles ripple the tissues of my flesh; a blazing fire shoots up through my bones. I begin to shiver until a cold sweat beads on my brow. I try to speak but I can feel the muscles in my jaw contract and lock shut. A force stronger than I'll ever be, has got a hold on transforming me. I pull in air through my nose and exhale the same way after three rounds of nasal breathing, words come my way.

"You ready Nila?" Mommy holds the passenger door open for me.

Three words and the conniption inside me stops; calm takes its place. As I put my right foot on the warm concrete my metamorphosis is complete.

***

The First Lady of Friendship Baptist Church had her office floored with candy apple red carpeting so she could have pomp and circumstance under her feet. The fabric on the floor is plush, expensive looking and probably imported from some country in the Middle East. I see a French influence in some of the furniture, and the walls are all textured with shimmery gold glitter.

The shine of the gold on the walls serve as a backdrop for the room's centerpiece: an ornate coffee table. The table is planted between one red and one gold sofa. It table stands four feet tall and was made from an oak tree that was cut down with the sole purpose of turning the woody plant into a piece of furniture. The woodworker did a masterful job with the hunk of nature they were given. The wood was preserved, petrified and the top of the table stained with a maple varnish. Adding an exquisite and timeless accent, the circumference of the truncated oak is encased in a single sheet of 24-karat gold.

"Is you goin' sit down or nah?" Andrea nudges as I realize I was lost in the majesty of the room.

Feeling honored to be in The First Lady's private sanctuary I take a seat in a gold tinted armchair upholstered in red velvet fabric. The chair sits in front of a three-foot wide vanity mirror bordered by twelve white light bulbs. I look at my reflection, wondering if what I see is really real.

"I left something out in the car ya'll. I'll be right back to help." Mommy says to Andrea and I.

Andrea responds to her as I turn my attention back to the looking glass. Looking at my own eyes, I ponder if the soul has a reflection as visible as the flesh. I peer deeper into the mirror, trying to dive in a river of self. Stepping outside myself, I watch myself trying to verify if I can see the changes taking place in me. Splicing between inside and out has me lost between moments and time.

"Ow!" My introspective voyeurism is interrupted by an external irritation.

"I'm sorry girl, my bad." Sister let the curling iron under her control make contact with the upper section of my right earlobe.

"Would you please hold still Nila? Shit!"

"Kiss my ass, and lick my crack An-drea. You keep nicking me with that curling iron and that shit hurts!"

"Do you wanna do your own hair?"

"Do you want me to break my foot off in yo' ass!?"

"Ladies!" Mommy exclaims. "We are in the house of the Lord and ya'll in this sacred place talkin' with the devil's tongue!"

Sister and I know better than to curse around our mother. Guess we didn't hear her come back into the room. The scowl on her face is strong enough to shatter the vanity mirror.

"Cut her some slack, Nomie- she's had a rough couple days, from what I hear." Scolds the woman who gave her life.

In the mirror, I see a woman I have adored since before I could say my first words, my grandmother, Inez Valentine. I almost catapult out of my seat to get to my Grams and put my arms around her, and shower her with love. Since she's already standing, Andrea has a few steps on me in the race to get to Grams. Luckily for me, Andrea forgot to put the curling iron down and has to retreat as I move closer to a pair of loving arms. Outstretched and entrenched, I am caught in a maternal love when Grams Inez wraps her branch-like arms me. My grandmother is what clothing designers would categorize as petite, two inches under five feet and probably 115 pounds, depending on how recently she's eaten. Even though she is petite, Inez Valentine is wiry and strong like rope that fastens a boat to a bay dock. The power in her grip becomes evident to my ribcage as she squeezes the flesh Allgood used for a punching bag. I grimace slightly and the subtle movement causes Grams to release me from her embrace. As we separate Grams interlocks her hands with mine and leans back a quarter of an inch to gaze at me with all three of her eyes.

"Look at my baby! Nila you are so beautiful, baby. I wish your Papa could be here to see you right now."

The words send a pain through my heart, causing a stinging sensation in my eyes from which a warm river begins to cascade down my cheeks. The tears are contagious as the other three women in the room shed tears for a magnificent husband, father and grandfather, Jerome Valentine. He blessed the earth for seventy years before a devastating heart attack on a scorching August morning left him in a coma, a week later he died in the midnight hour. My Papa loved in abundance and unconditionally. He was the first one to tell me I should marry Drian. Drian and I were still relatively new as a couple when I brought him to a family dinner. Papa pulled me to the side later that evening and told me to marry Mr. Yancy, because he said he could see Drian was a good man that would take care of me and wouldn't be intimidated by my bullshit. At the time, I didn't pay my Papa any mind because I wasn't thinking about marriage. I just wish he was here so I could tell him he was right all along and hug on him one last time. But the wishes from this living witness are a dream deferred, until I can make it to the place where streets are paved with gold. The pressure I feel at the corner of my right eye wrests me from my dream-like wish.

I blink and see Grams pulling her tissue-holding hand from my face. "Good thing you ain't put no makeup on yet." She says through a red eyed smile.

With my heart, mind and mouth not ready to produce words yet I stare at Grams in awe. The Creator blessed Inez with an unblemished complexion that is brown like the outer layer of a ripe kiwi depending on the circumstance her temperament can turn from sweet to sour just as quick as the fruit. Since I was a kid she has always worn eyeglasses that take up most of her face, the frames are square and oversized. Consequently her nose looks smaller than it is and her cheekbones are high and tight under the tortoise print frames. There is the head of a rose about where her navel would be. It's constructed from metal and decorated with rhinestones. The rhinestone rose bridges both sides of her off-white silk blazer. The skirt and camisole she pairs with the blazer are also off-white and made from silk. From the way the fabric forms on her physique I can tell the ensemble was stitched by her own hands. What I can't see is the extravagantly flamboyant church hat that I know Grams has to match her ensemble. She must be waiting until I walk down the aisle to surprise me with her bejeweled headdress.

"How I look?" Grams prances left to right, her hands still holding mine.

I answer from the soul. "I love you."

"With your whole heart?"

"All the way down to the veins and arteries."

Grams smiles using only her eyes, and I try to keep more tears from developing in mine as I go and sit back in front of the wall of lights to let Andrea finish my hair. Once seated I feel energy on my left. Switching my head in that direction I see Mommy has a comb and a jar of Press-n-Curl wax. I also notice she has on a red t-shirt with the Colorado flag patterned on the front of it.

"Ya'll know two hands are better than one." Mommy reminds.

"Yeah, and one drink is better than none!" My mother from another laughs as she enters The First Lady's Lair.

"Reese, what you doin' here so early girl?" Mommy turns to the woman who saved my life a few hours ago.

Through the mirror, I see Lady Reese fan both hands at

Mommy.

"Nomie you know I had to come see 'bout my baby. I already missed one daughter's wedding. I ain't about to miss another."

Before Mommy can respond, Grams steps in. "I don't believe we've met before, but you look familiar to me, Inez Valentine."

I turn around in my chair and see Grams extend her right hand to my executive assistant. Lady Reese eschews the olive branch and wraps both arms around my Grams. Lady Reese is dressed casual in a pair khaki Bermuda shorts and a yellow short sleeve V-neck. With the way everyone except Grams is dressed, I'm becoming less sure a wedding is supposed to take place today.

"Ms. Clarice Ellis, I'm from Dallas originally."

Grams perks up. "You from Dallas you say?"

"Ummm hmmm, sho' am, got some folks in Shreveport too."

"You don't say? That's where our family is from too."

"Ohhhh!" Lady Reese fawns, "I wonder if you know any Thomas's or any Guions?"

I don't know who leads who, but in less than an eye blink Grams and Lady Reese are on the red sofa, fast friends, chatting about the deep South. Lady Reese doesn't know it yet but she has won Grams' admiration. She's always had a soft spot for Southern transplants.

"How does your head feel where the stitches are?" Mommy combs out my locks.

"It's still a little tender."

"Iight. Well, you let me know if we start to hurt you, because we about to go work on this untamed mane."

I nod and the women go to work like termites in a lumber yard. They become forces of energy, blurs in the haze of time. Currents spiral round me delivering the precarious sensation of soft bristles on my skin. Someone instructs me to keep my eyes until they finish my face. I hear the women laughing and chatting around me, their distraction with one another gives me a chance to meditate and find a quiet place in my center.

When the inward silence becomes an outward hush my eyes open instinctually, out of fear that something might be wrong. Looking through glass I see the women in the room now dressed like they're going to a wedding and gathered around the 24-karat table. Whatever has captivated their attention is obstructed from my view. I clear imaginary particles from my throat and the party of four turn around anxiously, like they've been waiting for me. Rising from my Rococo throne, I turn and head to the women. I take note that even though the three women have turned to face me with anxious faces, their legs and thighs still obscure what they were hunkered over on the coffee table. Grams stands in the center of the women with Mommy and Sister on her left and Lady Reese flanking her right.

"Which one of ya'll is playing Effie?"

"What?" Three of the four women ask.

"Well with the way ya'll are posing, I assumed the Dreamgirls were gonna be performing at my reception."

"And I am telling you..." Everyone except Grams sings out before the five of us dive into laughter.

Grams finally stops laughing. "Well baby it's about that time. My mama wore this dress at her wedding. I wore a part of it at mine, and your mama wore at part of it at hers. Now it's your turn."

Grams and the ladies back up from the table slowly, and part, allowing me to behold the regalia laid out on the golden wrapped platform. I see a magnificent blend of satin fabric and Swarovski crystals sewn together perfectly. The gown is ivory, in its purest form like the dentine from African elephant calf whose tusks have just started to sprout. I finesse the gown from the garment bag; the satin fabric is seductive to the touch. Tingling with awe at the dress, something in the embellishment lures my eyes. There are several small beads artistically interspersed between and around the Swarovski crystals. A close look reveals those beads to be pearls. Mother-of-Pearl to be exact. I don't remember the transition from visually ingesting the Mother-of-Pearl beads to wearing the gown, but I look down and find myself cloaked in the satin fabric. I step to the full length cross shaped mirror behind The First Lady's desk and check out the woman looking back at me. The ivory mermaid gown she's wearing doesn't make it over her shoulders. Her girls are outlined with crystals and pearls, and propped up behind a pedestal of satin and lace. Her face is flawless, the makeup applied in such a way that it appears that she's wearing none at all. Her locks are pressed, curly and frozen just above her collarbone. She looks radiant. Three taps on the door to the Lair distract me from my mirror-mirror moment.

The only door in the room opens and the man who gave me life enters. Tuskegee D. Montgomery Sr. is tall, soot-black and handsome. His nose and lips are thick and full, resembling those of King Tutankhamun. It's a safe bet to assume that he went to Drian's shop earlier to get a haircut. Daddy's head and facial hair have been recently trimmed and crisply lined up; his silver hued beard is a beautiful contrast against the darkness of skin. As he saunters over to me, I that observe the two tails flapping behind my father on his black tuxedo jacket. The white vest and bowtie he has on under the formal wear jacket reminds me of a penguin. His hug engulfs me like the sea. On an inhale I sniff a woodsy, floral and slightly sweet aroma coming from him. His grip is tight, but the adrenaline of the moment has me feeling little pain from last night's beating.

Separated and looking at only one another Daddy clears his throat before speaking. "Yenila Montgomery, you are simply beautiful and I love you. Me and yo' mama are so very proud of you. We knew this day would come, but what I didn't know is that I'd be in awe of you. Holding you from when you were no bigger than an ant's antenna…"

Daddy pauses to chuckle and so do the rest of us. "- - -to watching you evolve into the beautiful Black woman you are today makes me feel like I've accomplished something with my life. I'm proud of you."

After his final remark, Daddy pulls on a chain attached to his vest and out of his pocket comes a gold locket, hanging from the end of the chain.

"Me and yo' mama got this for you." Before I can turn around for him to put it on, Daddy walks behind me and fastens the locket around my neck. I look in the mirror and see that I am finally dressed and ready to walk down the aisle. But I have to have my epic wedding "usie" first. I ask sister for my phone and then call my parents, siblings, Grams, and Lady Reese to surround me as I take a photograph memory of the moment.

In the middle of smiles and flashing lights, an usher sticks her head in the open door. "They waitin' on ya'll out here."

Lady Reese answers for us. "Here we come." Like the Israelites who followed Moses across the Red Sea, we all trek out of the Lair behind Lady Reese. Walking towards the sanctuary, I try to focus on everything around me, but the scope of my attention is too broad. I end up focusing on just putting one foot in front of the other until I come to a complete stop.

The person who pats on my outer left thigh lets me know that my forward momentum has stopped

"Nila! Nila! You look so pretty." Adrianne holds a white wicker basket filled with the petals of a white flower in the crux of her left arm.

I bend down and kiss the little cutie on her cheek. "Almost as pretty as you little girl."

Drian's only child is wearing her Sunday best; a simple white dress made from material that imitates the look of crushed velvet. She has on white stockings to match and black patent leather shoes that buckle at the ankle and have a cubic zirconia bow above the toes.

The child giggles loudly before replying, "Thank you. Look Nila- I got flowers for you!"

She holds her basket out for me to get a good look at the plant petals.

"Oh! They are so pretty, just like you and me!"

"What about me? Am I pretty too?" Clarice's grandson Camiko stands to the right of Adrianne.

"No, Miko you are not pretty. You are too handsome!" I put my lips on his cheek at the end of my compliment and his face turns almost as red as the ring pillow he's holding. Juanita's son is dressed just like my father, except there are no tails on his tuxedo jacket.

"Come on little babies, ya'll ready?" The female usher who came to get us from the Lair asks the flower girl and ring bearer of my ceremony. The white glove wearing usher motions for the two children to start walking in the sanctuary. Leaving the father and the bride as the only two left in the foyer of Friendship Baptist

Church. Daddy and I remain peacefully silent as we wait for the usher to come back for us. I inhale fresh air, hoping to calm the nerves back flipping on my backbone. Tingles tickle every part of my flesh as I wait in sweet agony to meet the man I am to marry. As oxygen cycles through my lungs, the sound of an organ sound hums through my ears. I know the melody, but I can't recall the name of the tune.

"Yenila?"

"Huh? I mean yes Daddy." I stammer still distracted by the organ music. He squeezes my wrist slightly and I focus on the usher in front of my face. Even though I've seen her two times today, it isn't until she is standing before me with a medium sized white box that I truly look at her. She is a deep shade of brown I can only accurately describe as molasses. Her face has horizontal lines forming at the cheeks from the natural aging process, the same way an oak tree develops annul rings. Aside from the age lines her face is unwrinkled, and her eyes are small making it hard to decipher how hold she really is. I put her in the same age range as Cicely Tyson–ageless. Her smile is warm and puts me at ease. My legs start to move as Daddy guides me towards her and the open doors of the sanctuary. When we're an inch or so apart she opens the box to reveal a bouquet of roses. The assortment of flowers are arranged in a pattern of red, white and a deep blue that wavers between the color of deep sea and violet. The flowers are symbolic of the holiday my wedding falls on. Extending the box to me, I pick up the bouquet and smell the sweetness in the pedals. Switching my senses I notice that the melody on the organ has slowed down some. "You Are So Beautiful" flows from the instrument, soft and sweet like syrup on a short stack.

"It's time, baby." Daddy whispers.

Our feet move in unison as we begin our slow stride toward the aisle. The usher waves us over the threshold into the sanctuary, and bows before stepping out of our way. Ten feet stand between me and the man of my destiny. Waiting at the outermost pew in the back of the sanctuary I gaze at the sunlight shining in from the west through the four large pane windows in the triangle shaped church. As soon as Adrianne drops her last flower, Daddy and I start to head down the aisle. Weightlessness overtakes me as I float slowly to Drian. Looking from pew to pew I smile lovingly at all the friends and family that have come out to share in this joyous occasion. From altitude I see the sanctuary has been decorated with streamers of gold and maroon cloth; there are white flowers all about the holy space. Lights that look like raindrops fall from the ceiling, bathing the congregation in a soft white glow. There is a gold cross suspended from cherry hardwood on the wall behind the pulpit, where Drian waits anxiously for me. To the right and left of the cross are two flat screen monitors, aglow with a video montage of moments Drian and I shared together. With nine feet behind us, I stare at my fiancé one step ahead. My baby is Ebony, Essence, Jet GQ cover model fine. The best barber at his shop had the task of grooming him and the other men in the party, and he did his job well. His hair is tapered on the sides, with a starter curl and side part on the top. His sideburns don't make it past the middle of his ear, while his goatee is precisely sculpted; the hair under his lip has been carved into a straight line connecting with the hair on his chin. Drian is dapper in his two-button tuxedo jacket; its cream color is almost as ivory as my dress. His shawl lapels are black satin, his matching bowtie crafted from the same material. As waist transitions to toe, black slacks cover his legs and thighs. Vintage regality adorns his feet, his shoes have the high gloss shine of patent leather, under cream colored spats that match his jacket. As the beauty in the Billy Preston standard fades out, I find myself standing up next to my fiancé at the altar. I hand my bouquet to Daddy as he takes his seat next to Mommy on the right front pew. On the left front pew, I see Ms. Vivian with Robert Bland seated by her side. I catalog, but am unable to process the observation before Reverend Paul Burleson speaks.

"Brothers and sisters," Reverend Burleson has a slight, but smooth southern drawl in his tone. "We have gathered here today to celebrate the union of two of God's most beautiful children,

237

Adrian Oscar Yancy and Yenila Montgomery. The couple told me that they have been together four years. Last year they came to me for premarital counseling and by the time we left the session, they had taught me a thing or two about love and happiness!"

The reverend's words draw laughter from the congregation. After a few more chuckles, Burleson continues. "Yes, yes I wanna talk about some love and happiness for a minute. Is that all right, ya'll?"

More than a few people shout for the reverend to carry on with his sermon.

"Amen, amen. Yes brothers and sisters, love and happiness is more than just something that makes you come home early, and stay out all night long. Love and happiness are Siamese twins, bound at the hip. When one is absent from a relationship, it feels like someone or something is missing. Ya'll know what I'm talking 'bout!"

"Make it plain!" A baritone voice in the back of room shouts at the reverend.

Reverend Burleson wipes his brow with a white handkerchief before picking up. "Oh yeah, love is something that can make you do wrong and make you do right. But I'ma tell you right now this couple here, they goin' do right. Only the Bible can best describe the importance of love and devotion. In John 15:13 it says Greater love hath no man than this that a man lay down his life for his friends. In speaking with Yenila and Adrian collectively and in private, they both articulated a desire that only death would see them part. I was solidified after meeting with them that they would collapse heaven into hell if it tried to keep them apart. Now that's love ya'll, that's that strong biblical love. The kinda love God showed Daniel when he saved him from the lions' den. The kinda love God showed Abraham, Isaac and Jacob when he gave them the Promised Land. Or the kinda love God showed Job when he put that protective hedge around him. Oh yes God showed them a mighty love, a powerful love. A blessed love and God's love is pure and divine, God's love knows no one greater, because God is love! God is love! I said God is love! Can I geta amen?"

Every voice in the sanctuary erupts. "Amen!"

"Don't leave me up here by myself, I said can I get an amen!?"

"AMEN!" The congregation shouts loud enough for hell to hear.

Reverend Burleson flashes a boyish grin at the assembly of saints and sinners in the sanctuary. The man of the cloth adjusts the gold colored stole he is wearing over a black clergy robe with contrast white silk cuffs and collar. With wardrobe restored and spirits settled, the reverend speaks again.

"Ya'll gotta forgive me, ya'll know I get caught up in the rapture of the scripture and get carried away."

"That's all right!" Lady Reese exclaims from somewhere behind me.

"But yes," Reverend Burleson wipes his mustache with the handkerchief. "This ain't about me- it's about God and his two children that are gettin' ready to tie that knot. The couple has written their own vows, so I will turn the floor over to them."

Reverend Burleson nods at Drian, allowing the gentleman to go first. Drian takes three deep breaths and burrows those Bambi eyes into me before parting his lips.

"Yenila Montgomery, for a long time I always thought that if I revealed the all the emotions that I feel, I'd be vulnerable and less of a man. Standing before you, our family, friends and God I will confess that you and your love have made me a better man.

Because you have allowed me to open up, be vulnerable and exposed. Your love has melted some of my insecurities away. Yenila, you have shown me through your actions that love is an inspired quality. You have to give people reason to love you, and keep loving you. You are my reason for loving and my reason for living. On this day, I vow to be your reason as well. In both verse and form our mind, heart, body and soul are intertwined as one. I am you as you are me. With God given strength and resiliency I promise to love you through triumph and tragedy, best and worst until my dying day. It is with our combined hope, grace and faith that we continue to go out and transform dark yesterdays into bright tomorrows. It is on this day that you and I have achieved a new beginning as we embark on a future as one. With this ring, I Adrian Oscar Yancy present to you Yenila Montgomery a commitment to love and serve you through eternity as my lawful wedded wife."

I don't know how I contain the tears that love has flooded my heart with. My life preserver Drian squeezes both of my hands in his and I compose myself to speak.

"Adrian Oscar Yancy. Love is life's greatest gift, and with that gift comes responsibility. The responsibility of upkeep, we are tasked with best arranging our life space to benefit our survival and enhance our existence. We have the choice of believing in any number of simple and complex things. On this day with witness from our family, friends and God. I choose you. I choose you and the love that you have shown me over the four years we've been together. I choose you as the person I want to spend an eternity with until the breath of life is no longer in me.   Love as the emblem of eternity, made a promise to time to last forever and a day. On this day, I make that same vow to you. I vow to love you with my whole heart, mind, body and soul until eternity ceases to exist. Love is a multitude of things, but most importantly love is truth. And sometimes the truth hurts, but it stands the test of time. I vow to be true to you in both verse and form regardless of consequence. Together we will build a life of joy, love and happiness. I vow to be as good to you as you have been to me. As husband and wife we will walk in victory for the rest of our days.

With this ring, I Yenila Montgomery present to you Adrian Oscar Yancy. My eternal emblem, a band of gold that bonds us both together. I vow to love, honor and serve you until our dying day as my lawful wedded husband."

A few anxious hands clap vigorously after my last word. The officiator of the ceremony waits for the zealousness to dissipate before weighing in. "By the power vested in me by God, I now pronounce you man and wife. Husband, you may now kiss the bride."

The applause is deafening when Drian's lips touch mine, our oral exchange has a electrical charge. With the current of love flowing between us and the raucous salutations saturating the sanctuary in my periphery I see the lights above our heads start to flicker rapidly.

Who said fireworks couldn't go off indoors?

***

As the door to the Maybach limo opens, all I see is green outside the automobile. The grass at Stonebrook Manor is so green and vibrant that for a moment I feel like I'm in a Technicolor dream. I must have ignored it when Mommy and I came to visit a few days ago but the grass looks like Kentucky blue, manicured to replicate the quality of grass you'd see on a golf course. Two young blondes, one male one female, are waiting for me and my husband once we step out of the luxury automobile.

The female speaks first. "Hello I'm Taylor."

"Hi, I'm Taylor too"

Both of them extend friendly hands to Mr. Yancy and I. I take note that they both have female names.

"We'd like to welcome you to Stonebrook Manor for your wedding reception. We are glad and honored to have you with us." Male Taylor says.

"Yes, very honored indeed. It's my understanding that we are going to take photos first and then you two will make your grand entrance in the ballroom as man and wife. Is that correct?" Female Taylor follows up."

My husband nods. "Yes, that is correct. We're just waiting on the rest of the wedding party to arrive."

His words dart my thoughts to the limousine that was behind us. Mr. Taylor and Mr. Tyson hired two limousines, one for the bride and groom and one for the immediate family to be chauffeured to Stonebrook Manor. The last time I remember looking out the Maybach window the other limo was right behind us. Then again, I was a little distracted since hubby and I played a game of Beyoncé inspired "Partition" on the way up here.

"Is that them there?" The Taylors point at the space behind us.

Neither of us answer, as we turn slightly to the sight of a silver limousine gliding up into the lot. The luxury vehicle glides until it comes to a stop behind the Maybach parked under the Porte-cochére. After its complete stop the occupants exit, one by one each of them smiling or laughing free from inhibition. Once the fourth person, Caldwell Cornelius steps out the limo cackling I am sure of one thing.

"Ya'll been drinking huh?"

Mommy, Daddy, Sister and Caldwell laugh heartily as their response. Curious is the fifth person out of the limo and my best chance to find out what happened on their ride to The Manor.

"Curious what is everyone laughing at?"

He responds just like the four before him. I shake my head and continue to stare at the exodus of individuals. After Curious comes Lady Reese with Miko in her arms, Ms. Vivian with Adrianne in her arms and Grams steps out last. Seeing Lady Reese with Miko I wonder if she suspected her grandchild was sitting in close proximity to his father on the limo ride up here.

"Is this everyone in the wedding party to be photographed?" Male Taylor asks after a pause in the laughter

Drian looks at him. "Yes."

"Wonderful." The male Taylor nods at his female counterpart and she says something into the Bluetooth in her left ear. Five seconds later a body attached to a face known to me walks out of the entryway of The Manor with an expensive looking camera dangling from his neck.

"Uh, Mikal!?" I remember his name as it was forming to leave my mouth.

"Ahhh! Nila wassup girl! Good to see you."

The young man wraps me in a sideways half-hug, his respectful way of showing affection to a married woman.

"It's good to see you too. I ain't seen you or your brother in a good lil' minute. How is he anyway?

"J? oh J is good he's out chea writing books now an' err'thang so he's doing good."

"And I see you not doing too bad either, Mr. Photographer!"

A suspect cough comes from my husband, a subtle hint he'd like to be introduced to this unknown male.

"Oh, where are my manners. Mikal this is my husband Drian. Drian this is Mikal. I knew him and his brother from way back in the day."

The men shake hands and exchange pleasantries.

Male Taylor signals us. "Okay okay. If I may have everyone's attention please. We're ready to for the photograph session now. If you will follow me and Taylor, we'll get you all started."

The twelve of us follow the two Taylors from under the Porte-cochére out into the lush, sprawling gardens of Stonebrook Manor. The landscape of the event center looks like a forest and a botanical garden came together in the middle of the night and produced an offspring by morning. Tropical and exotic plants line the outdoor periphery of The Manor. Flowers from hundreds of species are planted between the tropical and forest sections of The Manor, and a koi pond sits under a man-made bridge on the property. I let the others know I want to start our photo shoot by the pond. The twelve of us are photographed all over the gardens in various combinations and poses. By the time we're through, I feel my stomach roaring and observe most of the guests have arrived for the reception.

Female Taylor claps her hands for our attention. Once we all look her way, she motions with both hands for us to come close and huddle around her.

"Okay ladies and gents, the photo shoot went great. Now we will head to the ballroom and join the rest of your guests for the grand entrance and first dance from the newly married couple. Then we will serve dinner, cut the cake and have a fireworks show later in the evening."

The energetic blonde bows and does a pirouette to lead us into Stonebrook Manor.

"Except you two." The male Taylor gestures at us with a clipboard. "If the two of you would please follow me."

The rest of the wedding party heads into the front doors that lead directly into the Grand Foyer where I see a few guests sipping beverages and chatting. Drian and I follow the tall, lean, blonde around half the length of The Manor. We stop at a door that has eight panes of glass each divided by strips of wood that frame the glass into individual squares. The blonde presses on a small black remote and the door opens of its own momentum. Taylor steps aside to usher my husband and I in first. Crossing the threshold, we are bathed in artificially cold air, the breeze feels spectacular for as sweltering as the fourth day in July has been. Once the young man catches stride with us, he leads us to an elevator at the end of the hallway were in. Inside the vertical transportation machine, we travel up one floor to waiting lounge, furnished with two brown leather couches, an oval glass coffee table that has six bottles of Fiji water sitting on a silver platter. Decorum aside, I snatch and guzzle the water like a little kid at a chocolate fountain.

Male Taylor smiles. "We were told that Fiji was your preferred brand of water, Mrs. Yancy, I'm glad you're enjoying it."

Instead of a verbal reply I grab another water, and sip this time.

"All right I just wanted to go over a few things with you two before you head down to the Grand Ballroom for your introduction and first dance." Taylor looks down at his clipboard for a moment and then back up at us. "It says here a Mr. Caldwell Cornelius is going to be the Master of Ceremonies, is that correct?"

Drian nods. "Yes."

"Good and it also says here that the first song that you two chose to dance to is "Let's Stay Together" by Al Green, is that also correct?"

My husband responds in the affirmative again. The young blonde nods, taps on the Bluetooth in his right ear says a few words, then turns attention back to us. "The guests are assembled and waiting for your grand entrance. As is customary for a newly married couple at Stonebrook Manor you will greet your guests by descending down our copper carpet staircase."

The blonde dreamboat opens a door in the wall of the lounge and ushers Drian and I through. The lounge must've been soundproof; as we stand in out of public view in the hallway that leads to the staircase I hear the sounds of conviviality and instrumental music being played by a live band.

"Excuse me ladies and gentlemen!" I hear Caldwell Cornelius

say to the room. "If I can have your attention please, the moment we've all been waiting for is upon us."

The Grand Ballroom fills with catcalls and claps.

"Ladies and gentlemen allow me to introduce for the first time, Mr. and Mrs. Adrian Oscar Yancy!"

The crowd in the Grand Ballroom erupts, and the opening horns of "Let's Stay Together" siren through the air. Arm in arm, Drian and I walk around the corner and head down the arched staircase lined with copper carpet. At the base the staircase opens into the Grand Ballroom. The ballroom has windows three of the four sides in the room. The sun is just starting to set, casting a beautiful backdrop of the botanical forest we took photos in earlier.

The room is furnished with fifty or so round tables. Several guests are seated in eggshell colored Victorian chairs that pair perfectly with the decor on the tables. The tables are covered in white and gold cloths with cream colored plates and gold dinnerware. In the center of each table are the centerpieces that Ms. Vivian showed me a few days ago, designed especially for the occasion. Along the wall without a window the bride and groom's table has been erected. The table is rectangular instead of circle, decorated like the other ones in the room. The ballroom has two full bars, positioned east and west, with plenty of guests occupying both. Looking from the altitude of the staircase, I'd estimate that the room has just over hundred people in here to celebrate Drian and I. Two of those people will help us celebrate by serenading the night away.

Near the bar on the west side of the room, brothers Vance and Duane Bingham collectively known as the R&B group Instant Klazique, stand on a portable stage, in front of their band. The band is intoxicating, lubricating the air with 70's soul grooves. My hips move with the music and the euphoria of the moment has me feeling pain-free for the first time today. I grip Drian's right bicep tightly, letting him know his wife is ready to dance. Stepping off the staircase, we hit the black and white checkerboard dance floor planted in the center of the room. Signaling the singers with the spin of his right index finger, Instant Klazique and the band restart "Let's Stay Together" with a jolt. Vance starts off the song with a scream I felt all the way down to the nail on my pinky toe.

The rest of the band follows the pace of the drummer, ratcheting up the mid-tempo love song until it's transformed into a Chicago-Style steppin' song. Tapping on my two step, I keep up with hubby as he moves fluidly with the melody. Hoots and hollers percolate through the ballroom at our gyrations and physical syncopation as we Ginsu the dance floor. Climbing to the chorus, the band stops abruptly and the lights in the room go out. Seconds pass and the room is re-lit with the same kind of icicle lights that decorated the church. The dim lighting gives the room a sophisticated feel and puts the spotlight on me and Mr. Bambi Eyes. Duane resumes the song, but at a slower pace, the kind of pace that makes a newly married couple want to slow dance. Drian pulls me close to him holding my right hand in his, putting his left on the small of my back. I lay my head on his chest and listen to his heartbeat between us I hear one cardiac cycle, at this moment we are in sync. As one, we groove to Duane's smooth and raspy voice as he reproduces vocals that emulate Al Green. Eyes closed, chest for a pillow I am blissful for my husband and the moment.

Three rapid taps awkwardly strike out though the air; the fireworks are starting early. Three more taps ring out, a split-second passes and my mind remembers the sound–gunshots, like the kind fired into the ceiling of the Ritz-Carlton suite. Before I can fight or fly, the ballroom is overtaken by a thick, billowing smoke. Gasping for air, I grab Drian and scramble for the exit. Our pursuit is severed as I feel his hand ripped from mine. I reach through darkness, mass blocking my path.

BANG!

That's the last sound I hear before thirsty screams and screeching alarms. A vociferous explosion decimates the ballroom; walls tumbling down, I search for my husband refusing to let death do us part.

ABOUT THE AUTHOR

Jamil A. Shabazz was born and raised in Aurora, Colorado. A graduate of Overland High School and Metropolitan State University of Denver, earning his Bachelor of Arts in African American Studies. His introductory novel Not Another Night was self-published in 2016. Hiding Behind The Night is its sequel.

www.ingramcontent.com/pod-product-compliance
Lightning Source LLC
Chambersburg PA
CBHW030129180626
46812CB00002B/613